What others have said about HIGH SIERRA:

"A good, rousing melodrama with its heart in the right place."

—The New Yorker

"You can go along with 'High Sierra' just for the ride, fast and exciting, but it will leave you something to remember."

—Saturday Review of Literature

"The story has all the thrills one can want, much brilliant hard wit in the creamiest American vernacular and more than a little of the common touch that no good novelist in America despises."

—The London Times Literary Supplement

"Presenting a gangster who is at once a Public Enemy No. 1 and a disillusioned artist in a doubtful profession 'High Sierra' is an underworld story with an entertaining difference."

—Books

W.R. Burnett titles available
from Carroll & Graf publishers

LITTLE CAESAR

W.R. BURNETT

HIGH SIERRA

Carroll & Graf Publishers, Inc.
New York

Published by arrangement with Scott Meredith Literary Agency, Inc.

First Carroll & Graf edition, 1986

Carroll & Graf Publishers, Inc.
260 Fifth Avenue
New York, NY 10001

ISBN: 0-88184-282-6

Manufactured in the United States of America

CHAPTER ONE

Early in the twentieth century, when Roy Earle was a happy boy on an Indiana farm, he had no idea that at thirty-seven he'd be a pardoned ex-convict driving alone through the Nevada-California desert towards an ambiguous destiny in the Far West.

Then he'd felt secure and the world had seemed like a simple place. Grandfather Earle, an old man, sat on the porch in the summer, swatting at the flies and telling long involved stories of his experiences as a Union Cavalryman fighting the Morgan Raiders. Grandfather Payson, another old man, would drive over from his son's farm and spend the long hot afternoons listening to Grandfather Earle, putting in a sardonic comment from time to time and guffawing in the wrong places. Uncle Wert and Roy's father, Charley, worked hard in the daytime, summer and winter, but in the evenings they played checkers or cribbage in the kitchen or sat on the porch, watching the lightning-bugs flashing under the big sycamore trees and repeating all the gossip heard in town on Saturday night. The womenfolk were always busy at something; but whatever their work was, it never kept them from talking. They talked, talked, by the hour, and the soothing sound of their subdued conversations would drift out to the men sitting on the porch or the lawn, giving them a sense of happiness and security.

When Roy thought of the past it was always summer. There were a few simple scenes he liked to recall, and the older he got, the more frequently he let his mind wander back to that far-off time, a generation ago, which seemed to a worried man heading downhill like the morning of the world, a true Golden Age.

There was the swimming-hole. It was deep and wide; a pool formed near the mouth of a creek where it swung round a bend on its way to the big river. The grassy banks were steep and lined with tall oak and sycamore trees, whose branches broke up the hot sunlight and cast cool blue shadows on the water. Screaming and yelling, the kids would rush along the bank, casting off their clothes as they ran, and the last one in was a dirty name. They flung themselves from the high bank violently, some of them taking "belly-smackers" which echoed up the quiet creek and scared the big kingfishers, which flew from the trees with a heavy beating of wings, scolded the swimmers, then veered off upstream. The water was warm and sluggish. Sometimes it was so clear you could see shafts of sunlight striking to the bottom, through which swam schools of tiny sunfish and an occasional crawdad, which scuttled backwards rapidly into its little cave in the bank. Fat Evans, known to the grownups as "that chuckle-headed, lazy good-for-nothing", would clash rocks under the water, and heads would bob up suddenly all over the pool. They swam and dived and fought and yelled till the light began to fade, then there'd be a wild scramble for the shore; and the last one out usually found his clothes tied in knots.

There was the Saturday afternoon baseball game. Both Roy and his brother, Elmer, were born athletes and before they were twelve they were competing on an equal footing with the men of the community. Roy played the outfield and Elmer played second base. The family was proud of them, and Grandfather Earle bragged about them so much that he made enemies. The sun beat down on the dusty baseball diamond; the crowds jammed along first and third base lines, yelled and whistled and called insults to the opposing team and the sweating, bedeviled umpire; the pop-boys had a field day; and when it was all over, the people drove back to their farms or to their little houses in town exhausted but happy. Roy was a slugger. He took a long hold on his bat and when he swung he kicked up his left foot. When he missed, he whirled round and round and the catcher ducked his bat, cursing. When he landed fairly, there was a solid crash and the ball flew way out towards the big red barn in right centre. Sometimes it was a home run and Roy would tip his cap as he crossed the plate, and the homefolks went wild. His father would pat him on the back and Grandfather Earle would caper and yell so violently that he'd get a twinge of "sciaticky" and have to dose himself with "medicine", which he drank from a pint bottle.

There was Aunt Minnie's. Roy liked her house even better than his own home. She was always cooking or baking something, and fine, sweet odours were always drifting out of the kitchen on those hot summer afternoons long ago. Ray sat in the dooryard waiting for the cakes or pies to be taken out of the oven; Aunt Minnie's troop of geese waddled past single file, irritable big fowl which hissed at the slightest provocation and were always ready to attack; Sport, the mongrel farm dog, harried them half-heartedly, poised for flight; and bumblebees, as big as a boy's thumb, buzzed and blundered among the tall hollyhocks, adding a bass note to the drowsy humming of the other insects. Aunt Minnie's face was pinched and rather pale, but she had a sweet smile and was the gentlest person Roy had ever seen. She had a remedy for everything and Grandfather Earle said that

6

the family didn't have to spend a dime for doctor bills with her around. On Sundays, after church, there was always a big freezer of home-made ice cream in the summer house, and every day there was lemonade and chocolate cookies. Roy even enjoyed doing chores at Aunt Minnie's. He'd water the stock, and feed the pigs and chickens, and milk Sarah, the big red cow. Aunt Minnie's was a haven of refuge for all the kids of the community; when they were hurt or put upon they ran to her. It was the nearest thing to heaven any of them knew.

And there were those long hot evenings when the moon was up over the countryside and all the sweet odours of a summer night hung in the air. Down by the river the bullfrogs plucked bass strings, the crickets strummed, the tree-toads shook their rattle high overhead, and night birds, flying low, cheeped eerily under the trees. A distant freight train whistled at a far-off crossing, the melancholy sound carrying a long way in the still night. The farm dogs barked loudly, answering one another, and some of them, like wolves, bayed the moon. Bats blundered out from under the eaves of the barn and flew low, squeaking and chasing invisible insects and scaring the women, who put their hands over their hair and ran. And under the big sycamore trees of the dooryard the lightning-bugs began to appear, dotting the darkness with their tiny sulphur-green flares. Roma Stover, the yellow-haired girl from across the road, came sidling over shyly, and she and Roy and Elmer swung on the big farm gate and laughed at nothing. Sometimes she'd catch a lightning-bug and put it in her hair. One night Roy caught a lot of them and put them in a bottle, and the girl held it to her face so Roy and Elmer could see her features by this weird intermittent light. After a while Elmer would wander away into the darkness. He was no fool. He knew who she'd come to see. And Roy and the girl swung on the gate and whispered, and sometimes kissed, while the victrola on the porch played the latest tunes and the grown-ups called to them ironically from time to time, and Grandfather Earle went into a long, loud discourse on the technique of "sparking".

To Roy a few simple scenes represented the "past". Everything else escaped him. He forgot that he'd been a problem to Ed Simpson, the schoolteacher, and that at one time Ed had told his father that he was a bad, rebellious boy, with an evil temper and a wide streak of meanness which would get him in trouble some day. He forgot that he'd stuck a penknife into a bully named Bub Cowalter, a big fat fellow who had been kicking Roy and some of the other boys around; he'd done worse than that:

he'd gone on stabbing him, excited by Bub's calf-like cries of fear, till Elmer and another boy pulled him off. He'd forgotten that Elmer turned green with horror, and that some of the boys began to avoid him. He never knew that his mother and Aunt Minnie used to lie awake nights worrying about him and speculating on what his end would be. His father told the other relatives: "Roy's not like the rest of us. Damned if I know what it is. He's restless and won't settle down. He has to be running into town every night. He ain't a thing like Elmer or Anna or me. I swear I don't know where he gets his nature. Except maybe from Uncle Will. Remember? Ain't seen him for ten years. He may be dead. Nervous as a cat. Got so he couldn't stay in any one town over a day or so. He was a good workman, too; best lather in Brookfield. But just a bum and never was anything else. Last time I saw him he was dirty and stinking. I gave him a hat and pair of shoes and two dollars. 'Charley,' he says, 'I've seen many towns and missed many meals'; then he laughed."

The relatives all shook their heads over Roy, and nobody knew what to do with him.

CHAPTER TWO

As a young man Roy was tall, heavy-shouldered, hard, and muscular. His face was swarthy and his hair was coarse, dark, and wavy; he had heavy brow-ridges, a thick nose, and a firm wide mouth which, at times, was compressed into a thin cruel line; his eyes were dark, but, unlike most dark eyes, they weren't soft; he gave an impression of virile ugliness.

One of Big Mac M'Gann's women (or maybe it was one of his wives) meeting Roy (aged about thirty) was very much impressed. "You know," she said to Big Mac afterwards, "that Earle fellow reminds me of a cross between a farmer and a refined gorilla. I don't mean a strong-arm guy. I mean like they have in zoos."

"Yeah," said Big Mac, rubbing his chin and carefully studying the woman out of the corner of his eyes, "he's a big ape all right."

"You don't get me. I mean he's kind of like an animal. He's got a look out of his eyes – well . . ."

"I get you all right," said Big Mac, and this woman never saw Roy Earle again.

CHAPTER THREE

It was lonely driving across the desert in the dark, but Roy was used to being lonesome. Yeah, ever since his cellmate, poor old Barmy, cashed in he'd been alone. Nobody to talk to; nobody to share things with. That last year in clink had sure been hell without Barmy. Imagine the guys thinking that Barmy was a fink. Why, he'd cut his right arm off to the shoulder before he'd sing. But Barmy was smooth and clever and knew how to get around the screws; and he knew how to do time, a real "easy-doer"; and the fellows couldn't get on to it. They thought he was getting favours for snitching. Roy had to cool off a couple of the tougher ones and ended up in solitary for his trouble. But nobody was going to shove old flat-chested Barmy around.

"Yeah," said Roy, "I went in stir a punk and I come out with an education. What Barmy didn't know wasn't worth knowing. Smartest confidence man that ever lived. He got old and they caught up with him, that's all. Everybody gets caught up with sooner or later."

Roy remembered the day he came out. Full pardon. "The best money could buy," Big Mac said, laughing about it. Big Mac had sprung him, but not because Big Mac loved him like a brother. He had plans.

Roy came blinking out into the sunlight. He had on a neat blue serge suit Big Mac had sent him. He didn't look so bad except for his prison-bleached complexion. But his coarse dark hair had silvery streaks in it, and his dark eyes were weary and sad. Mac's driver was waiting for him. Mac was busy. Couldn't get away. Roy laughed ironically to himself.

All the way through the city he kept jumping and shaking and trying to put his foot through the floorboard of Mac's Packard. The traffic scared hell out of him. He'd been in clink nearly six years, and the world outside was now a strange and terrible place.

Mac was waiting for him in his office up over the shore-dinner joint. Mac had at one time been handsome; women went for him at sight. But he had sure slipped. His belly hung over his belt and he had about four chins. His hair was a dirty white. He was about six feet three and probably weighed over three hundred pounds.

Roy sat down. Mac was so upset for the moment by the change

9

in Roy's appearance (having no idea that Roy was equally disturbed by the change in himself) that he didn't even shake hands or speak. He just shoved a paper across the desk. On an inside page was a paragraph or two stating that Roy Earle, the Indiana bank robber and last of the old Dillinger mob, had been pardoned. No headlines. No fuss.

"That's that," said Mac, recovering a little from his shock and beginning to discern behind the hard, grim prison masks, swarthy-faced, grinning, tough young Roy Earle of the old days.

"Yeah," said Roy.

"I want you to leave for California in a week or so," said Mac. "Big job. Three punks on it. It needs a real guy. You're it."

"Yeah?" Roy did not feel "it" at all. He had an allgone sensation in the pit of his stomach, and he put his hands into his coat pockets so Mac wouldn't see how they shook. What he needed was a long rest, but Mac was the doctor.

"You're a sight for sore eyes," said Mac. "Nothing but punks nowadays. Little soda-jerkers and jitterbugs. Think they know everything, too. You'll find out when you get to California. One guy's name is Joe Hattery. Done time for a filling-station stick-up. The guy with him got so scared that when Joe yelled for the boys to reach for the sky, Joe's pal put up his hands, too. How do you like that? Joe's got a greaseball with him now. What's his name? Panek or some such heathen name. Small-timer, but tough, I guess. The other guy is a Mexican. It's his job. He's night clerk in the joint."

"What joint?"

"This hotel we're going to knock over. It's the Tropico Inn at Tropico Springs. Swank joint. We need a rodman and a boy who can kind of hold these jitterbugs down. Ain't one of 'em over twenty-five. Punks. You're it."

"Tell me some more."

"Hell, you're in whether I tell you anything or not. I got to protect my investment. I'm paying all expenses and I want service."

"What's your angle?"

"What do you care? You just do what I tell you, that's all."

"Look, Mac —"

"I sprung you, didn't I?" Big Mac grinned, took his feet down from his desk, and lit a cigar. "Oh, hell, Roy," he went on, "I keep forgetting you're folks. I been dealing with so many screwballs the last few years! Look, this is a big thing. God knows how big. Your end is going to run into four figures sure. I wouldn't steer you wrong. This is the swellest joint on the west coast. Everybody goes there from all over the world: dukes and rajahs and Lord knows what all. The safety-deposit boxes are lousy with glass, or they will be when the season gets going. The Mex gives us the tip-off when she's full. We walk in, take all the dough in sight, and bust open the boxes with sledge-hammers. I'll take all the rocks and give you a fair price for them."

"I didn't know you was a fence, Mac." Roy stared. He remembered Mac in the old days, hobnobbing with the big politicians and racing his string of horses at all the swell race-meetings.

Mac flushed slightly.

"A guy has got to do what he can."

"Well, I'm in," said Roy. "Sounds all right to me. The stir croaker says I'm not in such hot shape, so maybe the trip would do me good. Who knows?"

"It won't hurt you none, that's a cinch. And, listen, Roy. This is a soft spot. They've never had a knock-over in Tropico Springs. They got no police force to speak of. It's like taking candy from a baby."

After a while they got to talking about the old days. Big Mac had been one of Johnny's undercover pals. He thought Johnny was the best there was, and so did Roy, for that matter. Roy laughed, recalling how Dillinger used to lap up the chicken gravy. "Yeah," said Mac, "that boy could eat anything just so it come out of an egg."

Later Big Mac said:

"You was the lucky one, Roy. The F.B.I. couldn't hang a Federal rap on you, so here you are loose. Otherwise, pal, you'd be cussing the fog up at Alcatraz or planted by now."

"Sometimes I'd just as soon be there."

"Cut it out," said Mac with a laugh. "Quit kidding me." Mac remembered how Johnny had said to him one day: "You see that hick over there with the big shoulders and the ugly face? Well, keep your baby-blue eyes on him. He's folks." Big Mac would think about Roy Earle that way till he died. When Johnny said something it had a punch to it, and it stuck.

. . . . Recalling the past, Roy sat hunched a little forward and kept his eyes on the road. Since moonrise a chill had descended over the desert, and from time to time a cold wind blew from the north-east, ruffling the sagebrush. The moonlight lay over the flat land like a pale-blue carpet. Dim black shapes of mountains loomed ahead of him. He was like a man lost in a vast lunar landscape, the last human being in a dead world.

From time to time he had faint qualms which he didn't understand. Once he said aloud:

"Good God! Don't nobody live here?"

Not a light. Not a trace of human habitation. Nothing but a wide black road rushing towards him, vague brute hulks of mountains, weird blue moonlight, and a chill wind. Finally a pair of eyes gleamed at the side of the road and a coyote streaked across in front of the headlights.

"Brother," said Roy, "you can have it!"

He sighed with relief when a faint yellow light began to touch the highest peaks of the mountains westward, though it was still dark on the valley floor. Little by little the world turned blue, then lavender. Pretty soon Roy saw the eastern glow in his rear-view mirror. He sighed again and pushed his hat back.

"That sun's a funny thing," he said. "You never give it a thought, but, brother, it'd sure be hell without it."

CHAPTER FOUR

On one side of the road was a big faded signboard, reading: *Last Chance for Fifty Miles*; on the other side a run-down filling-station with two gas-pumps, an oil pit, and a tiny screened-in sandwich-stand. The lettering on the signboard was almost obliterated, and the weathered wood was scarred and pitted. Underneath it were scraps of newspapers, tin cans, and broken bottles.

Beyond the filling-station the desolate flat wasteland stretched in all directions, under the hard brassy glare of the desert sun, to the far-off ragged, blue hills. There was no wind. Nothing moved except for a huge red hawk which flew leisurely over the signboard, banked, turned, and disappeared eastward.

A tall man in a dirty khaki shirt and denim pants stood in the doorway of the filling-station and stared out across the mile after mile of greasewood and sagebrush. His eyes were narrowed against the glare and his long face sagged. Behind the screen of the sandwich-stand his fat wife fanned herself and groaned from time to time.

Finally the man said without turning:

"Stop groaning."

"I can't help it," said his wife. "It's so infernal hot and then I'm worried."

The man spat out into the highway, absentmindedly trying to hit the white line.

"It's early in the season yet," he said. "Folks ain't going to cross that desert, unless they have to, till it gets a little cooler. Stop worrying."

"I ain't sold nothing to eat today. We'll never make it this way, Ed."

Ed shrugged, then turned. He heard the faint hum of a motor. Would this car, too, flash past with that insolent swishing roar he'd come to hear in his dreams and to hate? In a moment he saw the car, a tiny dot lost in the immensity of the wasteland, its windshield flashing like a heliograph in the sun's glare. It came on at a high rate of speed, getting bigger and bigger. Ed glanced up. The hawk had come back; he was perched on the top of the signboard, his lean, predatory head raised slightly and his cat-eyes staring fixedly off into the sagebrush. "Spotted something," mused Ed. "Like me." He shrugged and watched the car as it roared towards him, held his breath as it came nearer and nearer, then exhaled as it streaked past towards the line of jagged blue mountains on the western horizon. It was a new coupé and there was a lone man in it.

Ed's wife groaned. Flushing with rage, Ed reached into the filling-station and got his rifle, which always stood beside the cash-register. "I'll get me that goddamn bird," he said.

But his wife cried:

"Look! He's coming back."

Ed lowered the rifle. The coupé had made a U-turn.

"O.K., hawk," said Ed, grinning. "Maybe you brought me luck."

The hawk flew off and sailed low over the sagebrush, but Ed forgot to watch him. The shiny black coupé was driving into the station. Ed's wife opened the screen door and stood leaning against the jamb, smiling.

Ed felt like a new man. It wasn't just that he was worried about business and wanted a customer; he wanted a man to talk to. He was sick of trading monosyllables with a wife who did little but groan.

"Howdy, pardner," he said. "What can I do for you?"

Ed was trying to be gay. But the man in the coupé was not at all responsive. He had a pale, tight-lipped face. His eyes were dark and hard.

"Fill her up," he said. "She'll take about ten. Take a look at the water and oil."

"Yes, sir. You bet," said Ed, bustling about. "Hot day, ain't she? Ain't many cars coming through right now. Little early, I guess. We've sure had some summer and here she is last of September and still she's hotter than the hinges of hell. A guy's got to be a regular Gilly monster this year. Oh, I see you got an Illinois plate. Brother, you're a long ways from home, ain't you?"

The man in the coupé pushed his hat back from his forehead and, turning, stared across the road at the signboard.

Ed's face fell. He shrugged and went silently about his work. Nice friendly fellow this was! Imagine a guy taking a trip like this alone, and then not wanting to pass the time of day with a man who really didn't give a damn and was just trying to be neighbourly.

Ed's wife walked up to the car.

"Hot, ain't it, mister?"

The man turned. His eyes did not look hard to Ed's wife; they looked sad.

"Yeah."

"Got some pop on ice. Coke, too. You like a sandwich or something?"

The man hesitated.

"Yeah. Got ham?"

"Yes, sir. My husband – this man here – his name's Ed – well, last winter business got pretty good, so he bought me an electric ice-box. We keep everything cold and fresh and we –"

"Ham sandwich. Got any beer?"

"Yes, sir. We got two-three kinds. We got ..."

"Just beer, and step on it."

"Yes, sir," said Ed's wife. "I baked a cake this morning too. It's pretty good. And I think I got some apple pie left. We ..."

"Lady," said the man, "a ham sandwich and a bottle of beer."

Ed's wife vaguely felt that she had been rebuked. She flushed slightly and glanced at Ed, but he was staring stonily in the opposite direction. When she had gone, Ed said:

"Ain't women awful? Talk, talk. They all talk too much. Ain't that so?" Ed was still trying to get some conversation out of the man in the coupé. As a matter of fact, Ed's wife was less talkative than he was, and when they were alone she had very little to say. But Ed could see that his wife had annoyed the stranger, so he said what he thought would put some kind of bond between them, even at his wife's expense.

"If you say so," said the man, turning and looking across the road.

14

Ed laughed. He pretended he thought the man was kidding and not just trying to shut him up.

"Yeah. Talk, talk. All day nothing but talk. Ed this and Ed that. Sometimes I get plumb fed up. You married, pardner?"

"Look. All I want is some gas and a sandwich."

Ed swallowed. The man was looking straight at him. He had a mighty unfriendly and chilling eye.

"Sure, sure, pardner," said Ed. "You got to excuse me. I just get kind of lonesome once in a while." All of Ed's defences were down. He had dropped his sad jocularity. He almost sniffled, he was so disappointed in this customer.

"Lonesome, eh?" said the man; then he yawned and ran his hand over his face. "Yeah, I guess a guy would get kind of lonesome out here."

Ed glanced at the man's eyes. They didn't look unfriendly now. They looked kind of soft.

"Yes, sir," said Ed. "I get mighty lonesome, especially this time of year when the winter travelling ain't started yet. Why, little while ago I almost shot me a hawk just to have something to do."

"Kind of hard on the hawk," said the man shortly.

Ed swallowed. This was sure a touchy kind of man.

"Almost, I said. Yes, sir. I just got to thinking it was a dirty trick to play on a hawk."

Ed carefully watched the effect of this lie. The man's face twitched slightly and the right side of his mouth was raised about a quarter of an inch. "I guess that's supposed to be a smile," Ed told himself. "This guy is sure an iceberg."

"When I was a kid," the man said, "I was always banging away at birds and rabbits. I was raised on a farm and there was always a lot of small game around. Now I don't like to hunt. I don't know . . ."

The man seemed to shake himself. His lips closed like a steel trap. Ed opened his mouth to say something, but his wife came out with a tray and interposed herself between him and the man in the coupé.

"Here you are, mister," she said.

"How much do I owe?"

"You ask Ed. Pay all at once. I mean, for gas and everything."

Ed told the stranger how much he owed and was paid.

"You notice I charge only a cent over town prices for gasoline. Farther on, they have a job trucking it in and you'll have to pay robbery prices. Now if you had a ten-gallon can – but I guess you ain't."

15

Ed stood with his foot on the running-board, trying to think of something to say that might interest the man.

"Look," said Ed's wife, "here comes another car."

Ed whistled.

"Brother, is she boiling!"

A Model-A Ford was limping into the station. The radiator cap was off and a jet of white steam was rising three feet into the air. An oldish man with a grey moustache was at the wheel and a plump, grey-haired woman was sitting beside him, staring rather anxiously at the column of steam.

"We made it," said the old man.

"You just did," said Ed, hurrying over. He was delighted. Here were folks he could talk to. The hell with snooty guys with solemn white faces who got riled up because a man was going to take a shot at a damned good-for-nothing bird. These were folks!

"Ain't that the car there, Pa?" said the woman, pointing at the coupé.

"Yes, it is. I'll go tell that fellow I . . ."

A girl sat up in the back seat and rubbed her eyes. Her thick, rather coarse blonde hair was tied carelessly with what looked like a red candy-box ribbon. She had on a yellow blouse and denim pants.

"Where are we?" she demanded.

"I don't know, pet. But we're safe. The old car got to boiling out there in the middle of nowhere and . . ."

"Why didn't you wake me up?"

"You ain't been getting your rest, child, I thought . . ."

"Where's Grandpa?"

"He went over to talk to that man. Good thing you was asleep. Pa hit a stone or something just when that man was trying to pass us. The man just whirled his car off the road and went bumpty-bump into the desert. Funny thing. He never even turned around or even looked at us. He just got back on the road and went on."

The old man had his foot on the running-board of the coupé.

"My name's Goodhue," he was saying. "I'd sure like to shake hands with you, sir. You sure saved our bacon."

"Saved my own, too," said Roy. "My name's Roy Collins. How are you?" The men shook hands. "I didn't know you had a girl in that car."

"She was laying down in the back seat, sleeping. She ain't been sleeping well on this trip and we was getting worried about

16

her. She's my granddaughter. It's on account of her I wanted to shake your hand. Me and Ma, we're old. Don't matter."

"Come far?"

"Clear from Ohio. You?"

"Chicago."

"Well. I'm proud to make your acquaintance. You sure can handle a car. Me, I'm kind of shaky at it. Velma's a good driver, but she gets tired, so I won't let her drive much. I'd have Velma come over and thank you, but she wouldn't, I know; she's too shy."

Roy nodded in reply, but he was paying very little attention to what old Mr. Goodhue was saying. He was looking at Velma. He was thinking what lovely hair she had; what a pretty, sulky face; and how well the red hair-ribbon and the bright yellow blouse became her. She was tidying up a bit now, combing out her thick hair. Every move she made attracted Roy; even the quick sideways tilt of her head and the pucker of her face as she pulled at a snarl. Spoiled, that was it! It was plain from her grandfather's tone that he thought Velma was one in a million, and from her actions and her sulkiness Velma thought so too.

"Guess I'll be on my way," said Roy, but he lingered. Velma was opening the car door. He wanted to see her move; he wanted to see what kind of build she had. He was surprised at himself for taking such an interest in a sulky-faced young hick who probably thought she was pretty as a picture.

The car door opened. Velma got out and walked slowly towards the rest-room. Roy's hands got cold. She was crippled. One leg was shorter than the other or else she had a clubfoot.

"You see?" said old Mr. Goodhue. "That's why she's so shy. Poor pet! Otherwise I'd have her come over and thank you."

"Don't worry about that. Well, I'm on my way."

"Going far."

"Going up in the mountains for my health."

"I thought you looked a little pale. Well, I'm going to Los Angeles, God willing. I lost my farm back home. Velma's mother's married again and she sort of invited us out. I don't know . . ."

"Goodbye," said Roy. "Hope you make it all right."

"Goodbye to you, son."

Driving slowly out of the station, Roy turned to look back. A hawk was sitting on the top of the battered signboard. Old lonely Ed was talking a mile a minute to Velma's grandmother, and Mr. Goodhue was staring dubiously at his still steaming car. Velma had disappeared. The afternoon was waning. The mountains were casting long blue shadows across the interminable flat land.

Roy stepped on the gas.

"Funny," he told himself. "I thought I was as dead as this country. I thought I was just walking around without sense enough to drop down."

Such a powerful feeling of sadness came over him that he could hardly stand it. Jesus! A sweet kid like that with a gimpy leg. What was it about her face that attracted him so? On his trip west he'd seen hundreds of dames; some of them pretty keen, too. There was that red-haired babe in Kansas who tried to thumb a ride. Not interested. All he could think about was how much of a jam a tough kid like that might get him into. How about the chili queen in the hamburger-stand who practically invited him into the backroom? Good-looking kid, too, with nice curly dark hair and big black eyes. Not a flutter. And here he was with the bottom dropping out of his stomach because an Ohio hick had a red ribbon in her hair and a gimpy leg!

He looked back again. Nothing but desert. The filling-station had been swallowed up.

"Well," said Roy aloud, as he stepped on the accelerator, and the speedometer needle moved from 62 to 75, "I hope the old guy makes it. He's sure all right."

CHAPTER FIVE

Roy woke with a start. He sat up and stared blankly into the darkness, sweating clammily. Outside, a faint clinking sound was repeated, and suddenly the immediate past rushed back over him in a sordid grey inundation. Still groggy from a heavy sleep, he glanced up high on the wall, looking for the small barred window; motionless he listened for the loud breathing of Barmy and for the faint but unmistakable pulsation of the huge prison where thousands of men slept fitfully, turned, tossed, and moaned. He had a dull paint in his chest, and his hands were shaking. Fully awake at last, he swore under his breath and got up to get a towel. Damn these night sweats! A man might just as well die and get it over with. The croaker in stir had told him it was nothing; just unhealthy nerves due to long confinement. Not T.B., like some of the poor bastards had.

Roy took off his pyjama coat and wiped his face and torso dry, then he powdered himself. The window was open and a cool breeze was bellying his curtains. He smelled the desert; there was a heavy odour of dry vegetation.

Outside his door he heard the clinking again. Some late arrival was being shown to a cabin in the little auto-court. Roy compressed his lips and shook his head. Even now, knowing what it was, the clinking made his flesh creep. If he lived to be a hundred he'd never be like other people. He was prison-conditioned! That's what the highbrow croaker from the university told him – the fellow that went around with a thing like a compass measuring the guys' heads. What was it poor old Barmy called him? A conk-feeler! Even the croaker laughed at that. Later he sent Barmy a copy of his book. Barmy was such a smart bird that even a university professor couldn't miss it. The book was all about the American Criminal. How wide his head was and what kind of eyes he had. Stuff like that. Malarkey!

Roy lit a cigarette and lay down. He had stopped sweating now and felt pretty good, except that the usual night-depression had settled over him. But he was getting used to that. Hell, you could get used to anything, even being without women and doing a long whack in solitary.

He flicked the ash from his cigarette and took a long drag, then he winced slightly. A picture had sprung up before his eyes: Velma, in her yellow blouse and red hair-ribbon, limping slowly across the tamped gravel of the filling-station. He lay back and stared at the faint pattern of light on the ceiling. "I don't know. It must be the trip. It must be getting out into this funny country. I thought I was dead inside; stir really fixes you up. But I feel just like I used to when I was a punk in overalls."

Down the row there were screams of laughter. Dames! How they could carry on when they once got going! These auto-courts! Nothing but call-houses, most of them. Police never bothered them. They got away with murder. Nobody had to worry about luggage or things like that. Perfect joints for the one-night stand. It sure was a break for the married men in the locality.

The noise got worse and worse. A loud, drunken argument started. Roy got up and flipped his cigarette out of the window. "Yep," he said, "I guess that's the reason I feel that way when I think about Velma. She looks like the girls I used to know when I was a punk. And then her grandparents. Just like my people. They got a kind look around the mouth and out of the eyes. They're not thinking what a so-and-so you are, or how much

19

can they get out of you. You're just a human being to them. Yeah, that's it. Just a human being."

He switched on the lights and began to dress. He'd had all the sleep he was going to get. The sooner he got where he was going the better.

CHAPTER SIX

Roy pulled over to the side of the road and got out his type-written instructions. He was up in the mountains now, and although the sun was blazing in a cloudless sky, a chilly wind was whistling down through the draws and ravines. All about him towered huge rocky peaks, scarred and fissured, their summits covered with snow. Roy felt very small and helpless; almost as small and helpless as he had felt when Barmy, one night at the Prison Farm, made plain to him that the earth was no more than a "wart on a pickle" and that the sun wasn't even a forty-watt bulb in the universe. He was used to flat farm country, or to cities where the end of the street was the horizon. This was his first encounter with real vastness, aside from the times he'd been star-gazing with Barmy, and he didn't like it.

". . . turn left at Jud's Place five miles and a half beyond Broken Creek Summit. Follow the road to Anderson's Camp, then inquire."

Roy looked up Broken Creek Summit on a road map he'd got in a filling-station. Altitude, 7,800 feet. He whistled and studied the map patiently, trying to figure out exactly where he was; finally he discovered a familiar place-name: Edison's Camp; altitude, 4,400 feet.

"Why, I passed that place half an hour ago. I'm really getting up there. I got to make this joint before dark or I'm in the soup."

He put his map on the seat beside him, where it would be handy, and drove off. In a short while the road began to climb steeply and he could get little speed out of his car in high. But there were no hairpin turns as the road wound off across a vast tableland, skirting the shoulders of the big mountains.

"Why, this ain't bad. Nothing to this," said Roy, loudly reassuring himself as his chronic sense of loneliness was enor-mously increased by this bleak and deserted country with its barren snow-covered peaks and its endless, empty blue vistas.

Roy drove for an hour, still climbing. He could see the road curving off ahead of him, rising gently towards a mountain northward which seemed to stand directly in its path. The mountain came closer and closer until it filled the horizon and cast a long cold blue shadow across the floor of the tableland. Huge towering pine trees began to appear. Above his labouring motor Roy heard a rush of water and saw a mountain stream plunging down in a precipitate fall around a rocky shoulder, churning the water into a white froth and throwing spray high into the air. Now the mountain was directly in his path and he sighed with relief when he saw that the road skirted it.

He saw other streams, streams you could jump across, tumbling swiftly along at the side of the road through tangles of birch and low underbush. The scattered big pines had turned into a forest now, darkening the road and increasing Roy's feeling of isolation. The road climbed steeply, then turned. Glancing up, he saw the cuts where the road lifted itself over a high shoulder.

"Ain't bad," he said dubiously.

The wind was blowing harder now. He felt cold and cramped. He wanted a cup of coffee; he wanted to sit in front of a fire and talk to somebody; his nerves badly jangled from the long trip, he wanted a little repose. He slowed down too suddenly for one turn and, as the road lifted sharply upward from that point, he had to shift into low. The gears whined and stuttered, and Roy cursed them, putting all the blame on them. But in a moment he came out on a windy plateau, where snow, fine as powder, was blowing, and he shifted back into high. He saw a sign at the side of the road and felt better. Even a sign was a little company. After all, some guy had put it up. This couldn't be the jumping-off place. The sign read: *Broken Creek Summit. Altitude, 7,800.*

The road wound off ahead of him, apparently as level and straight as a street-car track, and he settled back with a sigh. But he felt very depressed and began to wish that he'd never come into this God-forsaken country on such a wild-goose chase.

"Any bunch of guys that would pick a place like this for a hide-away, well . . . I'll end up on a marble slab and that will be the end of it. All right," he argued with himself, "then your troubles will be over. I'd like to know what you think you got to live for?"

The road took a turn he hadn't foreseen. For a moment a broken-shoulder of rock hid it and Roy swept round the bend faster than he had intended. He gave a gasp and turned white. Ahead of him was nothing. He'd come onto a hairpin turn, the first he'd encountered, without the faintest warning. With his tyres screaming he skirted the edge of the abyss and managed

21

to hold his car on the road. On his right hand was a two-thou-sand-foot drop, full of blue and lavender shadows.

As the road straightened out again, Roy leaned limply against the wheel with his teeth chattering.

Roy drove into Anderson's Camp a little before sundown. Between the tall trees he saw the blue glimmer of a mountain lake. Three men were walking along the dusty road in hip boots and plaid shirts; one of them had a string of fish. Roy honked at the gas-pump in front of the general store and a tall redheaded man came out.

"Howdy," he said. "Gas?"

"Yeah, fill her up." While the man worked, Roy leaned back in his seat and stretched, then he took out his handkerchief and mopped his face. He was dirty, hungry, and tired. When the man was through he said: "How much?" And when he found out he whistled.

"Well," said the man, "we got to truck it in, pardner. We just charge a fair price. Looking for a cabin?"

"No," said Roy. "How do I get to Shaw's from here?"

"Going to do some fishing? Why don't you stay here? I got better cabins than old Shaw has. I'll even take you out on the lake myself and charge you nothing for it. I treat my customers right. Anyway, Blue Jay Lake's a better lake than Eagle. We get bigger ones."

"Look. I'm trying to find a couple of guys. They're friends of mine. They invited me up."

"Couple of young guys, eh? Got a girl with them? Has one of them got red hair like mine?"

Roy stared. Hattery did have red hair, Mac said! Do you suppose these screwballs had a dame with them?

"Yeah. One of them's got red hair."

The man bent down to laugh.

"Pardner, I pity you. You sure are hooked up with a pair of swell fishermen. Why, that redheaded guy's already fell in three times. Yeah, they're at Shaw's. Take the first dirt road to the left. It's only a piece. Can't miss it. If you get tired of them fellows, you come see me. I'll take you out where you can get a three-pounder. They ain't over three-quarters at Eagle."

"I'm no fisherman. I'm up here for my health."

"Yeah? I was thinking you looked a little pale. Well, come down and pass the time of day with me when you get a chance. Thanks for your business, pardner."

Roy found Shaw's Camp after a short but exasperating ride over a rutty dirt road. The first person he saw was a rather tall

22

girl with long hair, hazel eyes and a well-shaped, firm mouth. She was leaning against the front of a little shack with her arms and legs crossed, smoking a cigarette. She had on a plaid shirt, skin tight jean pants, and boots. Her eyes sought Roy's as he hesitated and came to a stop.

"Hattery here?" he asked.

"You Roy Earle?" she demanded, studying his face.

Roy nodded, then compressed his lips. He was tired and nervous, and muscles in various parts of his body were twitching with fatigue. The girl irritated him, she looked so young and strong.

The door of the shack opened and a tall, good-looking young fellow with curly black hair stepped out. His eyes were pale and a little furtive under black eyebrows which met above his nose. His arms were long and he handled himself rather loosely. He had an irritating air of conceit and a sort of "devil-with-the-women" smirk. He was wearing his fishing uniform, too. He put his hand possessively on the girl's shoulder and glanced indifferently at Roy.

"Mac sent me," said Roy.

The young fellow called over his shoulder:

"Red! Here's the guy we're expecting."

Hattery came out. He had on corduroy pants and a checked cowboy shirt. His sleeves were rolled up and Roy saw tattooing on his forearms. His red hair was coarse and bristling; he had the dented nose and the flattened profile of a prize-fighter. His face was covered with freckles, and in spite of an engaging grin he was extremely ugly.

"Hello, Earle," said Red. "Glad to see you. Shake hands with my pal, Babe Kozak. And this is Marie Garson. I guess we look kind of crummy. We been fishing all day. We done all right. Smell 'em cooking? Pretty fair eating."

"Where do I sleep?" asked Roy, nodding to Babe and Marie.

"That cabin next door," said Red, his grin fading as he became aware of Roy's unfriendliness. "We was figuring that a big shot like you might be kind of exclusive. Anyway, we're full up."

Roy thought he detected irony and ran his eyes carefully over these three kids, none of them over twenty-five; all of them members of a generation which was not his own; all thinking probably that he was an old phutz and a has-been. His mouth tightened and he looked at them coldly.

The three of them exchanged glances. Roy's attitude made them uncomfortable.

"Yeah," said Red, "I think the porter has got your cabin all set. Now about chow. Marie could bring you over some stuff. We got plenty. Course you can go down to Halley's on the lake, but it costs a buck and it's nothing to shout about."

Roy got out of the car.

"I'll take the grub over myself. Then I'm going to hit the hay."

"Sure," said Red, shrugging. "O.K. Course you could eat with us."

"I don't feel like company," said Roy with a short laugh.

Babe and Red glanced at each other and shrugged. Marie kept staring at Roy, but he ignored her. Tough little tramp, probably; couldn't be much, running around with a couple of ten-cent heist guys, hardly dry behind the ears. They all helped Roy get his stuff out of the car and Marie unlocked the cabin for him and turned on his lights. She lifted the stove-lid and peered in.

"Yeah," she said, "Algernon's got you all fixed up. All you have to do is throw a match in. You sure need a fire up here at night."

"Well," said Babe, rubbing his chin and studying Roy out of the corner of his eye, "I guess we got you settled in, Earle."

"Yeah. You two beat it. I want to see Red a minute."

When the door closed, Red grinned sheepishly at Roy.

"Don't like the idea of the dame, hunh?"

"I'm crazy about it. Even guys like you ought to know better."

"Well, Babe's hell for women. He picked her up in a dime-a-dance joint in L.A. She's strictly oke. Sort of looks after things for us."

"The other guy's girl, hunh? All the same to you, then. Give her some dough and send her back to L.A. I've seen soreheaded dames spoil too many good jobs."

"Well, look. . . ."

"I get it. Just waiting your turn. Is that it, Red?"

"Well, ain't she a pip? But she's on the level with Babe as far as I'm concerned. He don't treat her so well either and I been figuring . . ."

"Nice set-up. First thing you know, you and your pal'll be fighting over her and go gunning for each other. We can't take no chances on stuff like that. Give her the dough and let her go. If you ain't got it, I'll give it to you."

"But look, Earle . . ."

"Beat it. I'm too tired to argue. Get her out of here tonight."

Red stood scratching his head. Several times he started to speak, but hesitated. When he felt Roy's hard dark eyes on his face he flushed slightly and cleared his throat.

"What's the matter?" cried Roy. "Does this dame know something? Have you punks talked?"

"It ain't that."

"All right. Beat it, then. This food's getting cold."

Red walked to the door, but hesitated and stood fiddling.

"I sure heard a lot about you, Mr. Earle," he said. "We sure feel like we're getting in fast company with you in on it. One time when I was nothing but a punk kid I seen your picture in a Chicago paper . . . yeah. . . ."

Red went out, shutting the door softly. Roy took off his shirt and scrubbed himself, then he sat down and started to eat. The coffee was good and after a few swallows he began to feel better. But the trout was a disappointment. He picked at it, then pushed it away.

When Red came in, Marie and Babe were sitting at the kitchen table staring at each other. Babe had an irritating sardonic smirk on his face. Marie's lips were compressed into a thin hard line. They had been fighting. Red glanced quickly from one to the other, hope in his heart. This Marie baby was some girl!

"You can have your Roy Earle," sneered Babe. "He may be a powerhouse to some people, but he's a blowed-out fuse to me."

"You'll see," said Marie. "Get out of line and you'll see."

"Yeah? All right. We'll see. And let me tell you something. You better quiet down. You're getting so you just go around asking for a smack on the nose. Stop arguing with me all the time."

There was a short silence, then Red said:

"Can you feature him being Roy Earle! Why, his hair's getting grey around the edges and he looks sort of old and he's kind of fat around the middle. Only he ain't exactly fat, just kind of soft. Boy, he sure is a surprise to me."

"I say he's got a hard eye on him," said Marie. "He's tough, don't you worry."

"Maybe he was once," said Babe.

Red sat down and scratched his head.

"Boys and girls," he said at last, "I got bad news for you. Roy says we've got to send Marie back to L.A."

Babe jumped up as if somebody had stuck him with a pin.

"What! Why, that broken-down old son-of-a-bitch, I'll—" He hesitated and stood rubbing his chin.

Marie threw him an ironic glance.

"Yeah? There's your chance. You don't want me to go back to L.A., do you, Babe? You go tell him off."

Babe stood staring for a moment, then he sat down.

"I don't know. We need that guy. Anyway, Louis says Big Mac spent a fortune springing him. But that's no reason why he should come up here and start pushing us around." He jumped up. "Yeah, That's right. He's not the boss, no more than we are. I'll go tell that twerp he can't—" He hesitated and sat down again.

"Keep it up," said Marie. "I think you're going to win this argument."

Babe swung at her with the flat of his hand, but she drew back sharply, then got up. Red grabbed Babe by the wrist. He had a grip like a wrestler. Babe winced and tried to pull away.

"You leave Marie alone," said Red. "You go smacking her around and I'll cool you off."

Babe jerked his hand away.

"Some day I'm going to call your bluff, Red."

"Call it right now. That'll suit me."

"Cut it out," said Marie. "You won't get nothing out of fighting but a black eye. Course if you was Joe Louis . . ."

"I don't care what you say," said Babe, "Marie's not going back to L.A."

"That's what you think," said Red. "He means what he says. Another thing. He had me. He's smart. He asked me if Marie was in the know."

"Yeah?" demanded Babe, eagerly leaning forward. "What did you tell him?"

"I told him she wasn't."

"Good."

"Sure. But don't you get the idea? If she don't know nothing we can send her back and nobody's hurt. But she does know something. She knows plenty."

"I got an idea," said Marie. "You stay right here. I'll go talk to him. He's not going to send me back to that dime-a-dance joint if I can help it."

When the door closed behind her, Red said.

"Smart girl. Babe, you dope, why don't you lay off that rough stuff? You got a swell kid and don't know it."

"You're just a sap about dames, Red. You got to keep 'em in line. They get out of line mighty easy, especially the sharp ones."

Roy was sitting with his chair tipped back, smoking a cigarette, when Marie knocked and came in. The coffee and the food had revived him. He felt more like himself and had even been humming an old dance tune of the twenties. But his irritation returned at the sight of Marie. From self-consciousness she was putting on her boldest front and looked predatory. She wasn't

26

his type at all, he decided, in spite of her good build and her brunette handsomeness. She was the kind Johnny went for in the old days. Yeah, and look what it got him!

"I want to see you a minute, Mr. Earle. Can I sit down?"

"Help yourself."

He noticed that her skin was clear and that she had a shallow dimple in her right cheek when she smiled. She had a small mole on her left cheek, like a beauty mark; even, white teeth; and long black eyelashes. There was a sultriness about her looks that disturbed him, and he sat staring at the floor.

"Red says you want Babe to send me back to L.A."

"That's what I told him."

"Why? I like it here."

"Don't play dumb."

"I do. Anyway, you don't need to worry about me. I'm no fool."

"I'm not worrying about you. I'm worrying about them jitterbugs you got with you. They'll be throwing lead in a week or so. Babe's got you and Red wants you."

"Oh, I can handle them all right. Babe's tough and gets up on his ear at the least little thing, but he's afraid of Red and I can make Red think black's white. So what are you worrying about?"

Roy smiled slightly.

"Got it all figured out."

"In a way. I can give you a tip that might help."

"I'm listening."

"Louis's the one for you to worry about. He talks faster than a horse can trot and all he does is brag. That's how I got wise."

"Got wise to what?"

Marie smiled and put her hand on Roy's arm.

"I know what's coming off. I know all about it. But I didn't get it from the boys. Babe talked big money to me, that's all. But Louis thinks he's a bearcat with the women and made a strong play for me behind Babe's back. I just kidded him along, and he bragged what a big shot he was and said we'd all be wearing diamonds."

"Yeah?"

"That's the truth. So Louis's your headache, not us."

"O.K.," said Roy, beginning to understand that Marie was no chump. "We'll see how it works out."

Marie got up and stood looking at him. Her eyes had a certain power which he resisted. He compressed his lips and picked up a newspaper.

"Thanks," said Marie, then she turned and went out.

Roy threw down the newspaper.

"Yeah," he muttered. "A nice set-up. But that dame's got something on the ball. She may be more use to me than the punks."

CHAPTER SEVEN

ROY woke up sweating. Groggy from sleep, hardly conscious where he was, he began to swear under his breath. Another night sweat! Long hours of wakeful loneliness! He was getting to the place where . . . but no! He was sweating because he had three heavy blankets on top of him. It was morning. He glanced at his watch in unbelief. Nearly eight o'clock. He'd slept almost twelve hours. Outside, a perky little bird was singing in a bush and a cool gentle breeze was blowing in through the open window, stirring the curtains. Roy flung off the blankets and sat up, the bedsprings making quite a noise. The little bird cocked his head at the sound, then flew away. In between the huge trunks of the pine trees Roy could see a pale blue sheet of water: Eagle Lake. The sun turned the small ripples to silver. Gulls were flying low above the water, screaming, their parrot-like cries carrying a great distance in the thin, sparkling mountain air.

"I feel swell," said Roy to his reflection in the mirror as he shaved. "By God! No fooling! I feel swell. Nothing like sleep to set you up. And then this joint ain't bad. Not bad at all."

He began to hum a tune, a scrap out of his past.

> *Nothing could be finer*
> *Than to be in Caroliner*
> *In the mor-hor-hor-ning.*

Roy used to sing baritone to Johnny's tenor. At one time he'd thought he was quite a singer. But the prison ironed all that out of him. You didn't sing with bars in front of you. That took a canary. He lingered a little over the high notes. . . . There was a guarded knock at the door. Roy started as if he'd been caught in some shameful act.

"Yeah?" he said toughly.

There was a short silence, then a piping, drawling voice called:

"Mawnin'. This is me. Algernon. I'm the cullud boy who wuks fo' Mistah Shaw. Jest going around to see if people want anything."

Roy wiped the bits of lather off his face and opened the door.

There stood a short, saddle-coloured Negro with oiled, kinky hair, and a dog.

"Hello."

"Hello, mistah. I ain't seen you yit, but I heard you got in. Anything I kin do fo' you this mawnin'?"

"You can rustle me up some breakfast."

"The lady next do' got yo' breakfast all ready. She thought maybe I just sort of ought to see if you was stirring around. Yessuh."

Roy had put on his shirt while Algernon talked.

"Boy," he said, "where did you ever get a name like Algernon?"

"The old lady thought it up. Pip, ain't it? Yessuh. It kind of gives me class. Most cullud boys is named Tom or Ed or something like that. I'm Algernon. How you like this dog?"

Roy glanced at the dog, which was sitting patiently on its haunches, staring into the cabin. It was a mongrel, a small white dog, probably half fox-terrier and half bull-terrier, with faint light tan markings on its head and very pale, shrewd eyes of a yellow cast.

"Just a dog, ain't he?"

"Nossuh. He's a mighty fine dog, he is. Watch now." Algernon turned, looked off towards the lake, and cried: "Ducks! Ducks!"

The little dog was instantly alert. He jumped to attention and raised his ears. Roy saw the muscles rippling under his fine white coat.

"Down," said Algernon. The dog dropped. "You see? He's a mighty fine animal. Yessuh. Some of the men take him hunting with 'em. He'll get a duck no matter where he lights. Swim right out in the lake after him or anything. Yessuh."

"Kind of proud of your dog, eh?"

"Oh, he ain't my dog. He ain't nobody's dog. He's kind of took to me and follows me around. Sometimes I get kind of worried about it."

"Why?"

"Well, you see, this here dog – his name's Pard – he used to belong to a woodcutter who stayed up here.the year around. Most people go away. 'Tain't no place to be in the winter. Gets colder than Greenland, yessuh, and snow! You never seen nothing like it. Well, last winter a big snow-slide come down, bam! right on this here man's house and killed him. Didn't kill Pard, though. So a man saw Pard kind of wandering around lonesome-like in the snow and took him in. Damn, if that man don't up and die with pneumonia. Big strapping man, too. So Pard he gets to hanging around the lodge up there – that was in the spring – and doggone if Mis' Tucker don't come down with heart trouble. Fell plumb over and I hear yesterday she ain't going to live. Nossuh. So folks around here is getting scared of Pard. They feed him and take him hunting, but they don't want no part of him fo' their dog. Yessuh it's kind of sad, now, ain't it?"

Roy squatted down and called the dog over to him. Pard came warily, studying Roy with his pale, shrewd little eyes.

"He's no fool, that dog," said Roy. "He's got a keen look."

"Yessuh. He sho' has. But it's kind of sad, all the same. I don't know what he's going to do this winter. There's a man wuks fo' the State Highway Department; he's going to stay up here all winter, so I guess I'll just have to give him a buck or two to look after Pard. I won't be here, myself. I get out in November while the getting's good. Yessuh. It's going to cost me two bucks; but what I say is, I love this here little ol' dog."

Roy was rubbing Pard's ears.

"Sit up," said Algernon.

Pard sat up. Roy smiled slightly.

"Looks to me like you two have a real good pan-handling act."

"Nossuh," said Algernon, looking hurt. "I'm just telling you all about Pard in case you might want him fo' yo' own dog. I declare I get kind of scared sometimes at night when I think what happened to all them other people. Doggone! Little ol' Pard follows me around all day long."

"Are you in again?"

Roy glanced up. It was Marie. She was carrying a tray of food. Algernon quickly relieved her of it and took it into the cabin.

"Hello," said Roy.

"Hello. Is Algernon breaking your heart with that story about this mutt here?" She indicated the dog with the toe of her shoe.

"It's the God's truth," said Algernon, arranging the dishes on the table, then hesitating.

Roy gave him a quarter. Pard came in quickly and when Roy sat down at the table he ambled over and stood looking up expectantly.

"A born panhandler," said Roy, giving Pard a piece of toast.

"He won't eat that," said Algernon as Pard dropped the toast on the floor.

"Everybody around here stuffs that mutt till he's getting so high-hat he won't eat anything but meat," said Marie.

"That's the truth," laughed Algernon.

"Pard," said Roy, "I got a real appetite myself this morning. you're out of luck."

"Excuse me," Algernon interposed. 'If they ain't nothing else I kin do fo' y'all I better be getting up to the store. Pard'll stay, won't you Pard?"

When Algernon had gone, Roy said:

"Where's your boy friends? Sit down. Have a cigarette or something?"

Roy was surprised how amiable he felt; and it wasn't only that; Marie looked mighty good to him this morning. She had on a pink house-dress and not very much make-up; sort of domestic, as a matter of fact. Her bushy black hair was shoved carelessly back over her ears and she looked fresh and young.

"They're out fishing," said Marie. "About all they do is fish. Can you imagine guys like that! They fish all day and lie all night about big ones that got away. Yeah. It's sure funny."

Roy bent down and gave Pard a strip of bacon. Pard sniffed it for quite a while, then ate it condescendingly.

"Spoiled," said Roy. "Lives on the fat of the land, that dog."

Marie laughed.

"Algernon's really kind of scared of Pard. No fooling. All them people died or something, and Algernon gets to thinking he's next. But he sure gets a lot of money out of people with that story. Pard's his meal ticket."

Pard knew they were talking about him. He looked from one to the other, then solemnly sat up. Roy gave him another piece of bacon.

"Last night," he said, "I was feeling lousy. I'd've fought a bear if he'd spit at me. This morning I feel O.K."

"Yeah," said Marie, sitting down and lighting a cigarette. "You sure looked kind of all in. What you want to do is get out in the sun. You're awful pale."

Roy glanced at her. She was studying his face and he thought he noticed concern in her eyes. The old business? Maybe. All the same, Marie wasn't a bad-looking kid.

"Yeah," he said with a short, grim laugh. "They wouldn't let us out in the sunlight where I been staying. Afraid we'd spoil our girlish complexions."

"Stir must be awful."

"It ain't a picnic. Sometimes it's worse than others. Get a mean screw down on you and unless you got plenty guts you might just as well get up on tier 2 and jump off. Some of 'em did."

"I don't get you."

"Top row of the cell-block. It's a forty-foot drop and you land on concrete. I seen one guy take the dive. When the parole

31

board meets it's hell. This guy thought sure he was going out. But the board thought different. Five years more for the guy, and five years in that joint ... well, so he does a jackknife on to the concrete. Made quite a splash."

Marie shuddered and winced.

"That's awful."

"He just couldn't take it. I was doing the book, myself."

"Life?"

"Yeah. But I got a break."

"The boys said Big Mac got you out."

"That's right. It was sure good news and I wasn't expecting it, which made it better. It's when you expect it and don't get it, it really hurts."

Marie looked at him with interest. Between her parted lips he saw her even white teeth. He liked her mouth. It was pretty but firm. Nothing babyish, loose, or sappy about it. It had character. He noticed how slim and well cared-for her hands were. But suddenly he remembered Velma, poor kid, in her yellow blouse and red hair-ribbon; he saw her thick blonde hair and her pretty blue eyes; he saw again that sad, wistful something in her face he couldn't express to himself, and Marie was obliterated. She was just another girl. Keen, maybe. But not one in a thousand.

"What did you do?" asked Marie.

"What do you mean, what did I do?"

"Well, you knew you were in for life. I'd think you'd just go nuts."

"Some of 'em do. Lots of 'em. A lot more than the people outside ever know about. But not me. I got the jitters bad, I'll admit. I still got 'em. But all I thought about was a crash out. I tried it once at the Prison Farm when they moved me out there for good behaviour. But the fix slipped and a screw put the blast on me. Yeah, and what was worse, they moved me back behind the big walls. We was just getting ready for another crash out when I got pardoned."

"I get it. You always hope you can get out. That keeps you going."

"Yeah," said Roy, looking at her with interest. "That's it. You got it."

"I know. I been trying to crash out all my life."

"What do you mean?"

"Well, we got nothing in our family but no-good men. My old man's on relief up in Frisco and so's one of my brothers-in-law. The old man used to get drunk a couple of times a week and kick us all around. My old lady would just grin and bear it. But not me. I just waited for my chance and beat it. I crashed out."

Roy grinned.

"Yeah. I get you."

"I come down here to L.A. and got a job in a dime-a-dance joint. It was a living, but I got pretty sick of being pawed by Mexicans and Filipinos and a lot of stinking old men. So Babe came along and I crashed out."

"Thinking up another crash?"

"Maybe."

Roy ate in silence for a long time. When all the meat was gone, Pard opened the screen door with his nose, went out, and lay in the tall grass in front of the cabin.

"You know," said Roy, "Pard's some dog at that. He knows what he wants, and when he gets it, he scrams."

"You like it up here?"

"I sure do. That's the best night's sleep I've had in six years."

"It got me at first."

"What did?"

"The altitude. It's around eight thousand feet. My heart done tricks. I was short of breath all the time. Couldn't hardly walk around. Now I'm O.K."

"Well, it suits me. Say, whose idea was it in the first place to come up here?"

"Louis Mendoza's. You see, it's handy to Tropico Springs and there's no cops. Hick peace officers, that's all. Nobody bothers you up around the lakes. It wasn't a bad idea."

"Maybe not. I thought it was daffy when I was driving up here."

There was another long silence. Marie kept studying Roy covertly, but he paid no attention to her and seemed sunk in thought. Finally she got up with a sigh.

"Well, I guess I'll take the dishes back."

"Might as well. Thanks for the chow."

Marie glanced at him, hesitated, then went out with the tray.

CHAPTER EIGHT

After a brief talk with Babe and Red that night, Roy went to his cabin about nine o'clock and got ready for bed. It was a cold clear night; there wasn't a cloud in the sky. The stars sparkled brightly in the thin mountain air. From time to time the cry of a gull drifted up from the lake. A sudden feeling of loneliness

33

came over Roy. Here he was a mile and a half up in the air, on the roof of the world; the thought of it made him a little dizzy. The heavy silence of a remote place pressed on his eardrums. Shivering in the chilly night air, he opened his window, then jumped into bed, pulling the blankets up to his chin.

In the darkness, in a vivid flash, he saw old Barmy's thin wise face. Dead and buried now, poor guy! What was it he'd said about being buried? Yeah. Barmy said when they planted him he'd be wearing "the turning globe" for an overcoat. Now, who'd think of a thing like that but him? It made you see the little earth lost in space, turning slowly through the night.

Roy shivered.

"Sometimes," he told himself, "I wish I'd never talked to Barmy so much. The things he said kind of upset a guy. They sure do."

He lay there trying to go to sleep but wakeful through dread. He was afraid the night-depression he suffered from at irregular intervals was going to attack him. It was something a guy couldn't fight against.

He heard a sudden noise he couldn't identify, and sat bolt upright. Something had jumped through the window into his room. He felt a movement at the foot of his bed. Some small animal – Pard! Roy laughed and reached down to pet the dog, which had already curled himself into a warm ball of fur. Roy lay back, sighed and fell asleep. In a little while he and Pard were both snoring.

CHAPTER NINE

When Roy came in, the three of them were playing pick-up rummy with Louis Mendoza. Roy held the screen door open for Pard, who was right at his heels as he'd been all day. Algernon had noticed the dog's attachment to Roy, and while it hurt his feelings a little, he felt relieved. He told some of the men loafing in Shaw's general store that the new fellow'd better fish the banks and watch his step. "He better never go out in no boat. That little ol' dog has put the hex on him fo' sho'." The men all laughed and Algernon laughed too, as if he was kidding, but in his secret heart he had a dread of the supernatural. "Sometimes," he told old Shaw one night. "that little ol' dog's eyes git a funny kind of shine to them."

Red was winning and there was a wide grin on his ugly face;

Marie was yawning over the game; Louis played with elegant indifference, throwing his cards out with studied, very genteel movements of the wrist; but Babe, who always played to win, was losing and his face was pale with suppressed rage; his lips were set in a peculiar way as if his teeth were on edge, and there was a mean look in his eyes.

Red splashed, then rubbed his hands with glee. They were playing a penny a point and he'd caught them all with plenty.

Babe jumped up and slammed down his cards.

"Such goddamn dumb luck," he cried.

"Boy, oh, boy!" crowed Red. "Am I good or am I good!"

"Just plain dumb luck."

Louis Mendoza stood up to shake hands with Roy. He was a tall, slender Mexican about twenty-five years old. He was dressed in the Tropico Springs manner and Roy whistled under his breath at his finery. He had on a yellow polo shirt, a red and brown striped, V-neck pullover sweater, cream-coloured, balloon-legged slacks, and oyster-white buckskin shoes. He had patent-leather hair, a wisp of a moustache, and air of bored superiority. He irritated Roy, who quickly pulled his hand away from the Mexican's grasp and nodded curtly.

What Roy didn't know was that Louis, who had been working as a night clerk in the swanky Tropico Inn for three seasons, had been disorientated by the impact of the very "smart" and the very rich.

The first season Louis felt so inferior to the people he waited on, people who thought nothing of spending fifty dollars a day just to live, that he could hardly look anybody in the face, and he got so silent and morose that none of the other help would have anything to do with him.

The second season he spent all his money on clothes, paying as high as seventy-five dollars for one sports coat. It didn't help much. His coat of Harris tweed, cut in the most fashionable style and beautiful to look at, was no armour against the unconscious insolence of the big-time actors and actresses or the California and New York socialites who made their headquarters at the Tropico Inn. He might just as well have had on a fifteen-dollar ready-to-wear.

At the close of his third season he got a job, for the summer, as croupier on a gambling boat off the southern California coast. He was big stuff out there. He high-hatted the mugs with impunity and bragged at length about his Tropico connections. Little Ed Seidel, one of the biggest gamblers, fixers, and shady promoters on the Coast, got interested in him and introduced him to Big Mac M'Gann, who was in Los Angeles looking around.

In spite of his bragging, Louis hated Tropico; he hated the smugness of the rich people who frequented it; he was filled with malice and envy; he wanted to hurt and astonish the men and women he served every night, who barely nodded to him, never looked directly at him, didn't know he existed. One evening he drank a little too much in Big Mac's company and began to talk about what an easy knock-over the inn would be. Big Mac always knew when to listen.

Roy was thinking: "Marie's right. This guy won't do. He's got no business in a big-time job like this and he may gum the works. He needs a jolt. All you got to do is look at him. He thinks Loius Mendoza's a pretty slick article. I've seen his kind before. He'd brag about killing a guy if he burned for it."

While Louis talked, Roy was watching Babe out of the corner of his eye. Babe had squatted down and was fooling with Pard. He had a cruel light in his pale eyes. He began to rub the little dog's ears. Suddenly Pard cried out with pain, but Babe laughed and wouldn't let him go.

Roy kicked Babe's feet out from under him and Babe sat down heavily.

"Let that dog alone."

Babe sprang up with a murderous light in his eyes, but hesitated. Roy's face was hard as flint and he was carrying his strong, big-knuckled hands loosely, ready for a quick, crushing blow. He stared Babe down.

"I was just rubbing his ears, that's all," Babe said at last.

"You got licked playing cards and you took it out on the dog. I saw you."

Marie watched the scene with a peculiar expression on her face. Roy was tough all right; she'd known it all along.

There was a long silence, then the tension gradually relaxed. Pard had effaced himself. He was sitting in a corner with his pale, shrewd little eyes fixed on Roy. He knew trouble when he saw it. He'd been in and out of trouble all his life. Men were unpredictable creatures who fed you one day and kicked you the next. Pard had a low opinion of men. They didn't even smell good.

Snapping his fingers, Red cried:

"I almost forgot. Louis brought us a present, and, Roy, I guess you're the engineer."

Marie made a circuit of the room to see that all the curtains were closed. Red disappeared into a bedroom and came out with a suitcase, which he opened, grinning; it had a sub-machine-gun in it.

"O.K., Roy?" he cried, holding it up.

"Mr. M'Gann's in town," said Louis. "I was in to see him today. Got a night off. He gave me the gun. Know how to work it? Red don't and neither does Babe."

Roy said nothing. He ignored Louis. Red burst out laughing.

"That's a good one," he roared. "Roy, do you suppose you could learn to use one of them things if you studied about a year or two?"

"What's so funny?" demanded Louis, flushing, hating to be laughed at.

"Why, he eats guns like that for breakfast," said Red. "Ain't you never heard of Roy Earle?"

"No, I never have," said Louis. "Anyway, I thought his name was Collins."

"Skip it," said Red. "You're so dumb you don't even know you're dumb."

"I don't like that crack," said Louis.

"You know," said Roy, pretending to pay no attention to what was being said, and gently fitting the loaded drum into place, "this reminds me of one time about six or seven years ago. We were getting ready to knock over a bank in Iowa. It rained pitchforks. We had to call it off because we never used anything but the cat roads on a get-away and they had mud two feet deep on 'em. One of the guys, a bird nobody liked, had the shakes. We couldn't figure it out. But the rain saved our bacon. We get word that this guy with the shakes has talked too much and that a bunch of coppers are laying for us down at the bank. Nobody says anything. But Lefty Jackson gets out his machine-gun. He sits down and holds it in his lap like I'm doing with this gun here. The boy with the shakes is sitting across the room from him. Pretty soon Lefty just touched the gun a little and it went 'Tut! Tut!' quick like that. The fink fell out of his chair dead, and we drove off and left him there." Roy sighed, took the drum off the gun, and put it on the floor, then he took a screwdriver and began to take the gun apart. "Yeah," he said, ignoring the long silence, "the gun just went 'Tut! Tut!' like that."

Red and Babe stared at each other uneasily. Marie smiled slightly and glanced out of the corner of her eye at Louis, who looked as if he might jump up and run at any minute. His long, coarsely handsome face had turned very pale.

"This sure is a nice gun," said Roy. "Got lots of improvements on it. I'll have to study it up a little."

There was another long silence. Marie got up and made some coffee.

Without looking up from the gun, Roy asked:

"What did Mac have to say? I didn't know he was coming out. I thought he had a guy handling the fence end for him out here."

Louis shook himself slightly as if recovering from a bad dream, then he cleared his throat and said in an unnatural voice:

"He wants to see you, Mr. Earle. He said to tell you to drop down and take a look at the Springs, then drive into Los Angeles and see him. He's at the Berwyn Arms Apartment."

"Where's that at?"

"That's in Hollywood. I guess he got sort of worried about the deal and figured he'd better come out. He flew out. Hit some mighty nasty weather. He's still sick and kind of wobbly."

"I'll go tomorrow."

"He figures you'd better make your get-away straight to Los Angeles and not come back up through here and go over the pass. The pass is mighty tough going. It's ten thousand feet up and you never know this time of year when they're going to close it. Snowed up there last night."

"I don't know," said Red. "Babe and I kind of figured the pass was the best way. Nobody'd ever expect us to cross the Sierras to get into L.A."

"Sure," said Louis. "But suppose they did get on your tail? You could never shake them off on a mountain road. Anyway, how're we going to find out in time whether you can get a car through the pass or not? Suppose it did blow up a storm while we were knocking over the place. If the pass got blocked up with snow you'd be in fine shape."

"Yeah," said Red. "That's right."

"What's your end, Louis?" asked Roy.

"I don't know what it'll amount to. Can't say."

"I don't mean the dough. You're supposed to stick, ain't you?"

"Oh, sure. I'll act like I'm scared to death if there's anybody around. When you guys get through I'll stick and report the whole thing to the police. The night bellboy won't cause us any trouble and . . ."

"You mean he's in the know?"

"Oh, good Lord, no, Mr. Earle. You don't think I'd . . ."

"I'm just asking," said Roy.

"No. I mean he's such a scary kid, anyway, he even hates

38

to go around the grounds late at night. He may be out on a call. . . ."

"We don't want him out on no call. We want him right there in the lobby. You think we want some scary kid looking through the window at us and yelling bloody murder?"

"I get you. I'll fix things."

"Don't forget it," said Roy. "You know, guys, when I first come out here I thought we had a screwball set-up, but it begins to look all right. The best thing is, none of us's wanted. Ain't that right?" Roy looked at each one in turn.

"Yeah," said Red. "You got the right dope. Louis was never pinched in his life. Neither was Babe except for 'contributing'. I'm out on parole and I ain't violated it. I mean I ain't left the state or nothing. Course I knocked over a couple of liquor-stores, but the coppers don't know it."

"How about Marie?"

"I'm clean," said Marie.

"And I was pardoned," Roy concluded. "Best set-up I ever saw that way. Generally speaking, in every mob at least one guy is wanted, and just when you got things ready to go, some dumb copper comes nosing around."

"Yeah," said Babe. " 'Contributing'! That was sure a bum rap. If it wasn't for that, no copper would ever know my name. Boy, did they hang it on me! This gal, see, was fifteen years old. But, hell, she'd been running around since she was thirteen. I got tired of her; she was a dumb rabbit; so I give her the air. She kicks up a fuss and tells her old man all about me. I was just twenty-one. That's justice for you. Why, she'd been with more guys than there are in the U.S. Navy. Swell, hunh? And I get sent to clink for 'contributing'."

"That old stuff catches up with you once in a while," said Red, laughing.

"You're telling me! No more jail-bait for this baby."

Marie put cups on the table and poured the coffee; they all sat sipping in silence. Pard came over and sat with his body pressed against Roy's legs.

"So you adopted the mutt, eh?" said Red.

"Yep."

When Roy had finished his coffee he got up.

"Come on, Pard," he said. "We'll hit the hay."

"Going?" said Marie. "Don't you want to play some cards?" Their eyes met. He thought that she looked at him more warmly than usual. He could see she didn't want him to go.

When he had gone Red said:

"Boys and girls, I'm beginning to get the idea that our boy-friend is no cream-puff."

"Yeah," said Babe. "He'd cut your heart out."

"All the same I'm glad he's in," said Red. "With him bossing things, we're a cinch."

"Who said he was bossing things?" Louis demanded.

"Nobody said so. He just is."

"Like hell he is. M'Gann's the boss. Earle hasn't got a dime. He just works for M'Gann." Louis ran a long thin hand through his greasy black hair. He felt resentful and envied Roy the impression he had created. Why couldn't he, Louis Mendoza, create an impression like that? He began to turn over in his mind what Roy had said and what he'd done. There was nothing outstanding. It was a question of manner. Louis decided that he'd cultivate quiet ways; then, suddenly, he'd lash out at people in a voice that cut like a whip.

"M'Gann's nothing but a fence, you dope," said Red. "Say, boys and girls, how did you like the little bedtime story about the gun that went: 'Tut! Tut!'? Did you all get the idea of that story?"

"You suppose he meant it that way?" asked Louis, plucking nervously at his hair.

"You bet he did," said Marie with conviction.

"Another Earle admirer," said Babe viciously, still smarting from his clash with Roy. "Who asked you to cut in?"

Marie lowered her eyes and poured herself a second cup of coffee.

"Why don't you lay off, Babe?" Red demanded. "Marie's a swell kid and you know it. Quit picking at her all the time. Start picking at me. That'll keep you busy, and that way you'll get cooled off quicker."

"Some day I'm going to call your bluff, Red."

"Right now's as good as any time."

Louis got up.

"I'm on my way. If there's going to be trouble I don't want any part of it. Why don't you fellows wait till we get this business off our chest?"

"That's what I say," said Marie. "Anyway, Roy won't like it. It will annoy him very much."

"Oh, my God!" cried Babe. "I'm fed up. I'm going to bed. Now we can't even annoy that twerp."

He flung himself into the bedroom and slammed the door so hard that a dish bounced off the shelf above the sink and fell with a crash.

"Goodbye," said Louis, opening the door quickly and going out.

"When this caper's over," said Red, "I'm through with that hunky so-and-so or whatever he is. If I don't get away from him, I'll bump him sure and I'm too young to die. Murder's against the law in this state."

"It won't be long now, Red."

"No, that's a fact. You know, kid, I like the life up here. Funny. When I first talked to Louis I thought this joint would give me the willies. But, say, if I was one of them rich guys, I'd stay up here every summer. Yeah, I sure would. And then when the snow began to fly I'd get on my yacht and sail down to the Islands where the babies shake a keen haystack and don't never say no. Look," said Red, getting closer to Marie, "why don't we blow for the Islands, you and me, as soon as we knock over the inn? We'll have plenty of dough; maybe twenty Gs. Yeah. That's a great idea. How about it, kid?"

"I don't know."

"It's a walk. You're always talking about big dough and what you'll do with it. O.K. In a little while I'll have plenty, so . . ."

"Look, Red. I don't want nothing more to do with Babe. Will you back me up?"

"Will I back you up! I'll say I will. Why, I'll spank that chump if he gets tough. Kind of falling for a certain red-headed guy, hunh?"

"Don't rush me. Don't get in a hurry. I don't know. But you're a good kid, Red," said Marie, flashing him a smile which brought a flush of pleasure to his homely face. "I like you."

"Mutual," said Red, laughing.

CHAPTER TEN

Roy drove into the outskirts of Tropico Springs at about eleven o'clock the next day. His ears were closed up and he felt irritable and uneasy. The road had dropped nearly five thousand feet in a little over twenty-five miles and this sudden change in altitude had affected him more than he had imagined it would. In fact, he'd scarcely given it a thought until he noticed that he could just barely hear the sound of the motor. He parked his car in front of an outlying drugstore and went in for a coke; he thought the act of drinking might open up his ears.

"Coke," said Roy so loudly that the counterman jumped and

41

a woman standing at the magazine-rack turned to stare.

"Yes, sir," said the counterman, moving with alacrity.

Roy was experiencing a new form of loneliness and he did not like it. His nerves on edge, he began to have visions of himself permanently deaf. That would be the final touch. But suddenly his left ear popped, then after a moment his right. The world rushed at him with its chaotic medley of sounds, sounds which ordinarily he wouldn't even be conscious of. Before the man came with his coke, he had re-adjusted himself.

"Is that all?" asked the counterman, covertly studying Roy.

"Yeah." Roy noticed the counterman's furtive glance and said: "I didn't know how loud I was talking a minute ago. My ears was closed up."

The counterman grinned, reassured. He'd been imagining things. Either this big, sort of farmerish-looking guy was nuts or he was sore as hell about something. At times Roy's face had an implacable look to it which marked him out from the ordinary run of citizens. He himself was but vaguely aware of this. Experience had taught him that men who were supposed to be tough quailed before him. He was used to his own weaknesses and fears, and was too contemptuous of them to realize that there was a streak of mercilessness in his nature which was only too evident to others.

"Yeah," said the counterman, "it's quite a drop. It bothered me some when I first used to come here, but I don't notice it any more. Did you feel the quake this morning?"

"Quake?"

"We had a little shake about nine o'clock. A glass fell down and broke. The floor did a shimmy for a couple of seconds. Wasn't much. But there was two women in here from New York sitting at the counter and, brother, they really took it big." The counterman bent down to laugh.

"Have many quakes here?"

"Yeah, we have 'em right along. But they never amount to anything. We didn't even get much of a jolt when they had the big one at Long Beach four-five years ago. It knocked me down at that, but there wasn't no damage."

Roy sipped his coke and smiled at the counterman. He was learning. When he first came out of stir he smiled at nobody. For years an impotent snarl had been his characteristic expression, and for this reason his mouth was higher on the right side. He didn't realize that even now his smile was wry and grim. He meant to be friendly, and that's the way the counterman took it.

42

"Driving through?"

"Yeah," said Roy. "Some place!"

"It sure is. Nothing like it in the world, I guess. People come here from all over. Tropico sure gets the publicity. Sometimes we're lousy with royalty. Last year an Indian Prince sat right where you're sitting now. I don't mean an Indian like we have around here. A what-do-you-call-it – Hindu. Nice fellow, too. I heard he had twenty trunks full of clothes, and it cost him a hundred and fifty bucks a day at the inn. I didn't see no harem, though. Those guys have harems, don't they?"

"You got me, pal. Well, I'll be moving."

"Going east, huh? Well, good luck. I hope your ears don't close up any more."

The counterman's friendliness pleased Roy and he thought about that guy out at the filling-station in the middle of the desert. What was his name? Ed!

"Yeah," said Roy to himself as he got into his car and drove off towards the centre of town, "I guess I could've been a little more friendly to him, but I wasn't thawed out then. I ain't yet, but I'm improving."

The magnificence of Tropico Springs awed Roy. He'd seen a lot of desert towns on his trip west, but they were all dumps. Crummy-looking, sun-baked, hopeless little places straggling along the transcontinental highway. But Tropico was like a dream-oasis. Towards the east there was mile after mile of burnt-up country, ridged with tufted sand dunes, a real desert which reached unbroken to the violet line of the horizon. North and south the desert floor rose gradually to the lower slopes of humped-up, barren foothills, which changed colour as the sun moved across the sky, red in the morning, an ugly brown at noon, violet at sundown, and blue in the swiftly descending desert twilight. At the western end of town a gigantic, stony mountain rose steeply nine thousand feet above the roofs of Tropico, dwarfing the place and making pygmies of its inhabitants. Enclosed by this burnt-up, hostile environment, the town bloomed like the oases of the Koran.

Tall palm trees lined the streets and drives; there was the welcome sound of running water; lawns were green; and the desert sun shone down on immaculate white stucco houses with red tiled roofs, on flagged patios where fountains played and time seemed to sleep, on smart shops and rambling expensive hotels, on people who dashed about on bicycles and on horseback, dressed in all the colours of the rainbow or in practically nothing.

43

Roy looked with awe at the almost naked, slender women and girls, most of them blonde; at the sunburnt, nonchalant men. He felt old and a rank outsider. What was Roy Earle to such people? Less than nothing. He could drop dead at the main corner and they would shrug and step daintily around him.

He parked in front of a sign which read: *Tropico Inn Coffee Shop*, and sat in his car staring at the big rambling hotel, its white stucco walls gleaming among the tall palm trees on its immense lawn. It was set well back from the street south of the coffee shop, which fronted on the sidewalk, where there were a lot of tables filled with smartly dressed people protected from the hot sun by big blue and red beach umbrellas.

Roy studied the hotel grounds for a long time, then he drove slowly up to it along its palm-bordered drive. There was a huge plaza in front of it parked almost solid with shiny new cars, many of them of foreign make. Roy tried to keep his mind on his business, but he couldn't help running his eyes over the parked cars. Some of them had hoods as long as his whole car.

Roy whistled.

'Well, boys, we really picked out a job for ourselves this time. I don't think the guys realize what kind of a noise this is going to make in the newspapers. Wow!"

Following Louis's instructions, he turned from the plaza into a narrow road which led to the polo field and to the driveway he'd seen on the get-away chart. Not bad; not bad at all. It led, without a turn or hindrance of any kind, to a smooth highway which wound off towards Los Angeles and safety, or to a cross-road where you could hit for the High Sierras if things got hot. Roy noded to himself. "The Mex's no fool at that. If the roads O.K. from here on, we got nothing to worry about. I'll look into that later, on my way in."

Roy had no reason to stay in Tropico any longer. Now was the time to take the Los Angeles road. But he was not ready. He wanted to get a glass of beer and stare at the sights. A guy didn't get into a joint like this every day. It was really something to write home about.

He drove out into the main street and started south. Idling along, he searched for a place among the bars and restaurants that didn't look too "swell"; he was in awe of the town and its inhabitants and was afraid of being stared at. Girls in shorts flashed past his car on bicycles; some of them were burned a deep tan and they surely struck the eye with their dark bodies and their pale blonde hair. They waved at people on the sidewalks, who waved back.

One of the girls was laughing and Roy glanced at her guardedly. She didn't know he was alive. She was talking to one of her friends.

". . . right in the middle of the street," she was saying. "Down there. Look at the crowd."

Roy saw a crowd at the next corner. The street was blocked. He wanted to avoid whatever it was, but there was no way to get off the main street without making a U-turn, and that was impossible as the street was cluttered up with bicycle-riders, people on horseback, automobiles, and pedestrians. He pulled into the curb and sat waiting, but the crowd increased. Muttering impatiently, he jumped out of his car and went to see what was wrong.

A model-A Ford was crossways in the street. Water was pouring from underneath it, flooding the pavement; one of its front fenders was crumpled up into accordion pleats. Three men were pushing a big, cream-coloured car over to the curb; it had a busted headlight and a lot of scratches on its immaculate body.

"Yeah," one of the men was saying, "people with cars like that don't care how they drive. If they hit you, they hit you! They've got no money; they've got no insurance. It's murder."

"Tough luck, Marty."

"He's just an old dod or I'll take it out of his hide. Back she goes into the garage and I'll get a bill a mile long."

"Yoo-hoo," called one of the bicycle girls, "how are you doing, Marty?"

"She thinks it's funny."

Roy stared. In the middle of a group of arguing men was a familiar figure. It was Pa Goodhue. His coat was off and he had sweat through the back of his blue shirt. He looked exhausted and bewildered.

"It was, the girl," one man was saying. "I was standing right over there on the sidewalk. You know you weren't driving yourself, Pop."

"I was. I was," said the old man, stubbornly nodding his head.

Roy saw Ma Goodhue sitting in the back seat with Velma. Ma's face was red and she looked as bewildered and exhausted as her husband. Velma was staring defiantly, but in a moment she put her head down and began to cry. Roy gritted his teeth. He knew what he should do. He should beat it. This had the makings of a first-class row, and he was in no position to get involved in something that might bring the police.

"What's an outfit like that doing in Tropico, anyway?" observed a man contemptuously.

45

Roy tried to restrain himself. But it was no use.

"That's a state road, ain't it?" he demanded, turning on the man.

The man recoiled.

"Why, I suppose it is," he said.

Roy shoved his way to the centre of the crowd.

"What's wrong, Pa?"

The old man gave a gasp and his stare of bewilderment changed to such a look of joy that Roy was glad he'd jumped in; glad he'd taken a chance on blowing the biggest opportunity he'd ever had in his life. The poor old boy was about at the end of his rope. Taking the rap for his granddaughter and getting hell for it from this bunch of smug bastards. The old man had guts. He was the right kind.

"I – we – I guess I wasn't quite . . ."

"Don't admit anything," said Roy quickly. "All right," he cried, turning to the men crowding round Pa, "some of you guys give me a hand. Let's get this car out of the street." Nobody moved. "Come on. What's wrong?"

A couple of men stepped forward uncertainly and together with Roy pushed the old car over to the curb behind the big cream-coloured car.

"Hello, Ma," Roy said, touching his hat. "Don't you worry. We'll get things fixed up." He felt a sudden rush of emotion. It might have been his own old lady; she'd had just such a patient expression. He glanced at Velma, who was wiping the tears from her eyes.

"Thanks," she said.

Marty, a dark-faced little man in a white polo shirt and green, balloon-legged slacks, came up to Roy.

"Friends of yours?"

"Why?"

Marty studied Roy's face.

"I just wondered. I know I've no chance to collect. But I'm just curious. You know. I pull out from the curb and wham! I get it. Is that cricket? Look at my car."

"Pa said he didn't see you make no signal. Talk about collecting, brother," said Roy, "you be careful or you might have to pay off."

Marty shook his head solemnly.

"I get it. A wise-guy in our midst. All right, boy. Have it your own way. We'll just write the whole thing off to experience."

Roy heard the scream of a siren and compressed his lips. Coppers! A radio car pulled up at the curb and a big red-faced policeman got out and pushed his way through the crowd.

"What's the matter, Mr. Pfeffer?" he demanded.

"I got clipped," said Marty. "But I'm satisfied as long as this big guy is. It's all right, Mack."

"What a jalopy!" said Mack. "Them's the kind that causes half the trouble on the road. Your car, mister?"

"No," said Roy.

"What's your angle?"

"Friends of mine."

"Oh. Well, if Mr. Pfeffer's satisfied, I am. All right, people. Break it up. Break it up."

"That's Martin Pfeffer, the big director," somebody said.

Marty laughed and turned to Roy.

"My public. Cigarette?" He was holding out his ornamented leather cigarette-case.

"Sure. Thanks."

"Interesting face that girl's got," said Marty. "She was driving, too, I don't suppose you'd know anything about that."

"Pa said he was driving. That's good enough for me."

"Well, all I can say is, Pa's lucky. You sort of got things straightened out in a hurry. Well, no hard feelings."

"Listen," said Roy, "these people got no dough. They're trying to get to Los Angeles. The old boy lost his farm. That car's all they got."

"Stop it. You're breaking my heart," said Marty. "Look, wise-guy. For fifteen years I've been listening to sob-stories. You know why I've got money? I always say no."

"It wouldn't cost much to get that car fixed up."

"Look. I've got influence around here. I could make it mighty nasty for your friends, but I'm writing the whole things off. Is that fair?"

"Fifty dollars ought to get it."

Marty looked at Roy for a long time.

"Where's your horse, Jesse James? I'll give you twenty-five dollars and that's that."

The big policeman stepped up.

"I wouldn't do that, Mr. Pfeffer. They tell me the girl was driving, and she's crippled. See? She just got out. Shouldn't be driving."

Roy gritted his teeth. A copper was a copper! Always on the side of the big dough.

"So the girl's crippled," said Marty. "And with a face like that. Never mind, Mack. I'll take care of this."

"It's your money, Mr. Pfeffer. But if you admit you're in the

47

wrong they may sue you later. I'm just doing my duty, that's all."

"I don't admit anything. Let 'em sue. They all get nothing but headaches."

He shoved a wad of bills into Roy's hand and got quickly into his car, slamming the door.

"Thanks, Mr. Pfeffer," said Roy.

"The name's Galahad."

"Yoo-hoo," called the girl on the bicycle, "are you still doing all right, Marty?"

"Listen, darling. Your mother went to a lot of trouble to raise you. Don't annoy me too much!"

"What does he mean his name's Galahad?" Roy demanded of the girl, who laughed, then hurried off to tell one of her companions what the big hick who took Marty for some money had said.

CHAPTER ELEVEN

Pa and Roy were sitting under the trees on the auto-court lawn. Things had got straightened out and Pa was smoking his pipe and sighing contentedly. Roy wasn't so tranquil. He was still smarting from the insolence of the two coppers, who had told him to get that "junk-heap" out of town, and when Roy had asked them where the folks could stay, one of them had said: "There ain't no government camps in Tropico," and the other copper had laughed. Roy finally got a tow-car and had Pa's old jalopy taken to a garage, where it was now being patched up for the trip to Los Angeles. Then he'd bundled Pa, Ma, and Velma into his coupé and taken them to a cheap court about three miles out of town.

"Pa," said Roy, "how did you ever happen to end up in Tropico? Get off the road?"

"No," said Pa. "It was Velma's idea. She'd read all about it in one of them movie magazines. She was dead set on seeing it. Poor pet! She was gawking around looking at things and smacked right into that fellow's car. I was sure surprised when he gave you that sixty dollars."

"I only asked him for fifty. Don't worry about him, Pa. He's got plenty. He's a director in the movies or something."

"What? He is? Does Velma know that?"

"I don't know. I guess not. She was too upset to do much listening. Is she coming out pretty soon?"

"Yeah. She and Ma are washing up. You know how women are. Ma's pretty bad, old as she is. But Velma won't answer the telephone without powdering her nose and putting that stuff on her lips." Pa laughed and spat.

"You know," said Pa, "I'm kind of glad to get out in this country. I've heard about it all my life and I always wanted to see it before I died. Now I'm getting my wish. I had an uncle who came out here in the Civil War days." Pa puffed on his pipe, stared off across the desert towards a pale-blue smoke-tree at the edge of the road, then went on talking.

"Yeah," said Roy, paying little attention to the old man and wondering why Velma didn't come out.

". . . born in '69 I was," Pa was saying, "and, Roy, that's a long, long time ago. My father fought all through the Civil War in the Ohio Volunteer Cavalry. I did a little fighting myself in the Spanish War. Fought mosquitoes mostly, however. That wasn't no war at all. That was a skirmish. I get a little pension, though, and it comes in handy. I had a couple of sons that would've been of age for the Big War, but we had a flu epidemic back in Springvalley and we lost 'em both. My daughter was a good bit younger. She's Velma's mother. You know," Pa went on, "I'd never pick you for a big-city fellow, Roy. You said you was from Chicago, didn't you?"

"I come out here from Chicago, but I'm really from Brookfield, Indiana. Was born there. Went to school there."

"Little town?"

"Yep."

"I knew it," said Pa, striking his thigh. "I told Ma out in the desert you was our kind of folks. Yes, sir. I can always tell. Son, I was mighty glad to see you down there on that damned street when everybody was yelling and pushing. Was you in business back in Chicago?"

Roy hesitated. If another man had asked him that question he'd have cut him off short. Pa was different.

"Yeah. I was in the plumbing business. Sold out and come west. My health went back on me."

Pa nodded slowly.

"Yeah. That time out in the desert I thought you was looking a little peaked. Now you look better. Getting sunburnt."

"I feel better."

There was a long silence. Pa smoked tranquilly and stared off across the desert, humming to himself. Roy got up.

"Pa," he said, "I got to be going. Got to drive into Los Angeles on business."

49

"Sit down. Sit down. We'll have supper by and by. Business can always wait. I want you to eat with us, Roy. Ma will cook us up a nice supper. It's the least we can do after you've been so nice to us. Why, son, you saved our life. When Velma smashed into that car I had thirteen cents in my pocket and a five-dollar bill in my shoe. We could have made it all right, only Velma wanted to see Tropico Springs. Course the women didn't know, and don't you tell 'em."

Roy laughed, the first real honest-to-God laugh that had come out of him in five years, and sat down.

"Pa," he said, "you're all right."

Pa grinned and winked.

"Two of a kind. That's us. I knew your quality the first time I talked to you. Matter of fact, you look sort of like the Goodhues. Same kind of stock, I guess. Got any foreign blood?"

"Not a bit," said Roy. "My folks helped settle Morgan County. I had two grandfathers in the Civil War."

"You see?" said Pa. "And between ourselves, while we're talking, I'm mighty proud I'm what I am. I don't do no bragging. But inside I feel proud, though we don't amount to a goddamn any more."

Roy sat smoking, glancing from time to time at the cabin where Ma and Velma were.

"Velma's not like the rest of us," said Pa. "She's pretty as a picture and sensitive. Her mother wasn't like us neither for some reason. Her father wasn't worth the powder to blow him up. He played the trombone in a circus band. I didn't want Mabel to marry him. That's my daughter. But she just would, no matter what I said. He died in a couple of years. Lungs. I'm glad she did marry him, though, on account of Velma. If Ma and I didn't have her we wouldn't have nothing."

Roy hesitated.

"Excuse me, Pa. What's the matter with Velma's foot, or should I ask? I guess it's none of my business."

"Oh, that's all right. It's a clubfoot. She was born that way."

"Can't nothing be done about it?"

"Well, one time a doctor told us we could get her operated on. That's when she was little. But Mabel's so scary, and so is Velma. They carried on so we just didn't do anything. Last few years I been so broke we just barely had enough to eat. I finally had to let my farm go. Charley Sutcliffe, at the bank, carried me as long as he could. I had a right nice farm. Good land. But farming's nothing any more, anyway . . ."

"Surprise," said Ma. "Come and get it."

Pa struck his thigh and laughed.

"Them women! They was in there so long I was pretty sure they was up to something. Come on, Roy. We'll eat."

"It's early yet," said Ma, "but we're hungry and we thought you'd be. Anyway, a little food never hurts."

Pa laughed.

"Ma's hell for food. She used to put me up a lunch to take on the train when I'd go to the county seat. It took an hour and a half." Pa bent down to laugh.

"Yes," said Ma, "and you'd start eating it before the train pulled out of the station."

But Roy was paying no attention. He was looking at Velma. She had on a blue and white checked house-dress, and her thick blonde hair was nicely combed and tied up with a white ribbon. She smiled at him shyly.

They sat down at the little table. To hide his embarrassment Roy picked up a spoon and began to polish it with a paper napkin.

"Those spoons are clean," said Ma. "I washed them myself."

Roy blushed and stared uncomfortably at the table. When he glanced up he saw that Velma was blushing too, and looking at him with some concern.

CHAPTER TWELVE

After supper they all sat out under the trees. Pa smoked his pipe and Roy lit a cigarette. He knew that he ought to go; Big Mac would be wondering what had happened to him; but he couldn't tear himself away.

"Look at the stars," said Velma. "I never knew there were so many stars in the sky. Back home you can't see them like that."

Roy looked up and began to rummage in his memory. The sky was a velvety blue-black covered with flashing diamond-points of light. Far overhead, lost in the dark immensity, curved the wide powdery path of the Milky Way.

Roy pointed to the zenith.

"You see that bright blue star up there? That's Vega. See how it sparkles? It's in a kind of a lop-sided square with points running up. See it? That's the constellation Lyra. . . ."

"I see it," said Velma. "How do you know?"

"A man I used to know, a pal of mine, learned me all about the sky. You see, we were out on a farm. There wasn't nothing much to do." Roy sounded apologetic; he was both proud and ashamed of his knowledge.

"It must be fun to know all about the sky," said Velma. "I used to wonder about it a lot. But I don't see how you could remember. Is that star always up there like that?"

"No," said Roy. "You see different stars at different times. The stars change with the seasons. See that other bright star sort of north-east of Vega? That's Deneb in the constellation Cygnus, I think. I'm getting kind of rusty."

"Yes, that's a beauty."

"We ought to be able to see Arcturus this time of night in September. It's west, I think. Can't find it. That mountain must be in the way."

"There's a big star farther south. See it? Do you know what that is?"

"Where? Oh, yeah. Wait a minute. That must be Altair. Yeah, I guess it is."

"Oh, they've all got such pretty names."

"Young fellow," said Pa, "you sure surprise me. You don't look like the star-gazing kind."

"It was because I didn't have nothing else to do," said Roy, very much embarrassed. "I was out on a farm and . . ."

"You hush, Jim Goodhue," said Ma. "Just because you're an ignoramus is no reason why everybody has to be."

"I never, never did see so many stars," said Velma. "It makes you dizzy just to look at them."

"It used to make me dizzy when this fellow I was speaking to you about would tell me how little the sun was and how the earth was no more than a wart on a pickle."

"Ha! Ha!" laughed Pa. "That's a good one. A wart on a pickle! But it's big enough for me. I never saw so much empty country in my born days on the way out here. I surely never did. Yes, sir. This little old earth is big enough for me."

"Good grief!" cried Ma, starting up. "What's that?"

They all stood up and stared. They heard people calling to each other in the little settlement beyond the court. A woman screamed shrilly. Low in the sky and moving slowly eastward, parallel with the earth, was a huge flaming ball of green and white fire.

"It's a plane," cried somebody. "It's burning up. It's falling."

"Good grief!" cried Ma. "We've sure seen some strange sights on this trip."

Pa's pipe fell with a clatter.

"That's no plane," said Roy. "It's a meteor, I think. But I

never seen one like that before."

"Look how slow it's moving and how bright it is," said Velma. "Do you suppose it will hit the earth?" She was standing close to Roy. He reached down and took her hand. Her fingers clung. "Oh, but it's scary."

"Now, don't you worry, honey," said Pa, his voice trembling slightly. "It will go right on past." Then, with a laugh, he added: "I hope."

Roy laughed, too, but he didn't feel like laughing. His old sense of insecurity returned. This might be the end of the world. Barmy said that stars and planets sometimes smashed into each other and busted all to hell. Just a puff of smoke and you'd be gone! He held Velma's hand tightly.

"Look," said Pa, "she's spluttering. Don't I hear a noise?"

They all stood listening, straining their ears. There was a roaring hiss, then the meteor flared up and went out. They all waited for it to hit, but nothing happened. In a moment the meteor appeared again far to the east, very low on the horizon and moving much faster, vanishing finally behind a high point in the desert floor.

Velma took her hand away and laughed.

"That's something for my memory book," she said. "Oh, I'll never forget that."

"Neither will I," said Roy.

"I got to go," said Roy after a while. "I got a business date in L.A. I sure enjoyed that dinner. It reminded me of when I was a boy back in Indiana."

"Now, Roy," said Pa, "we sure enjoy your company. I give you that address. Don't you fail to look us up. We'll be strangers, except for Mabel, and we may be lonesome, especially Velma. Some night you come and take Velma to a movie."

"Why, Grandpa!" said Velma. "You mustn't say such things. Maybe he doesn't like movies. And, anyway, why should he take me? I'm surprised at you."

Roy cleared his throat nervously.

"I'll sure do that, Pa. That is, if Velma would go with me."

"She'll go, all right," said Pa with a laugh. "She'd go to a movie with the devil himself."

"That's a nice way to talk," cried Velma.

"Pa," said Ma, "I declare to goodness the older you get, the sillier you act. Every time you open your mouth you put your foot in it."

Pa laughed and hit Roy on the back.

"Roy knows me. Roy and I are old-timers."

CHAPTER THIRTEEN

It was nearly midnight when Roy got to the Berwyn Arms in Hollywood. Big Mac had gone to bed, but he wasn't sleeping. Roy found him propped up on three pillows with a quart of bourbon on his night table, straining his eyes over the *Racing Form*.

"Hello, Mac."

"Hello, Roy. Sit down. I thought you'd get here earlier. But it don't matter. How does she look?"

"I can't see nothing wrong with it. If the boys don't blow up on me it's in the bag. But, Mac, it's going to be a big noise in the newspapers. What a joint that is!"

Mac laughed, his big belly shaking under the cover.

"Yeah. Headlines. But so what? The heat will be on for a while, then it'll die down. The insurance companies will pay off, and we'll be in the clear, enjoying life. How do you like your helpers?"

"The Mex is no good. The girl's the best man of the lot. Red's all right, too, but dumb. Kozak's a bad one."

"So they got a girl with 'em, the damn fools!"

"That's the way I felt about it at first, but take my word for it, she's all right."

Mac laughed.

"You're just out of stir. A cross-eyed dame with a wooden leg would look all right to you."

"Who said anything about looks! I mean, she's right. She's no loud-mouthed squawker. I'd take her on a caper any day before I'd take any one of the three guys."

"Well, you've sold me. Anyway, that's your headache. Roy, the pass is out. Come in the main highway unless you get a rumble, which you probably won't. Now, look. I want the glass. That's about all I'm interested in. You get your mitts on it and keep your mitts on it. Deliver it right here. If you're hot, telephone me. That's all. Now you got a free hand. You manage it. If you're sleepy, go hit the hay on the couch. I'm about ready to call it a day."

Roy hesitated for a long time. Finally he said:

"Mac, didn't somebody tell me that old Doc Banton was out here?"

"Yeah. He's out here. Why?"

54

"Used to be a pretty good doctor, didn't he?"

"Yeah. Used to peddle drugs, too, and God knows what, till they caught up with him. He's out here running some kind of a phony health service under a phony name. Never could get his licence back. Why? If you feel lousy, go get yourself a real doctor. Don't fool around with him."

"Wasn't he pretty good with a knife? Ain't he the guy that dug them slugs out of Lefty's chest after I was sent up?"

"Yeah. What's the matter? You carrying lead?"

"It's not me. I just want to ask his advice about something."

Mac turned to study Roy's face. He noticed the tightly clamped lips. When Roy didn't want to talk you couldn't pry anything out of him with a crowbar.

"I'll call up Ed Seidel for you tomorrow. He'll tell me how you can get ahold of the old Doc. Now go to bed. I can't keep my eyes open no longer."

When Roy woke up the next morning, Big Mac was already moving around, grunting and talking to himself, looking like an enormously fat woman in his dressing-gown. Without speaking, Roy lay studying him; Mac's face was pale, puffy, and lined; he seemed to have difficulty breathing; his movements were slow and laboured, and suddenly Roy realized that Big Mac, the resplendent big shot of other days, was an old man.

"... goddamn nigger!" Mac was grumbling. "Why don't he come with that breakfast? Not that I'm so hungry. Got no appetite. But, hell, I want to get it over with. Now where did I put all that change I had last night? Damned if I'm not getting . . ." His voice trailed off.

Roy shrugged. Mac had slipped badly. He was far along on that one-way street that has no turning; and yet here he was avid for diamonds, planning one of the most sensational knockovers in years, trying to recoup his fortunes. "Hell," thought Roy, "he's just going through the motions like me. It probably don't matter a hell of a lot to him one way or another. A guy just gets started and keeps on going till he runs down like a kid's toy."

"Morning, Mac," he said.

"Hello, Roy. I ordered breakfast sent up for both of us. I guess you can eat toast and bacon and eggs and coffee, can't you?"

During breakfast, Big Mac took a sealed envelope out of his dressing-gown pocket and handed it to Roy.

"I woke up about six o'clock. I couldn't sleep no more, so I wrote this out for you. I feel better now. That's the works. No

55

matter what happens you'll know what to do. I was careful. I didn't name no names and no places. But you'll get the drift all right. This caper means a lot to me, Roy. I spent a lot of dough setting it up and I spent a lot getting you out of stir. Is there anything hungrier than a crooked, conniving politician? A hog is delicate!"

"Thanks for springing me, Mac."

"Hell, Roy, I won't kid you. I thought you was the best there was. That's why I sprung you. I'm giving it to you straight, see? But when you get right down to it, I *did* spring you, so give me the best you've got. I need the dough bad. I'm paying alimony to two chiseling dames and I got other things I got to meet. I'm in to my ears. Look, I got the right boys behind me out here. Even if there's a rumble and they make it stick, you may not have to do no time. We got the right frame. But for God's sake, no killing. They won't stand for that and I don't blame 'em. Times have changed, Roy. Things ain't what they used to be."

"I'll watch it," said Roy. "I ain't one for blasting. You know that."

"It's them young guys. I wish I had four like you. It would be a waltz."

Mac belched and pushed his plate away from him with distaste.

"I just ain't hungry."

"How the young guys get by nowadays, I don't know," said Roy. "A bank robber is just a chump. Not like in the old days when Eddie Bentz was living on the fat of the land with not a rumble. The Feds fixed that. The city, and country coppers would listen to reason. You could talk to those guys. The Feds are different. They really go after you. And now most of the banks are Federal depositories and it's a government offence to knock one of them over." Roy shook his head slowly from side to side. "Yeah, it's getting so it's tough to earn a living."

"Yeah," said Mac. "Robbing banks is a chump profession now. You're right. Public attitude's different, too. When Johnny was running wild, a lot of people were with him. Back in Indiana, Ohio, and Illinois half the farmers were getting their farms took away from them. The bankers foreclosed till there was nothing left to foreclose. And when Johnny'd knock over one of them banks for a big wad, the farmers would yell: 'Attaboy, Johnny. You're doing fine'."

Roy laughed.

"That's no lie. Why, half the country people in the Mid-west were pals of ours. They'd never turn us up. Johnny used to go home and have dinner with his old man every once in a while, and he'd sit out on the front porch and pick his teeth and tell the old man funny stories right in broad daylight."

"Yeah. Times have changed."

Mac sighed and lit a cigar, took one puff, made a face, and put the cigar down.

"What's the matter, Mac?"

"I don't know. Nothing sets well with me any more. I'm getting so I don't even like bourbon. Yeah, times have sure changed. Now about that letter. If everything goes off all right, burn it up. But if things go haywire or if anything should happen to me, just read the letter and you'll know what to do. I used the old backwards code, you know. The one the boys used to call the Jump code."

"I got it." Roy pushed his empty plate away from him, lit a cigarette, and sat smoking and sipping his coffee. "Look, Mac. You going to find out about old Doc Banton for me?"

"Hunh? Doc Banton? What for? ... Oh, I remember. Sure. Do it right now."

CHAPTER FOURTEEN

Doc had heavy white eybrows and pale piercing grey eyes. He was running the Nu-Youth Health Institute in Hollywood and said he was doing all right. Doc was a kick.

"Roy," he said, "this is the land of milk and honey for the health racket. You go over on Hollywood Boulevard and pick out ten men, any ten. Four of them will be worrying about their health; a couple of them at least will be worrying about manhood. So I got six potential customers. Naturally, I got lots of competition or things would be too good to be true. Besides, you'd be surprised how many dames (mighty nice-looking ones and young) like to get their backs rubbed. I got a Swedish guy who really knows his holds. And then every woman in Hollywood thinks she's too fat. Of course there are plenty of fat dames out here like every place else. But half the girls who come here to get reduced are practically down to the bone as it is. You couldn't get a pound off of them with sandpaper, but we kid 'em along. Yeah, it's a nice racket, and no rumbles. Listen, if I'd come out here in the first place I'd be a pillar of respectability. You don't have to be crooked out here. You can gyp to your heart's content on the square. I got a couple of diploma-mill doctors that I wouldn't let work on my own dog. People are nuts about them. And the customer is always right. I happen to know something about medicine myself, so we manage to keep from killing anybody. Legally, I can't practice; that's why I've got these croakers. I wish I was thirty years younger. In ten years I'll be a rich man; I'll also be seventy. Life's a funny thing, isn't it? When you get what you want, you either don't want it any longer or it doesn't do you any good."

Doc reminded Roy of Barmy. He sat listening without a word.

"Now, Roy," said Doc, "I guess I've talked enough. What do you want? A massage? Or is it the old prostate? Whatever it is, I'll guarantee a complete cure." Doc bent down to laugh.

"It's – it's a clubfoot," Roy stammered.

"It's a cinch," said Doc. "We'll cut it off. Complete cure." He stared at Roy. "No kidding, Roy. Are you carrying lead? If so, I'm your man. You're one of the old-timers. A real guy. I wouldn't do it for anybody else, mind you!"

"Look, Doc. I wouldn't kid you. A good friend of mine has got a granddaughter. She's a mighty nice girl, but she's got a clubfoot. One time a doctor told the old man maybe an operation might fix her up."

"Young kid, is she?"

"Well, she's about twenty, I guess."

"Twenty! Oh, I see. Well, my advice, Roy, is to forget all about her foot. It's easy to do if she's good-looking enough, especially in the dark. Why, I used to know a woman . . ."

Roy's face reddened.

"Look, Doc. I'm not kidding. I came to you because you was one of the boys and I thought you'd steer me right."

Doc lowered his eyes and sat tapping on his desk. A chill had run up and down his spine. He'd always been a little afraid of Roy.

"Can't you take a joke?"

Roy laughed uncomfortably.

"Yeah. Sure. Excuse me, Doc."

"Now about that clubfoot. Some of them can be operated, some can't. It's mighty unusual for a girl to get to be that age with a clubfoot if anything could've been done about it. Did you ever see it?"

"Lord, no!"

Old Doc controlled his face with difficulty. Roy was actually blushing. Strange place, this world! A bank robber blushing over a girl's clubfoot.

"I can't help you without seeing it."

"Will you go take a look at it, Doc? That is, if I can talk her into it."

"Certainly, Roy. You understand I can't do any operating, but I'll tell you who to go to. It will cost you, though. You're paying for it, aren't you?"

Roy squirmed, then got up.

"Well, thanks, Doc," he said. "I'll be back in town in a day or so. I'll give you a ring."

"You do that. I'll make you a present of my fee. Old time's sake."

When Roy had gone, Doc stood stroking his chin and looking out the big front window. Absentmindedly he watched a couple of Hollywood blondes climb the steps to the Institute: reducing cases, probably, and both of them, by any normal standard, underweight now.

"Women!" thought Doc, then he laughed to himself. "Roy Earle blushing over a girl's clubfoot! Nuts about her, that's all that's the matter with him. Poor old Roy! That jolt in clink certainly aged him. Getting grey, too. Why, he can't be over thirty-seven or eight. Looks sort of hollow. Still got that something, though, whatever it is. Made me feel a little uneasy, all right."

A male nurse in a white coat put his head in the door.

"Excuse me, sir. Dr. Corson would like for you to come to Room 212."

"What now?"

"Something he wants to ask your advice about. The patient ..."

"Be right there." Old Doc chuckled to himself. Corson and his patients! They could have smallpox and he'd never suspect it!

CHAPTER FIFTEEN

After leaving Doc, Roy went into a drugstore, looked up Pa's son-in-law's number in the phone book, hesitated for a while, then called him up. Velma's mother answered. Roy tried to explain who he was, but she was not only dense but irritable.

"No," she snapped, "they're not here. Who did you say this was? Well, I don't know you. I tell you I haven't heard from them. They may be in Kansas for all I know. Oh, you saw them. Well, why are you calling? ..."

"I'll call later," said Roy. "Thanks very much."

He shrugged and drove back to the Berwyn Arms. Mac was more like himself. His lunch had digested well and he'd drunk a half pint or so of bourbon. His face had regained its colour and his expensive clothes helped the general impression. But Roy noticed how unsteady his hands were and how from time to time his head nodded involuntarily. Mac's obviously bad condition made Roy uneasy. After all, Big Mac was the boss and this was his show.

They talked about the old days for a while, and Roy drank a couple of highballs out of politeness. In prison he'd lost the taste for liquor. Finally Roy said:

"Well, Mac, I might as well be getting back if there's nothing I can do for you."

Mac grunted and handed him a sealed envelope.

"Some more dough. You may need it. Now keep them jitterbugs in line until we can get this thing off our chest, then the hell with them. They can go hang themselves for all I care. Louis'll keep in touch with me in case there's any heat, though I don't know where it'd come from. Louis'll let you know when to go for the dough. Now don't get impatient. It may be three days and it may be three weeks. You sit on the lid. That's your job. And don't let me down."

Roy was annoyed.

"I don't let nobody down."

Mac grinned hurriedly.

"I know. I know. I was kidding. How much do you think it cost me to spring you? I know all about you, son. Best there is." And after Roy had gone, he went on talking to himself: "And that's no rib, either. Things would sure be simple if a guy had four or five boys like Roy Earle working for him. Funny about Roy. He ain't like the rest of the bunch. Never was. First off you'd think he was a softy if you didn't know better. What do you suppose ever made him get wise to himself and stop being a sucker? All the rest of his family are chumps, or that's what Lefty told me. All of 'em are working two-by-four farms or else losing 'em to the bankers. Working for peanuts; getting nowhere; taking the usual pushing around that the honest little guy gets." Big Mac grunted, poured himself a drink, took a sip, and began to nod.

There was a knock at the door. Big Mac started and called: "Come in. Come in. It ain't locked."

Roy stepped back in, followed by a big man who took off his

60

hat hurriedly and smiled like a kid who wants to join in a game but knows he isn't wanted.

"Copper," said Roy. "Waiting outside for me."

"Just wanted to talk to him," said the copper. "I got nothing on him. You're Mr. McGann, ain't you? I'm Lieutenant Kranmer. Vice Squad."

"We don't want any," said Mac, and Roy laughed.

Kranmer grinned uneasily.

"A kidder, I see. Look, Mr. M'Gann, I'm no guy to butt into anybody's business, but I was thinking maybe I could do you guys some good. I seen Earle come in here once before and I got to wondering."

"Sometimes a guy's better off not to wonder," said Big Mac.

"Yeah. Sure. Don't think I'm trying to stick my nose into anything. Don't get me wrong. But, look, Mr. M'Gann, we got a D.A. that don't want guys like Roy Earle around. He's death on big-timers. Now I'm just figuring that you and Earle have got something up your sleeve. O.K. That's your business. I says to myself: 'Mr. M'Gann maybe has got a job for Earle to do.' Maybe, see? 'And if Earle gets hauled in by the D.A., Mr. M'Gann will be out of luck!' . . ."

"I got you," said Mac. "Of course, I could save myself dough by letting Roy take care of you . . ."

"Now wait a minute, Mr. M'Gann. I didn't . . .

". . . but I don't handle things that way. How much do you want, Petty Larceny?"

"Well," said Kranmer, "I figure it ought to be worth something to you, and then there's another boy I got to fix, so . . ."

"Thank God there's only one boy," grunted Mac. "There's usually six. Beat it, Roy. I'll take care of this. Wait a minute. Kranmer, my friend, I guess you know all about Roy Earle. Sometimes he gets a little annoyed when guys talk too much."

Kranmer grinned at Roy with exaggerated friendliness.

"You don't need to worry about me at all, Earle," he said. "I don't talk."

"Not unless you're paid for it," said Big Mac. "All right, Roy. Beat it."

CHAPTER SIXTEEN

Roy was surprised to find both cabins dark, for it was only about nine o'clock. But it was evident that Red and Babe hadn't gone far, as their car was parked under the big pine tree west of their cabin.

"Maybe they all hit the hay early," thought Roy as he got out of his car and searched his pockets for his door key. "Been out fishing all day, I guess."

He heard a sharp bark and turned. The moon was bright, and Roy could see, far off between the black tree trunks, the silver-blue glimmer of the lake. Pard was running towards him across an open space of meadow. He'd come out of a dark clump of bushes.

Roy bent down to pet him.

"What's the matter, pal? Been hiding out?"

Roy's door opened a few inches. He jumped back quickly and made for the side of the cabin. Pard barked and followed at his heels.

"That you, Roy?" It took him a second to realize that it was Marie speaking, there was something so unnatural about her voice.

"Yeah. What the hell! You had me scared for a minute. I don't carry no gun, so I powdered. I thought somebody was laying for me. What's the idea?"

"Pard with you?"

"Yeah."

"Come on in."

"Turn on the lights. What's the matter with you?"

Roy stepped into the cabin, followed by Pard, and Marie turned on the lights. Roy was shocked at her appearance and took a step backwards. Her left eye was nearly closed and it was surrounded by a swollen purplish bruise; there was a long gash in her chin, which she had painted with iodine.

"I'm glad Pard's all right," said she. "I thought maybe Babe killed him. I was trying to look after him for you, Roy, because I know you adopted him and . . ."

"Don't worry about Pard. Who give you that shiner?"

"Babe. He went nuts. Red tried to cool him off, but Babe fought like a wildcat. He got hold of a poker and hit Red over the head with it, and when Red was down he swung on me twice with his left hand. He could've used the poker, but . . ."

At the sight of Roy's grim face and compressed lips, Marie lowered her eyes and sat down.

"What started this brawl? Was them guys fighting over you?"

"Yeah," said Marie.

"Red was standing up for me. Babe's been getting meaner and meaner, so I told Red I wasn't going to have nothing more to do with him and Red backed me up."

"Sure, sure. Red's been waiting for the chance."

"That started the trouble. Babe come pawing around and I pushed him away. He just laughed and wouldn't let me alone, so I called Red, and Red told him how things was. Not that I care anything about Red, Roy, but ..."

Roy avoided her eyes.

"I got you. Go on."

"Babe was like a crazy man. He just lit into Red and knocked him back on his heels. My God, it was awful. Red smacked Babe down finally and kicked him all over the place. But Babe got hold of that poker some way – I don't mean a poker; I mean one of them things you lift the stove-lids up with – and he slammed Red on the head with it and then ..."

"O.K. When did this happen?"

"About dark."

"Where are they?"

"Red's got a gun hunting Babe. As soon as he knocked Red cold he beat it. He jumped in the car, but Red had the keys, so he jumped out and started running. I could hear Pard barking and I could kind of see Babe throw something at him; the lifter, I guess; then I didn't hear Pard any more and I got worried. Well, Red got up pretty soon and staggered around awhile, then he got out a gun and ..."

"For God's sake! Not the machine-gun!"

"No. They're both scared of that. An automatic. That's the last I saw of them. I run over here and locked myself in." Marie reached in the drawer of the kitchen table and took out Roy's .45 revolver. "I found this under your pillow. I figured if Babe sneaked back I could hold him off. He was like a crazy man. Makes me jittery just to think about it."

Roy jumped up, put the revolver down in the waistband of his trousers, and unlocked the door.

"Got the key to the other cabin?" he demanded.

"The door's open."

Roy gritted his teeth.

"What a bunch of screwballs! A chopper in there and two or three rods. You stay here. I'll be right back."

As soon as Roy closed the door Pard came out of his corner and sat up. Marie was different now. She was a friend. When Marie first came to Eagle Lake she'd even thrown a lump of dirt at him once because he was hanging around the cabin barking.

Marie got some cold meat out of the ice-box, and when Roy came back, carrying the machine-gun, a box of ammunition, and two automatics, she was feeding Pard, who sat up before each bite as if he felt that he had to perform for his dinner.

"Take this junk and put it away," said Roy. "I'm going out and get them guys."

Marie glanced up at him. He looked grim and hard, and his eyes had a vindictive light in them she'd never seen before.

"Take it easy, Roy," she said, jumping up. "You'll get yourself in a jam. Anyway, poor Red, he . . ."

"Shut up and lock the door behind me," he said, and went out.

It was a beautiful night, cold and clear. The stars had a frosty glitter and the sky looked vast and far away. The moonlight was so bright that he could see the snow on the barren peaks which surrounded the lake.

Roy walked briskly up the main road which led to the little settlement clustering around Shaw's general store. The door of the solitary bar-room was open, and Roy glanced in. Two fat men in fishing togs had their feet up on the rail. The mechanical Victrola was playing a plaintive Hawaiian tune. Behind the bar the baldheaded bartender was yawning.

Just beyond the bar-room Roy saw a man standing in the shadows, leaning against a telephone pole. It was Red. Roy slipped the gun out of the waistband of his pants and stepped up quickly to him.

"Roy!" gasped Red, and when he felt the muzzle of the gun presing against his side, he cried: "Wait! Take it easy. For God's sake, Roy, let me talk to you a minute. . . ."

"Where's Babe?"

"He's over in Halley's sitting around with the fishermen, scared to come out."

Roy frisked Red and took his gun away from him.

"Babe got a rod?"

"No. Not unless he glommed one some place. If he'd had a rod it'd've been curtains for me."

"You was going to bump him, hunh?"

"Well, he . . ."

"I thought so."

"Yeah, Roy, but . . ."

"You stay right here. If you scram I'll catch up with you and blow your guts out."

"Yeah – sure. . . ."

When Roy stepped into Halley's nobody looked up but Babe. A dozen men were lounging around in front of a big log fire, smoking and swapping lies about the big ones that got away. Pale and shaky, Babe got to his feet.

"Well, good night, fellows. Here's my pal. I guess I'll get going."

"Good night, son. I hope you get a ten-pounder tomorrow," said white-haired, kind-faced Mr. Halley, smiling benignly.

"Yeah, thanks," said Babe with a sickly grin.

Roy took Babe by the arm and smiled at him, but when the door closed behind them, he hissed:

"You dumb son-of-a-bitch!"

"Yeah," said Babe, swallowing hard, "I know, I know. I went nuts. Marie, she . . ."

"Blame it on the dame!"

"Look out!" cried Babe, jumping sideways. "There's Red. He's gunning for me."

"I took care of him."

Babe went limp.

"Oh, God! Thanks, Roy. He'd've set me over sure if I'd've come out."

Roy made them walk in front of him side by side. Nobody said anything. When they'd passed the last light and were heading towards the dark shadows of the pine trees they both began to lag. Without a word Roy kicked them in turn, then prodded them forward with the hard muzzle of the .45. Overhead, an owl hooted, three long ghostly cries; they both jumped, and Babe muttered:

"My God!"

Roy marched them up to the cabin and Marie opened the door. They went in reluctantly and both of them started at the sight of the machine-gun on the kitchen table. Pard, who had finished eating, stared at them for a long time, then he scratched to be let out. His hackles had risen slightly. He smelled fear. Roy nodded and Marie let him out.

"Good God! Your face . . ." cried Red, looking up at Marie.

Babe hung his head.

"There he is, Marie," said Roy. "Swing on him. Mark him up. Hit him with anything you can find. Here's a nice rough stick of wood."

Marie's eyes flashed as she looked at Babe, but in a moment her face fell.

"No," she said. "I don't want to hurt him."

"I ought to fill 'em full of holes and throw 'em in the lake," said Roy.

Marie looked at him. Little shivers of fear ran up and down her spine. She went over to him and put her hand on his arm.

"Now wait a minute, Roy. Don't hurt 'em. Let 'em go. They won't act like that again. It was my fault, I guess."

"What Mac wants with rats like this, I don't know," said Roy, shoving Marie aside. "Running around gunning for each other and taking a chance on blowing up the biggest job in the country. All right. I'll let 'em go. Listen, you numbskulls. Your car's right outside. If I was you I'd beat it. I guess you don't think much of this job. . . ."

"Jeez, Roy," said Red, "we been counting on it. We . . ."

"O.K. You still got a chance to blow. But if you stick, I'll shoot the first bastard that don't do what I tell him."

"O.K., Roy," said Red. "We get you. Come on, Babe."

They went out quickly. Roy heard them shut their cabin door, then there was a long silence. He sat down, tossed his gun on the table, and pushed back his hat. Pard scratched and Marie let him in. Pard sat looking up at Roy and after a while Roy reached down and began to rub the little dog's ears absent-mindedly.

Marie watched them out of the corner of her eye.

"I'm not going back over there, Roy," she said finally.

"No. That's no good. The trouble'd just start all over and this time somebody'd get hurt. I'll send you home tomorrow. You can get a bus into Ballard, then take the train."

"I found a cot in the woodshed," said Marie hastily. "I can fix it up and sleep here in the kitchen. I won't bother you, Roy."

CHAPTER SEVENTEEN

It was about three in the morning and the moon was just setting behind a gaunt, snow-covered peak when Roy began to roll and toss. He woke Pard, who jumped down from the bed, startled, and sat on the floor, looking up in bewilderment. Roy flailed his arms, kicked, groaned, and talked inarticulately.

. . . he was driving his black coupé at breakneck speed down a narrow, unfamiliar road full of dangerous, hidden curves.

There was an unknown girl with him, who smiled serenely, which struck him as strange, for he himself was terrified and filled with a sense of doom. He didn't know what he was fleeing from, but it was something so awful that he couldn't even force himself to think about it. The road widened. Trees and beautiful lawns began to appear. He saw big white houses set well back from the highway; children were playing and little dogs were rushing about, barking; it was a safe and happy place. Roy turned to say something to the girl. He felt fine now. The girl was very young and she had long yellow curls. "I thought you were dead," said Roy, terrified again. "I thought they buried you in the little cemetery at Brookfield." The girl's face crumbled. She had turned to ashes. It got dark. The road narrowed again. "Roy," said a sweet voice. He turned. Velma was sitting beside him, smiling serenely. "Velma!" he cried. "Where did you come from? What are you doing here? You got to go back." Suddenly a dead end loomed up. The road stopped at a blank brick wall. Roy jammed on the brakes in a panic, but machine-guns began to stutter all around him and he heard the sour whine of bullets. He turned to help Velma, but it was too late. She lay back dead, with her hands over her face. . . .

Roy woke with a start. He was sweating clammily. Little by little he oriented himself. The windows were open and a chilly breeze was blowing in from the lake.

Roy sat up and mopped his face with a handkerchief, then he lay back with a groan.

"Yeah," he told himself, "it might happen, at that. I got no business thinking about that kid, a guy like me. But wasn't it funny, me seeing Roma Stover? I don't get it."

He lay staring out into the darkness for a long time, awed by the senseless mystery of his dream.

Pard gave a little whimper and jumped up beside him. Roy patted him and rubbed his ears.

"You have 'em too, don't you, old kid? But where they come from I don't know. I sure don't."

CHAPTER EIGHTEEN

Roy rubbed his eyes and sat up in bed. Bright sunlight was streaming in the windows, little birds were singing and bickering in the bushes just outside, and from the jetty came the faint stuttering explosions of an outboard motor which was being tuned up.

Marie was standing in the doorway. She didn't have anything on but her stockings and a thin white silk slip.

"Roy," she said, "Red and Babe are outside. They want to know if it's O.K. for them to go fishing."

"Sure. Why not?"

"They look like a couple of school kids. You sure put the fear of God in them last night."

"Tell 'em it's O.K."

Marie ostentatiously wrapped a coat around her and opened the front door about a foot.

"Roy says it's O.K.," she said; then she started to close the door.

"How's your eye this morning, Marie?" came Babe's voice, very subdued.

"Better, I guess. All right, Pard. You can come back in."

Marie shut the door. Pard barked his morning greeting to Roy, then he jumped up on the bed and curled himself into a ball. Roy lay back and began to doze. He heard Marie moving around in the kitchen, getting breakfast. A pleasant feeling of contentment stole over him. Damned if it wasn't nice to be lying there in bed with Pard sleeping on his feet and a smart kid like Marie moving about in the next room. "Why, hell," he told himself. "I never felt this happy when I was a married man. I'm getting old, I guess. When a guy begins to get along, helling around don't seem so nice any more. A guy just wants to relax. Anyway, it never seemed like I was married at all when I was with Myrtle. She was out running around some place half the time. Always at me to make more dough, be a big shot, do this, do that. I don't know. Myrtle was a swell-looking dame, but she sure made a mistake when she got married. It's not her racket. Funny, though. As soon as she gives me the shake she gets hooked up again. And to a copper! I always thought Myrtle was a little screwy, but I never thought she'd marry a copper. Oh, well, that's all over and done with. It don't even gripe me any more. But I'll never forget that day in stir when I got tipped off she was going to get a divorce. If it hadn't been for Barmy I'd blowed my topper sure. A guy gets lonesome in clink. He likes to figure he's got somebody outside rooting for him. Yeah, it was hard to take. But it's all one now. I don't wish her no harm."

Suddenly he thought about Velma, and his soliloquy took a new turn. "Now take Velma. I don't know what it is, but I get to feeling all funny when I'm around her. Not like I did when Marie

68

come in here in a slip I could practically see through. It's funny. She has a look to her face that makes me feel like I want to do something for her. It's because she's a gimp, I guess. Sort of sad-looking. Like that Marty guy says: 'She's got an interesting face.' Only that ain't it either. Hell, I ought to stop thinking about that kid."

He lay remembering his dream, but it had lost most of its force now, owing to the brightness of the sunlight, the happy chirping of the birds, and the tranquil voices of the fishermen which drifted up from the lake.

"Hell," said Roy, "a dream's just a dream." He smelled coffee and toast and roused himself. "Pard," he called, "let's go see if we can't dig up some chow. Pard jumped down and stood waiting for Roy, who flung on his clothes hurriedly, then went out into the kitchen, which looked spick and span. The cot was neatly made up and shoved over against the wall out of the way; the table was covered with a red and white checked cloth, the dishes set; the curtains were tied back from the windows and the sunlight of a beautiful mountain morning was flooding the little room.

"All we need is a canary," said Roy.

Marie gave him a reproachful glance. She was looking mighty cute in her pink house-dress with a little white frilly apron tied around her waist. He patted her on the back.

"Stop kidding," she said.

"I'm not kidding," said Roy. "A canary wouldn't go bad in this room."

Marie studied his face.

"Maybe we can get one."

Roy laughed.

"Yeah. Can't you see me driving into Tropico for the knock-over with a bird-cage in the car? We may be leaving tomorrow or the next day, and when we scram we won't be back. But you're a good kid, Marie. How's chances for something to eat? Got some bacon for Pard?"

"You bet."

Roy sat down and Pard sat at his feet, waiting for his breakfast.

"I'm going to lay my ears back," said Roy. "This place really gives me an appetite."

"Here you are," said Marie, bringing the food. "Go to it."

She sat watching him eat. Pard was standing with his front feet on Roy's knee now, hungrily gulping the pieces of bacon Roy held out for him.

"That dog's got a real appetite," said Roy. "Used to be mighty finicky."

"He don't run around so much now. He stays close to the cabin. I guess he thinks he belongs to us and we got to feed him."

"Yeah. You know, Marie, I'm going back to L.A. in a couple of days if the blow-off don't come. You can go with me."

"Oh, can I? Swell. Will you take me to a movie? God, I'm hungry to see a show."

"You don't get me. I mean I'm taking you back to stay. You got no reason to be up here now."

"Well, I thought maybe . . ."

Marie lowered her eyes, took a sip from her coffee-cup, lit a cigarette, and pushed her plate away.

"I got business down there," said Roy, then he hesitated. He wanted to talk about Velma, and Marie seemed like a sympathetic audience. "Speaking about movies," he went on, feeling slightly embarrassed but urged on by an uncontrollable desire to tell somebody about Velma, "I got a date to take a girl to a show."

"Oh," said Marie.

"Yeah. She's a mighty pretty girl. Her grandfather's a good friend of mine. He asked me to take her himself."

"What's his angle?"

"He's got no angle. He's just a farmer from Ohio. Lost his farm."

"Figures you for some dough, I guess. You look sort of prosperous. You'd look more prosperous, though, if you'd keep your tie straight and get your shoes shined once in a while. Why don't you, Roy?".

"I don't know," he said, glancing down at his dirty, scuffed shoes. "My wife used to be always giving me hell. You think I'd look better? Girls notice them things, don't they?"

"Are you married, Roy?"

"No. I used to be. I'm divorced."

"I don't want to stay in L.A.," said Marie suddenly. "I got no friends there."

"You said you was from Frisco, didn't you? Well, maybe I could stake you to a ticket."

"I got no friends there either," said Marie. "I guess I just got no friends. Like Pard here. He's got us now. But we'll be going away soon."

Roy got very silent. He finished his second cup of coffee, jumped up without a word, and went out into the sunshine, Pard at his heels.

Marie bit her lip to keep from crying. She got up quickly and began to bustle about the kitchen.

The mountain lake was beautiful in the morning sunlight. A gentle breeze was blowing from the east and the water was covered with little golden ripples.

"Nice place," he said with a sigh. "Sure is."

He walked down to the jetty, where there was a lot of activity. Men were fishing from the boathouse landing and from the far end of the wharf; boats were coming in and going out; strings of trout, flashing in the sun, were being weighed; and from all points of the lake came the drowsy droning of the outboard motors.

A man getting ready to push off in a rowboat called to Pard.

"Come on, boy. Want to take a ride?"

Pard barked sharply, but didn't move.

"I guess he's adopted you," said the man, pushing off. "He used to be crazy to go out in this boat. Lots of company, too."

"Yeah," said Roy, watching the man as he rowed round the end of the wharf and headed for the far shore.

Pard barked loudly and Roy bent down to pat him.

CHAPTER NINETEEN

Roy woke with a start and reached under his pillow for the .45. The room was dark. He lay listening, wondering what had wakened him. But Pard was snoring on the foot of the bed. He was a pretty watchful little bugger. Must have been a dream.

Roy turned over. He saw something white in the darkness.

"Who is it?" he demanded.

"It's me," said Marie.

"What's the matter? Them guys rarin' again?"

"No. I'm cold."

"You got plenty of blankets.'

"No, I ain't. Feel me shivering."

"Hell," said Roy. "Naturally you're cold standing there in your shirt-tail with the window open. Go back to bed. Let me alone."

Marie began to sob. Her hand gripped Roy's tightly as if it was the end of the world and they were the only two people left.

"I'm cold and I want to die. I'm no good. Nobody wants me. Let me in with you, Roy. It's just because I'm so lonesome. Honest it is."

71

"O.K." said Roy.

Marie slid in with him. She was so cold that she shook the bed shivering. She began to cry and he lay listening to her sobs. He'd been dreaming about Velma again; and the dream was so real that it was as if she'd been in the room; he'd felt the touch of her small hand like that time when the big green meteor streaked across the sky, scaring them all.

Marie turned to him and put her arms around his neck.

"Don't take me back to L.A. and make me stay," she sobbed. "I want to be with you."

"Now look, honey. I'm giving it to you straight. I got other ideas. But I'm human. If you stick with me, you're just a lay. That's all. Did you hear what I said? Just a lay."

Marie didn't say anything.

"Pard," called Roy, "you get out of here."

CHAPTER TWENTY

Red and Babe stood at the side of the coupé grinning in at Roy. Marie came out of Roy's cabin, jumped in the car, and slammed the door.

"I got business in town, guys," said Roy. "I got to talk to Mac about you for one thing. You been doing pretty good lately and I'm going to tell him so."

"Thanks, Roy," said Red.

Roy wanted to laugh but carefully controlled his face. Red and Babe were looking at Marie respectfully. It was a kick. Just as if she was Roy's wife and they had only a bare speaking acquaintance.

"If Louis calls tell him to get in touch with Mac. And you guys stay off the booze and don't go moseying around the settlement trying to cut in on some guy's wife or daughter. Keep your noses clean."

"We got you, Roy," said Babe. "I'm sure looking forward to my cut at all that dough. Boy!"

Marie nudged Roy and pointed.

Pard was sitting on the steps in front of the cabin, looking a little forlorn.

"Hold the fort, Pard," said Roy. "We'll be back."

He turned the car in front of the cabin and started for the settlement road. Pard followed, keeping pace with the car with some difficulty. Roy turned to look. Pard was panting and his ears were flapping in a kind of pathetic way. He stopped the car and leaned out.

"Go back," he shouted, waving his arms.

Pard stopped and stood watching warily, his tongue hanging out and his sides heaving. Roy jumped out of the car, picked up a stick, and made motions with it.

"Go back. Go back."

Pard sat down.

"Oh hell," said Roy. "He'll follow us till he drops."

"Let's take him. It will be nice."

Roy scratched his head.

"I don't know. We got to leave him some time. He might just as well get used to it."

"Yeah," said Marie, "we got to leave him some time, so let's take him now."

Roy laughed.

"You sure changed. When I first come up here you didn't have no use for Pard at all."

"Pard and me are pals. Anyway, I'm happy. I hate to see Pard sitting there looking like that."

"Come on, Pard," called Roy.

The little dog gave a yelp of joy, streaked across the grass, and jumped into the car. Roy got behind the wheel, muttering to himself. Marie hugged Pard, then put him between them. He sat with his ears raised and when the car started he gave three sharp barks.

"Yeah," said Roy, "I'll be damned if I'm not collecting a family. Old Mac would think I was nuts. Who's going to look after Pard? I can't take him with me."

"Where you going?"

"You know where I'm going. I told you I had a date."

"Oh," said Marie.

"I wasn't kidding. I meant every word I said."

"Pard and I'll wait for you."

They drove along in silence, mile after mile. Roy took the dangerous hairpin turn on the way up to Broken Creek Summit with hardly a glance at the terrible abyss on his left, filled with bare, jagged red rocks and, far down, a dark green forest of pine trees.

"I'd hate to get stuck up here," she said.

"Yeah. I didn't like this place much the first time I crossed it. And that turn back there gives me the creeps."

"It always gives me the creeps," said Marie. "Before you come, the guys and I used to drive around in the car just to have something to do. You ought to see Babe take that turn. He's crazy. One time we went the other way from the l___ ___ear up to the top of the pass. I thought I was going to have to lay down on the floor or get in the rumble-seat and shut the lid. The wind was blowing up through them rocks, howling like ghosts around an old house. We was above timberline; nothing but rocks; and it was getting dark. We saw a big eagle sitting on a rock. Red took a shot at him with his automatic but never hit him. It was awful up there. I nearly died when Red and Babe stopped the car and got out and begin to climb around the rocks. They saw I was scared to death, so they made me look over the edge and I got dizzy and I would have jumped if they hadn't held me. Down below was Sutter's Lake, and it's about nine thousand feet up and it didn't look no bigger than a fifty-cent piece. That'll give you some idea how high that pass is. Babe and Red got a big kick out of me being scared, so they fooled around up there till it was pitch dark, and on the way back one of our lights went dead and there we was crawling around them curves! ... My God, it gives me a chill just to think about it."

"The dirty bums!" said Roy.

"Yeah," said Marie. "But I didn't think so then. I was just ashamed of myself for being such a panty-waist. I guess I never was really hooked up with any guys that wasn't bums, so I didn't know the difference, till I met you."

Roy glanced at Marie, then he lowered his eyes to Pard, who was lying asleep between them.

"I can't stand nobody mistreating a woman," said Roy. "Guys like that ought to be cut up for cat meat. If a guy needs a beating, O.K. Give it to him. I got nothing against that. But women – well, hell; they ought to be looked after."

"A woman that got you would be lucky, Roy," said Marie.

"I don't know. Some women like to be kicked around, I guess. But I'm no hand at it."

"It's funny," said Marie. "I never knew no real crooks till I met Red and Babe. I knew a lot of cheap chisellers and pimps. There's always a bunch of pimps hanging around those dance-halls trying to get a girl to go on the streets for them. Are they dirty rats! Red and Babe ain't like that. They're tough and when they want dough they go out and stick a gun in some guy's ribs and take it. So I thought all real crooks would be like them. When I heard you was coming and Red kept bragging what a big-timer you was, I thought you'd be like Babe and Red, only ten times tougher. I was kind of scared, but I wanted to see you, too. Well, you're just like any ordinary nice guy except once in a

74

while you seem awful tough. I used to know a guy like you up in Frisco. He was a longshoreman. He was a lot older than me and went with my sister. He thought I was nothing but a kid. Used to bring me candy. He got killed in a fight down at the wharves. Course I didn't know him very well. Roy, I don't like to ask questions; Red and Babe told me I never should; but I'd like to know how you ever got mixed up in bank robbery and stuff."

"Well," said Roy reflectively, "it's kind of hard to say. I just never seemed to fit in no place. I tried helping Elmer on the farm. But that wasn't no life for me, except a man was his own boss. I never could stand a boss. Even in school the teacher used to gripe me. And I got a bellyfull of bosses before I was through. I went three years to high school, so I had a pretty good education. I worked as a shop-clerk in Indianapolis for over a year. But there was a straw-boss over me named Crandall. He got to riding me. He rode everybody and they took it. But not me. One day I cooled him off and got canned. Same in Ohio. I worked in a chain shop and made pretty good money. But the boss didn't like me and began to give me the wrong end of the stick, so I told him off and quit. Them guys like you to be meek and mild, so they'll feel big. That was the trouble. I felt just as big as they did – bigger; even if they was the boss. Yep. I just never seemed to fit in. Pretty soon I was back working on the farm with Elmer. Elmer's steady. I ain't. I like to keep moving. I can't stand doing the same thing day after day. Lefty Jackson's brother, Angus, was working on the next farm. He was like me. One day Johnny Dillinger stopped in to see Angus. He'd just got out of stir and nobody'd ever heard of him at that time. I used to play baseball against him in high school. He was a good ball-player. We had a lot of fun sitting around talking. I don't know. Pretty soon I was with the mob. I missed the Arizona business. Angus and I got knocked over on a payroll rap. I was doing time before Johnny got bumped in Chicago."

CHAPTER TWENTY-ONE

When Roy drove up in front of a neglected-looking little frame house in the far south end of Los Angeles, Doc shook his head dubiously and shrugged.

"What a neighbourhood! You know, Roy, I'm a good friend of yours or I wouldn't be letting you waste my time like this."

"Take it easy, Doc. You're one of the boys. I couldn't ask nobody else to do this for me, could I?"

"This place gives me the jim-jams. Roy, I'll give it to you straight. You're just putting your neck out. What does a guy like you want to go and get excited over a little softy for? You got no future. You know what Johnny said about guys like you and him, don't you? He said you were just rushing towards death. Get yourself a hot young tommy you can keep moving with. And when they catch up with you, what does it matter? Outsiders are never anything but a burden. I ought to know. An outsider (nice woman, too) got me sent up. Didn't even mean to. I kept hanging around when I should have been moving."

"Oh, save it, Doc. I guess I talked to you too much. Told you my business or else you figured it out. You remind me of a con-man I was in stir with. Always giving me good advice. Maybe I ain't got a future. But I got a present and that's what I'm interested in."

Old Doc sighed and got out of the car. A heavy fog was rolling in from the west, almost blotting out the dim street-lights.

"I talked to the old man over the phone," said Roy. "He thought it was a good idea. He'd probably talked 'em into it by now."

The house looked dark and uninviting. A crack of light was showing behind a crooked window-blind. Pa opened the front door when Roy knocked.

"Hello, Roy," he cried, beaming. "Come in. Come in."

"Pa, this is Doc – this is Mr. Parker of the Nu-Youth Health Institute. He's kind of an expert. Knows his stuff."

"Proud to know you, Mr. Parker. Mister? Ain't he a doctor?"

"I'm a specialist," said old Doc, smoothly.

"Yeah? You are? That's fine. I might know Roy would do things right. He's that kind. Come in and meet the folks."

He escorted them into a dingy, badly lit box of a room filled with ugly furniture. Ma was sitting by the only light, with her glasses to the tip of her nose, darning socks. Velma's mother, a faded woman with a peevish face, which once must have been handsome, rose from a couch and stood staring suspiciously. Velma's stepfather, a big solid-looking man of forty-five, with a thick-set body, a bald head, and a ragged dark moustache, looked up from his paper, grinned, then got up slowly.

Velma had on a yellow dress and there was a yellow ribbon in her hair. She smiled shyly at Roy. When Doc saw her he nodded his head several times as if agreeing with some comment he'd been making to himself.

76

When the introductions were over, Velma's mother, Mrs. Baughman, said:

"Did you say *Mister* Parker? Isn't he even a doctor?"

"He's a specialist," said Pa. "Personal friend of Roy's."

"You keep out of this," said Baughman, turning to stare at his wife. "Seems to me you'd be thankful somebody was finally trying to do something for that girl of yours."

"Well, she's my girl. You got nothing to say about it, Carl. I was thinking if he wasn't even a doctor . . ."

"He can look, can't he? That can't hurt nothing."

"I don't think Velma wants him to look. Do you, dear? If Velma doesn't want you to look we won't pay you for this visit, Mr. Parker. We didn't tell you to come all the way out here. It was just that man's idea."

Velma blushed and tried to hide behind Ma.

"Pa wants me to," she said. "So does Roy."

"Funny thing to me," said Velma's mother. "I never heard of this Roy before, and yet on account of him you're going to let this stranger look at your foot when you won't hardly let me look at it. Who is this Roy, anyway?"

"I told you all about him, Mabel," said Pa, who was a little agitated.

"If it hadn't been for him . . ." Ma put in.

"I know all that. But why would he go to all that trouble to help perfect strangers? He must have some reason."

"Maybe he likes Velma," said Baughman. "And you better thank God he does. She's past twenty and not married yet and not likely to be. If you want my opinion . . ."

"We don't," said his wife. "Look. You've got Velma all upset talking that way. Don't you worry, honey. If you don't want him to look at your foot, you don't have to."

"I do," said Velma.

"Well, then, that's settled," said Baughman. "And, Mabel, I don't want no protests. She'd protest if somebody was going to give her fifty dollars. I swear I . . ."

"Well," said Velma's mother, "if the child's made up her mind, I'll say no more. Only I don't see – All right. Step in here, Mr. Parker. I'll go along with you. I guess I'm allowed to do that."

She flounced into a bedroom, and when Velma and Doc had followed her in, she slammed the door.

Roy took out a handkerchief and wiped her face; then he sat down and offered Baughman a cigarette.

"Thanks," said Velma's stepfather. "Don't you pay no attention to Mabel, Mr. Collins. She just has to put her nib in. That's all. Can't let anything pass without putting her nib in."

Roy cleared his throat. He was all at sea. Pa and Ma were not like themselves at all. They seemed shrunken and very old. It was this room maybe. Or maybe they were beginning to feel their dependence. Folks used to a free existence didn't take to living off of people or being handed charity.

"Foggy out," said Pa, stroking his face uncertainly. "First time I ever see a fog in my life."

"We don't have 'em in Ohio," said Ma. "A little mist maybe, but nothing like what's rolling in out there now."

"We have a God's plenty of fog in the fall," said Baughman. "If I didn't have my business out here I'd move away. Not that business is worth worrying about. A man can't make a dollar at nothing nowadays. I've cleared as high as three hundred a month out here in the old days. Now I can't pay my bills hardly."

"Yeah," said Pa hurriedly, lifting the window-blind, "that sure is some fog. I've heard tell of London fog and how bad it is, but it can't be worse than that."

"When the little fellows, working people and such, haven't hardly got enough to eat they're not going to spend money for gasoline, and they'll run on a tyre till it just naturally falls apart, and won't buy a new one. They just buy those damned reconditioned ones, if they buy any. As far as repairs are concerned, they work on it themselves, no matter how much harm they do. It's getting so . . ."

"Yeah," sighed Pa, "some fog."

"Why don't you hush about that fog?" snapped Baughman.

Roy got up and began to pace the floor. He avoided Pa's eyes entirely. This was sure painful!

When Velma came out of the bedroom she was so wrought up that she didn't know whether to laugh or cry.

"Pa! He says it can be fixed. He says in a little while I can walk as good as anybody."

"Dust my buttons!" cried Pa, the old Pa of the desert, slapping his thigh and grinning. "You hear that, Ma? Ain't that wonderful? Honey, you just thank Roy. Roy's the one. It was his idea. He thought up the whole thing."

"I've got to go, Roy," said old Doc. "I'm late now."

"I don't know," said Velma's mother "It don't sound logical to me. We're poor people. Where's the money to come from?"

"Not from me certainly," said Baughman. "I can't hardly pay my bills as it is."

There was a short silence, then Roy said:

"I'm going to lend Pa the money. Now I got to take Mr. Parker back to town. How about that movie, Velma? I thought maybe you'd like to ride in with us and go to a movie."

"Why, sure she will," said Pa.

"You let her make up her own mind," Velma's mother put in. "It's a long ways in and back, and it's nearly seven-thirty now. I don't know if I want her riding around with somebody she . . ."

"You keep still," said Baughman. "This man's all right or he wouldn't be worrying about Velma's foot. He'd be worrying about something else. Pretty girl like her!"

"And maybe he is," snapped Mrs. Baughman.

"People! People!" said Ma. "I declare I'm ashamed of you. Talking like that in front of Roy."

". . . and not being far wrong," old Doc whispered to Roy, who was pale with rage.

"All right," he said in a voice that chilled everybody and made them stare at him. "I'll be going. I guess I know how I stand around here." He turned and started for the hall, but Velma hurried across the room, stumbling a little, and took him by the arm.

"Roy! Don't pay any attention to what they're saying. I'd go any place with you and be glad to do it."

Roy waited in the hall while Velma got her coat and hat.

In the living-room Baughman was saying to his wife:

"No wonder Velma never had any beaux, if that's the way they got treated. I swear sometimes you act like you haven't got good sense. Don't you know an operation like that will cost around three or four hundred dollars? Why, he's crazy about Velma, that big fellow!"

"Three or four hundred dollars!" gasped Velma's mother.

"Oh, if we only had that! We could pay all our bills and take that vacation you been talking about."

"Well, do a little pushing then instead of pulling. He's got swell friends, hasn't he? I'll bet the diamond ring Mr. Parker had on cost him five hundred dollars. And did you notice his clothes? It wouldn't be a bad idea for us to have a man like Mr. Collins in the family. I don't give a damn if he's a burglar or what he is!"

"He was in the plumbing business in Chicago and sold out, Pa said. Maybe he's retired. A man that would spend that much money on a – Wait a minute. He's not gone yet." She hurried out into the hall.

Roy glanced at her, but said nothing.

"Mr. Collins," said Velma's mother, "I hope you'll excuse the way I acted. But I been so worried about Velma. Poor child, she's always at such a disadvantage with that foot. After all, I'm her mother and . . ."

"Sure. Sure," said Roy, a smile breaking slowly over his grim face. "I got sore over nothing. You don't know me from Adam. I . . ."

Doc looked on sardonically, humming a little tune to himself, and thinking: "The eternal comedy. Baughman probably put her wise how much the operation might cost and now she's figuring Roy for a millionaire. I'm old enough now to laugh. But I've been a sucker in my day. I've had mothers talk to me like that. It always cost me, too."

Velma came out into the hall, hurrying, her mouth slightly open with excitement; she had a cheap little fashionable hat perched up on her blonde head. Doc thought she looked pathetic, but Roy didn't. His face lit up at the sight of her.

"That's some hat, Velma," he said.

"You like it?"

"It's swell."

"Where are we going? What movie?"

"You name it."

"Claudette Colbert's at the Paramount. We'll go there. They've got a stage-show, too."

"Swell."

"Is Mr. Parker going with us?"

"Sorry," said Doc. "I can't make it. But I certainly hate to miss that show." He chuckled sardonically to himself.

Roy glanced at him, wondered what he was chuckling about; then he took Velma's arm.

"I don't mind limping now," said Velma, "when I know that pretty soon I won't have to any more."

CHAPTER TWENTY-TWO

When Roy drove up in front of the Institute, Doc told him he wanted to talk to him, so Roy politely asked Velma to wait (Doc chuckling to himself at the bank robber's formality) and followed the old man to the foot of the steps.

"It's criminal," said Doc, "that nothing's been done for that girl before. It's a simple operation, and she ought to be walking around in no time. Now, Roy, I'm going to arrange everything myself. I got an in with the best surgeon in town. I've sent him cases before. On the side, you know. Of course I operate my gyp-joint on the assumption that surgery isn't necessary. Most of the screwballs I get want to think that way. Know what I mean? But once in a while the going gets too tough and I suggest that they talk to this guy. I don't want any rumbles. We never sign any death certificates if we can possibly avoid it. All right. Naturally I work on a fee-splitting basis with this surgeon. But I'm going to make you a present of my end. I've got plenty of dough and what the hell good is it to me? The whole thing is going to set you back about four hundred. Satisfied?"

"Sure. I can raise it."

Doc chuckled.

"I'd like to see poor old Mac's face when you put the bite on him for that four hundred."

"What makes you think it's Mac?"

"We'll skip that. I guess I'm getting old. I never used to talk out of turn. Well, Roy, it's your funeral. That's a nice girl. All you're going to do is get her fixed up for somebody else. I told you tonight you didn't have any future and you know I'm right. You may catch lead any minute. If you're so nuts about this kid, marry her the way she is and worry about the foot later. No matter how you look at it she's going to throw a fit when she finds out what kind of a guy you really are."

"Yeah, I thought of that," said Roy. "Oh, what the hell. Her grandparents are people like my people. They got nothing in the world but her – so . . ."

"I get you. You're crazy as a loon, but you're all right. See that I get that four hundred tomorrow and I'll take care of everything for you. I may be able to save you a little dough, even."

"Thanks. Doc."

They shook hands, then Doc turned and walked up the steps slowly and thoughtfully. The good impulse which had animated him was already fading. He was beginning to wonder if after all he shouldn't chisel out a hundred for himself. Money was money!

As Roy got back in the car he said:

"It's all set, Velma. Don't be scared, now. You just do what they tell you."

"I am scared. But I don't care. If it will make me well, I'll do it. You don't know what it means to have everybody looking at you and feeling sorry for you. Sometimes I'll be sitting in a drugstore or some place and when I get up I'll see the funniest looks on people's faces. And then I can't dance and I just love music, and, oh, gosh, sometimes I used to wish I was dead."

"Yeah, it must be awful."

When they got down into the centre of town and began to pass the big buildings and the blazing neon lights of the restaurants, movie houses, and cocktail bars, Velma got so excited she could hardly talk.

"It's the first time I've been downtown," she said. "Gee, I didn't know Los Angeles was so big."

Roy got a bang out of showing Velma the sights. He felt like an old settler, though he was practically a stranger himself. But he was used to big cities and took them for granted, while Velma was a small-town girl who had lived on a farm a good part of her life.

Velma was a little bewildered, and held tightly to Roy's arm after they left the parking-lot and started towards the brilliant lights of the big movie house.

"I'd sure hate to come down here alone," she said. "I wouldn't know which way to turn. I'd get run over or something."

Roy saw men glancing at them curiously. Velma was a pretty girl and the men looked at her in spite of the limp. Probably thought he was her old man, although God knows he wasn't quite that old. Or was he?

"How old are you, Velma?" he asked in such a strange voice that she glanced up at him and studied his face.

"I'm twenty-two. Twenty-three in December."

"I'll be thirty-eight my next birthday."

"Oh, will you? My mother's thirty-nine. She got married young."

"My God!" thought Roy.

CHAPTER TWENTY-THREE

After the show, Roy took her to an all-night drugstore and they sat at the counter and drank chocolate sodas Velma laughed when she made a loud noise with her straw, and Roy laughed too. He was having a swell time. On the way out he saw the counterman staring at her foot and frowned at him. The counterman averted his face self-consciously, then walked over to the cashier.

"Funny people," he said. "Did you notice?"

The cashier yawned.

"I thought it might be her old man. The clothes she had on didn't cost her over five dollars. And, my God! That hat!"

"Pretty kid, though. Got a clubfoot, I guess."

"I'd think that'd turn a man's stomach. But if a girl's just young enough men don't give a damn."

"You should've seen the look that big bird gave me when he saw me looking at the kid's foot. I'll bet he'd cut your heart out and show it to you."

"Looked like a big country twerp to me!"

All the way home Velma talked about the movie they'd seen. Roy agreed with everything she said, although the picture had bored him so that he could hardly keep awake.

"And the clothes!" said Velma. "Did you ever see such beautiful clothes in your life? And the way she wears them! It's just a gift, I guess. It must be wonderful to have clothes like that."

"You know, Velma," said Roy, "you ought to be in pictures. I'll bet you'd look mighty pretty on the screen."

"No, I wouldn't. Anyway, I couldn't walk around and, oh, that's silly!"

"You'll walk like everybody else in a little while. You know that fellow who had the big white car you bumped into?"

"At Tropico?"

"Yeah. His name was Marty Pfeffer. He was a big director, somebody said."

"Yes, I know. Pa told me. Wasn't that awful, me running into him like that and scratching up his beautiful car!"

"Well, he told me himself you had an interesting face."

"He did? Martin Pfeffer said that?"

"He sure did."

Velma thought for a long time.

"Oh, I guess he saw me limping and felt sorry for me. Just wanted to say something nice. Why, he's been married to two stars already. He couldn't think that about me."

"The hell he couldn't. Excuse me. But why couldn't he? I do, and I'm just as good a man as he is. Better maybe."

Velma laughed.

"Oh, Roy," she said, "you're so funny."

Roy had a sudden picture of the dark ugly little man in the green, balloon-legged slacks.

"I guess you think I'm not!"

"Pa thinks you're the best man that ever lived. And I guess I do too, when I think what you've done for us."

They got home all too soon to suit Roy. He hesitated at the foot of the front steps and took Velma's hand.

"Well . . ." he began.

But the front door opened and Pa came out.

"I was waiting up for you. I want to see you, Roy, before you go. Anyway, Ma told me to give you this loaf of home-made bread. She baked today, and she said it might go good with them trout you been catching. Only thing is, it'll spoil you for baker's bread."

"Thanks, Pa."

"You better be getting to bed, pet," said Pa. "It's way past your bedtime and Ma's been kind of worrying about you. Not on account of Roy, I don't mean. She says you been losing sleep lately. You know you don't feel well when you don't get your rest."

Velma put her hand on Roy's arm.

"Thanks ever so much for a lovely evening, Roy. Gee, I had such a swell time."

"We'll go again. Some night I'll come out early and take you to Hollywood."

"Oh, will you? Oh, I can hardly wait."

"Hollywood! Always Hollywood!" said Pa.

"Good night," said Velma, patting Roy's arm. Then she turned and kissed Pa on the cheek. "Night, Pa."

"Sleep tight," said Pa. "Don't let the bedbugs bite."

Velma laughed and closed the door behind her.

"It's late for me," said Pa. "But I wanted to see you for a minute."

They sat down on the top step. Roy put the loaf of bread under his arm and lit a cigarette.

"First," said Pa, "what about Velma?"

"It's all fixed. Mr. Parker will take care of everything."

"What's all this nonsense about you lending me the money. I could never pay it back. I didn't say nothing because there was trouble enough. But, Roy . . ."

"I'm not going to worry about that money, Pa."

"I know. It's on account of Velma, ain't it?"

"Partly. It's on account of you and Ma, too."

"I don't know. It seems so unlikely. You ain't figuring on marrying Velma, are you?"

"I ain't got that far in my figuring."

Pa sat for a long time carefully scratching his head, then he said:

"I don't know what's the right thing to do. We're old-timers, we are, Roy. I think I'll tell you about Velma. You got a little age on you. You know about things. Well – we come out here mostly on Velma's account. Ma and I could've stayed in Ohio and made a go of it some way. But Velma . . . you can see how awful it is for her to be crippled. She wasn't like other girls at all. She never had any beaux. All them young fellows wanted a lively girl that could dance and run around; you know. They felt ashamed to be seen with a cripple even if she was pretty. And the poor pet didn't help herself either. She's too sensitive, and she got to thinking nobody wanted nothing to do with her. She stayed by herself most of the time. All of a sudden she was wanting to run over to Barrowville every day. Barrowville's close and it's a right good-sized town, about seventy thousand; got a lot of movies and a big public library and other city stuff. Velma was always talking about a new movie she wanted to see or some new book she wanted to get out of the library. I was tickled at first, till one day a friend of mine asked me if I knew my granddaughter was running around with a divorced man in Barrowville. A fellow named Lon Preiser. He owned the biggest movie theatre in the town: the Palace; managed it, too, I guess. Got quite a bit of money; not rich, but comfortably off, I heard. Fellow about thirty. I used to know his granddad and he was an old bugger. Came in from Cincinnati in the late eighties. Was so Dutch the sauerkraut was hanging out of his ears. Not my kind of people. It didn't look right. Here was a divorced man, who had a good bit of money, running around with a crippled farm girl. See what I mean? Well, Ma and I did our best to bust it up, but it was no use. I didn't know a sweet girl could be so contrary. So finally I wrote her mother and I told Velma that fellow would either marry her or I'd take her to California. Well, I guess she must have told Preiser because she come home crying one day and cried for about a week; then we lit out for California. . . . She got a letter from him today, though. And she seemed right set up about it. I don't know much about women and girls, Roy. I was always kind of a one-woman man, being's I met Ma early. But I'm a pretty good guesser and I'd guess Velma's still thinking about that Dutchman and will keep on thinking about him." There was a long silence. Roy never moved or offered any comment. "Now, course I don't say there's anything wrong. I'm always telling myself there ain't; makes me feel better; but I wouldn't take no affidavy to that effect. You see, Roy? I want the poor child to be sound as much as I've ever wanted anything in this world, but I made up my mind I wouldn't let you spend all that there money without telling you how things stood."

Roy got up and shook hands with Pa.

"I guess I'll be on my way."

"I hope you ain't sore at me, Roy."

"I ain't sore at nobody. We'll just go right ahead. And don't you ever let Velma find out you told me anything."

"You mean you –?"

"Yeah. Mr. Parker's going to look after the works. You sit tight and say nothing."

Pa swallowed and scratched his head.

"Don't forget the bread, Roy," he said finally.

"It's right under my arm." Roy turned and walked towards his car.

"Damnedest fellow . . ." Pa was muttering as he opened the front door.

CHAPTER TWENTY-FOUR

Big Mac was highly irritated at being disturbed. He had a woman with him. Roy saw her hat on the couch and Big Mac had carefully shut the bedroom door behind him.

"Yeah? What do you want?" he demanded belligerently.

"Take it easy, Mac."

Big Mac stared foggily at Roy, whose face looked pale and sort of haggard. Roy's eyes were narrowed to slits and a hard, dangerous light glared out of them.

"I'm busy, Roy. Mighty busy," said Mac, not too tight to realize that Roy was in no frame of mind to stand any pushing around. He smiled placatingly. "Even old Mac's got a little business to tend to from time to time. Even old Mac!"

"Yeah? I want some dough. I'll pay it back."

"Dough? I just give you a wad the other day. What's the matter, you in a jam?"

"I need four hundred dollars."

"You what? My God, Roy, be reasonable. This thing's beginning to cost me too much. I got a chiseling copper on my neck; I got three guys and a girl eating me out of house and home. Now you come rarin' about four hundred dollars. All right. You got me in a spot. But you're the last guy that I ever expected to put the bite on me for that reason." Mac fell down into a chair and groaned.

"I'm not trying to put the bite on you, Mac, and don't say I am. I need the dough, that's all. I'll pay you back double if you say so."

"Easy to say. Trouble, nothing but trouble." Mac groaned, went to a desk, and took out a big black billfold. When he handed Roy the money he said: "Don't come back again or I'll call the whole thing off. You're getting as bad as the rest of them. All right, good night."

He turned his back. Roy went out gritting his teeth. He'd stood enough for one day. He hoped that he could get back to the auto-court, where he'd left Marie and Pard, without getting into a jam of some kind. You never knew. Some drunk might get smart with him. Some guy might scrape fenders with him. He might even get a rumble from the police.

"I'll just cut loose if I do," said Roy. "I'm all tied up inside."

Unable to stand it, he drove to a cocktail bar and drank three straight whiskies in quick succession.

The bartender stared at him, then laughed.

"That's what I call loading up. You just got under the wire, brother. It's two o'clock. Closing time."

Roy threw some money on the counter and went out without a word.

But when he unlocked the door of the little cabin in the auto-court, Pard came to meet him and for the first time licked his hand. Roy patted him, feeling better already, then he glanced into the bedroom. Marie was asleep. He could hear her measured breathing in the darkness. It was like coming home. There were his pyjamas laid out across a chair, also a note which read:

> *If you are hungry you will find a sandwich I bought for you in the dish cupboard. Coffee is on the hot plate. Good night. I got too sleepy.*
>
> *Marie*

CHAPTER TWENTY-FIVE

Roy was pacing the floor, burning up half an inch of cigarette at every puff, and swearing under his breath. Red, Babe, and Marie were playing pitch for a quarter a game on the kitchen table and quarrelling loudly. Red and Babe found that Marie was not the girl they remembered at all. First place, she was getting respectable; didn't like rough talk; wouldn't stand for any foolishness of any kind, not even in fun. Second place, she quarrelled on an equal footing with them now and she could certainly hold her own in a word-battle. Violence, of course, was out; and Marie knew it. Roy would kick them all around the room if they laid a hand on her.

"Not because he gives a damn about her," Babe grumbled to Red one day, "but just because he's got to be the big shot."

"I don't know," said Red. "He's mighty nice to that girl."

"Sure," said Babe. "I used to be nice to my aunt. So what?"

"You never went to bed with your aunt, did you? Or did you?"

"Course not, you ape. All the same, I can tell. She's just like his sister to him or any other dame that don't matter to a guy."

"I don't get it."

"No? What makes you so dumb? He's picked himself up a gal in town. Look how he prances around since Mac told him not to come to town no more. He never used to be like that."

"Yeah," said Red, "that's right."

Roy went to look out the window. It was a grey morning. Thick dark clouds hid the stony peaks. A wind was whistling in from the east, bending the tall pine trees, and a light snow was falling. The lake was full of jagged little waves and looked slaty and bleak.

"A week or so more and we'll be snowed in," said Roy. "I'm about ready to pull up stakes. I don't think the business's ever going to come off. First one thing, then another. Maybe Louis's stalling. Maybe when we go for it, we'll just be walking into a trap. I don't like it, and if the blow-off don't come soon, I'm out."

"Come on, Roy," said Red. "Take a hand."

"Don't like the game."

"How about rummy?"

"Don't know how."

"Come on. We'll show you."

"Oh, shut up," said Roy. "Let me alone."

Things had changed. Not so long ago Roy had been the responsible one, trying to keep them all together till it was time for the knockover. Now Red, Babe, and Marie spent half their time soothing him.

Suddenly Roy turned.

"Where's Pard?"

"You let him out a long time ago. Right after breakfast."

"It's cold out there. Why didn't somebody remind me?"

Marie glanced at Red and Babe and shrugged. Roy opened the door. Pard was sitting on the top step shivering.

"Why didn't you bark, you dope?" Roy demanded. "I'll bet you've got icicles hanging on you. Where you been?"

Pard stared shrewdly at Roy, then sat up. Roy laughed and squatted down to pet him.

"Wise-guy, hunh? Little old Pard, the wise-guy."

"He ain't so dumb, that dog," said Red.

Roy sat down on the floor to play with Pard. Every day they had a sham battle, with Pard snarling and snapping and Roy swinging at him with his fists, neither connecting.

The three at the table watched the battle with interest. In the middle of it Pard miscalculated and tore Roy's shirt. There was a loud ripping sound. Marie held her breath, but Roy burst out laughing, cuffed Pard a couple, then picked him up and held him in his arms.

Roy yawned.

"I'm going to lay down," he said. "Me and Pard. There's only one thing to do in this joint, and that's sleep."

He slammed the door behind him. There was a short silence, then Red said:

"Roy is sure hell for dogs. If I was half St. Bernard he'd think I was wonderful."

"I'll bet Marie wishes she was a bitch of some kind," said Babe with a laugh.

"Just for that, you go home," said Marie. "I'm tired of this game anyway."

"She's tired," said Red. "How about us? Why, you've got horseshoes all over you. I never see anybody hold such hands. The last deal I had the queen, trey, and ten of diamonds and she makes high, low, jack and the game. She's tired!"

"Quiet," said Marie. "You just go on and on, Red, and don't say nothing."

"What are we going to do with that guy, Marie?" Babe demanded. "This is a big one. We may get enough out of this to go honest. As long as a guy's got plenty of dough he might as well go honest and stay out of trouble. That's what I'm figuring on. I got no record except for 'contributing', and what the hell's that! I could open myself a cocktail bar with dancing on the side and make myself more dough and have a lot of fun besides. . . ."

"Smoke up. You're going out," said Marie.

"No kidding. I don't want to blow this one, and if we've got Roy with us we can't miss."

"Yeah," said Red. "This is it. I got ideas myself. I'm going to take a trip down to the Islands and take a bang at some of them sealskin babes. I always was curious about them. Boy, there I'll be laying in a hammock eating oranges and drinking coconut milk. . . ."

"Coconut milk stinks," said Babe. "I've drunk it. It's nothing. . . ."

"You keep out of my dream," said Red. "It ain't no nightmare."

"I know what we better do," said Babe. "We better find out who the dame he's got on the string in town is and bring her up here. Then he'll be satisfied."

"He's got no dame in town," said Marie, colouring. "He takes me in with him, don't he?"

"Yeah. And probably parks you some place so you can look after the dog. You're not kidding us any, baby."

Marie jumped up.

"You get out of here, both of you. I'm tired of looking at you."

"Hit pay dirt there," said Babe. "If he's got no dame what are you so all worked up about?"

"Sure he's got a dame," said Red. "Come clean, Marie."

"Ask him."

Red and Babe got up.

"No, thanks. We'll take your word for it."

"He's just nervous," said Marie. "He got nervous in stir and he never got over it. He told me so one night. Sometimes his hands shake. He's nervous over nothing happening now He's got no dame and don't you go saying he has."

Marie's eyes flashed; she had turned pale. Red and Babe glanced at each other, then shrugged.

"O.K., honey. Don't yell so. You'll have him in here."

The bedroom door opened. Roy put his head in.

"What the hell is all this noise? Who hasn't got any dame and what of it?"

"We were just arguing," said Marie.

"What about? What's this about a dame?"

"They say you've got a girl in town. And I say you haven't."

Roy glanced at Marie. She was looking at him pleadingly.

"Course I haven't," said Roy. "Marie's my girl. Now stop yelling."

He slammed the door.

"All right, wise-guys," said Marie. "How do you like that?"

"Nice guy, Roy is," said Babe.

There was a knock. It was Algernon. He had a stocking-cap pulled down over his ears, and his teeth were chattering.

"Man at Ballard phoned in a telegram fo' Mr. Collins. How y'all, people? Ain't it cold? Where at's Pard?"

Roy opened the bedroom door and came out with the little dog at his heels. Algernon handed him a note written in pencil, then he bent down to pet Pard.

90

Roy read the note, smiled and nodded.

"Good news," he said.

"Doggone," Algernon was saying, "I sure miss this little ol' dog. He used to come and sleep in my room nearly ever' night. I don't never see him no mo'. He sho' is this here man's dog now. Mistah, you better look out. He's done took to you fo' sho'. That's might unlucky."

"Got to drive into town," said Roy, a wide smile spreading over his face.

"Yassuh. He sho' is yo' dog. Don't care nothing fo' po' ol' Algernon no mo'. Y'all got plenty wood? Going to be mighty cold night. Need lots of wood."

"You better load us up, Algernon," said Red.

"Yassuh, I'll do it, Mr. Red."

When Algernon had gone, Roy said:

"Mac wants to see me. Something's come up. Louis's coming in, too."

"I'll get ready right away," said Marie. "I wish we had a blanket for Pard. It's going to be cold till we get down to the desert."

"I was figuring I'd go in alone," said Roy. "You could stay and look after Pard and the boys."

"I'm going," said Marie firmly. "I got to buy some things."

"Well . . ." said Roy, scratching his head.

CHAPTER TWENTY-SIX

It was hot in Los Angeles, and the air was full of dampness. The change in altitude and atmosphere had made Roy irritable; he sat at the wheel with his coat off, sweating.

"You want to stop at the same place?" he asked Marie.

"I don't want to stop at all. I'll stay with you till you get through."

"I'm not supposed to see Mac till tonight. I got to go some place else. Business."

"Yeah. Monkey business. Well, you're not going to park me in no auto-court with Pard. I'll go to a movie and you can look after Pard yourself."

"All right," said Roy. "Tell me where you want out and where I'll see you later."

"I want out right here and you're not going to see me later."

"O.K." Roy reached into his pocket and took out a roll of

bills. "Here. If you want to beat it, I'll stake you to a ticket to San Francisco."

Marie began to cry as Roy drew up to the curb.

"I got money enough for the movie out of that last you gave me," she said.

"Stop crying," said Roy. "And stop trying to high-pressure me. It's no use." He sat waiting for her to get out. Marie glanced at him. His face was stony. She knew. Couldn't wait to get rid of her. Just dying to hurry off to Grandpa's girl, the big dope! She bent over and kissed Pard on the head.

"Pard loves me," she said, as the little dog licked her cheek. Roy was so crazy about Pard, she thought this might soften him up a little, and it did.

He reached over and patted her on the shoulder.

"See you tonight?"

"Yeah."

"Same court?"

"Yeah. I'll take the bus out after the movie."

" 'Bye, Marie. I'd take you along if I could."

" 'Bye, Roy. Take good care of Pard."

He drove off. He felt sorry for Marie, but it wasn't his fault. He'd never tried to kid her, not for one minute. She was a swell kid and all that and she was nuts about him, but as far as he was concerned she could go to San Francisco this minute and he'd never turn a hair.

The farther south he drove, the damper it got. The sun was blotted out by the mist and a pale, wan, silvery light was over everything. A heavy sea-fog was rolling up the street where Velma lived, blotting out landmarks and making everything unfamiliar. He idled along, straining his eyes to find the house. He came to a dead end he'd never noticed before and, making a sharp U-turn, he almost collided with a yellow taxi which loomed up suddenly out of the fog. Roy glanced in his rear-view mirror. The taxi turned at the dead end and followed him.

"Who'd tail me in a taxi?" said Roy. "What am I thinking about? The fog's got me jittery." He remembered Kranmer and wondered if the copper might be trying to find out something. Just a check-up, maybe. A crooked copper was a crooked copper. Turn you up in a minute after taking your dough. If it was Kranmer he might use a taxi so no one would think he was a copper. It might not be a bad idea to forget all about Velma till he could lose the taxi. No use getting the family in a jam if things blew up. But the taxi roared past him and disappeared into the fog.

92

Roy shook his head and laughed.

"I'm getting as bad as my Aunt Minnie. Couldn't sleep a wink. Used to walk through the house all night long, fooling with the gas-fixtures. Scared she'd get asphyxiated in her sleep. Yep. I get more like Aunt Minnie every day."

He found the house finally, parked his car, and locked the doors on account of Pard; then he went up the front steps. Pa answered his knock and almost kissed him.

"Hi, Roy. We were getting worried about you."

"How's Velma?"

"Fit as a fiddle. She wasn't in the hospital but ten days. You wouldn't know her. She even looks different out of the eyes."

"It's O.K., then?"

"Yep. Thanks to you."

"You mean she's walking around? Can she dance?"

"She has to stay in bed," said Pa. "The doctor comes every day. He says in a little while she can walk from here to San Francisco if she wants to. She can dance or do anything and nobody will ever know she was crippled."

"Boy! That's great."

Pa shoved Roy into the house. Ma was waiting for him, and when he took off his hat and grinned at her, she put her arms around him and kissed him on the cheek.

"You cut that out, Ma," said Pa. "Roy's a darn nice-looking fellow and I'm jealous."

Ma ignored him.

"Thank you, son," she said.

Pa laughed.

"Carl's at work and Mabel's uptown gadding around. We got Velma all to ourselves today."

Ma took Roy by the hand and led him into the bedroom. Velma was sitting up in bed with three pillows at her back, reading a movie magazine. She was fully dressed, but she had a comfort drawn over her knees. Her face lit up when she saw Roy and in her excitement, she dropped her magazine, the comfort slid down, and Roy saw her bandaged foot.

"I hear you're all right," said Roy.

"Oh, I'm fine. I'm a different girl now. You just wait. I'll make you take me dancing."

She was holding out her hands towards him in an awkward, embarrassed way.

"She wants to kiss you," said Ma, nudging Roy with her elbow.

"Oh, Ma!" said Velma, but when Roy bent down she put her

93

arms around his neck and pressed her soft little mouth against his cheek. Roy turned and kissed her on the lips, and Velma drew back and laughed.

"There," she said. "Now I feel better. We were wondering what had happened to you. My goodness, Roy, you never even called us or anything."

"I've been busy." Roy's face was red as a beet. He dropped his hat on the floor, and bending down to pick it up, he bumped his head on the bedpost.

"Good grief, Roy!" said Ma. "I'll bet that hurt. If it swells I'll put some butter on it. That'll fix it."

Pa laughed.

"She's always got a remedy. Used to make a goose-grease salve that she thought would cure anything from a split lip to smallpox. Uncle John had a wen on his head and Ma used to get mad at him because he wouldn't put her goose-grease salve on it."

"Would've cured it," said Ma. "Sit down, Roy."

Pa pulled up a chair for him and Roy sat down beside the bed.

"How did you like the hospital?" he asked, to make conversation.

"Oh, it was all right. Of course I missed Pa and Ma at night. They came over every day, though. They sure have nice food in that hospital. I gained three pounds."

"Did it hurt much when they fixed your foot?"

"Didn't hurt at all. I didn't even know it. Sometimes now I get sort of a twinge."

Pa stood looking on, grinning. Ma took him by the sleeve and led him out of the room.

"Excuse me," said Ma. "I want Pa to help me in the kitchen."

There was a long embarrassed silence, then Roy bent over and picked up Velma's movie magazine.

"Thanks," said Velma. "Do you ever read magazines like this, Roy?"

"Not me."

"What do you read?"

"The sports page," said Roy with an embarrassed laugh.

"Don't you ever read books?"

"Well, I read a few books when I didn't have nothing else to do. I don't like to read about doing things. I like to do them."

"Yes. I know what you mean. I'll be more that way now. I read an awful lot back home. We had a nice library in Barrowville."

Roy remembered what Pa had told him and flushed slightly.

94

"You're right," he said. "You won't be reading so much now. You'll be dancing and running around. Well, that's what you ought to be doing."

"We'll never get through thanking you, Roy. It was wonderful of you."

Roy hitched his chair up closer, but when Velma looked at him he lowered his eyes.

"Velma," he said, "I got a big business deal coming up. I figure if it goes through the way it ought to I can retire for life."

"Oh, that's fine, Roy. Did you tell Pa? He'll be tickled to hear it. You don't know how much Pa talks about you. Sometimes he talks about you so much that Carl gets jealous." Velma laughed. "Really he does. Isn't that silly?"

"Pa and Ma are all right. I sure like them. They remind me of my own people. They're my kind."

"That's the way Pa feels about you."

"Yeah. Well, look, Velma, did you ever think you'd like to go around the world?"

"Round the world! Oh, I don't know if I'd like that. It's so far. Takes so long to get back."

"I was figuring if this deal goes through I'd like to go around the world and I was just –" Roy hesitated and flushed. He glanced up. Velma was looking at him very strangely. He couldn't make out what she meant by the look. "You see what I mean, Velma?"

"Yes," she said, "I see."

"Well, I was just thinking ... if you wouldn't want to go round the world, what would you like to do?"

"I'd like to stay here; only I'd want to live nearer to where things are happening. Away out here we never see anything but fog."

"I'll bet you'd like to get in the movies."

"I couldn't. I never acted in my life. Of course I don't have to worry about my foot any more. But, oh, that's silly!"

"You know, Velma," said Roy, suddenly, "I'd sure like to marry you. I'm not so old and I'm going to have plenty of money."

He kept his eyes averted for a moment, then he looked at her. She was blushing and smiling at him very uncertainly. It was a weak smile and Roy wished she wouldn't look that way; it wasn't like his idea of her at all.

"I don't know ..." said Velma, lowering her eyes and fooling with the comfort. "You've sure been wonderful to us. And Pa says there's no better man than you, but Roy..." Her voice trailed off. She stared steadily at the comfort. He saw tears glistening on her long black eyelashes.

"You've got somebody back home, I guess."

"Yes," said Velma. "In a way I have. Yes...." She began to cry and, lowering her head, she hid her face in the comfort and sobbed.

"He figuring on coming out here to marry you?" Roy demanded.

"I don't know. I may go back there. I ought to be hearing from him any day now. He writes a couple of times a week."

"Are you nuts about him, Velma?"

She didn't answer for a long time. Finally, hiding her face from him completely, she nodded vigorously three times.

Roy cleared his throat and pulled at his hair. Little beads of sweat were standing out all over his forehead.

"Well," he said, shrugging, "I guess that lets me out."

Velma glanced up and smiled at him weakly, but her smile was immediately erased when she saw how pale and grim Roy looked and noticed the hard, ruthless light shining out of his eyes.

"Roy! What's the matter? I told you the truth. You mustn't be mad at me."

He saw fear in her eyes and wondered. He didn't know that he was looking murder at the thought of the wise-guy back in Barrowville who had made a lay out of Velma and was now giving her the runaround. Pa was probably right. She'd go on thinking about him.

"Did you tell him your foot was cured?" Roy demanded.

Velma didn't know what to say. Roy was a stranger to her now. She'd felt so comfortable with him before. He was the kind of older man who took you around and was nice to you, and you never had to worry about him getting rough. He'd seemed gentle and easy-going. She'd liked him the first time she'd talked to him. Of course she could never feel about him the way she did about Lon. Roy was rough and farmerish; his hair looked shaggy, and he was rather ugly except when he smiled. But he was mighty easy to like and any girl would consider herself lucky to have him looking after her. But now she was afraid of him.

"I wrote him about it," she said. "I had to. I mean, I thought – Oh, Roy, it was so wonderful of you to pay for everything and it's awful for me to act like this. But, at first, I just thought you liked the folks so well ... and then you said Pa would pay you back. I didn't know you – I mean, I wasn't sure. Maybe we

96

shouldn't have let you do what you did."

Roy got up, went to the window, and stood staring out.

"Roy! Please don't be mad," said Velma. "Let's be friends. I'd like to have you for a friend, Roy. All of us would."

He said nothing. He felt hurt and humiliated. Suddenly he started. The fog had lifted a little. He saw a yellow taxi standing at the curb. He was furious.

"I'll be back," he said in such a harsh voice that Velma jumped, then sat staring after him. What did he mean? What was he going to do? "Pa," she called, "oh, Pa! Come here!"

She heard the front door slam. Pa came hurrying in. He had sensed apprehension in his granddaughter's voice.

"Why, pet! What's wrong? You've been crying. You look so scared. What's Roy been up to?"

"He wants me to marry him, Pa, and I said I couldn't on account of Lon."

"Did you tell him about Lon?"

"In a way I did. And Roy looked so awful I got scared. He didn't look like himself at all."

"How did he look?"

"He just looked awful. I don't know. Like he could kill me."

"Why, Velma! You mustn't say a thing like that."

"It's true. Feel my hands, how cold they are. I've got goose-pimples all over my arms. I hope he doesn't hate me now, Pa. He might do something."

"He won't do anything. What would he do? Velma, you're getting so you try my patience. Dog it! If you ain't careful you'll get as scary as your mother. Mabel was the scariest girl I ever see."

Velma hid her face and began to cry again.

"I can't help it. I been through so much lately, the hospital and everything, and then I don't know what Lon's going to do and . . ."

"There, there," said Pa, patting her shoulder. "I don't know what got in me to talk like that to you, child, except maybe it was on account of Ma. She's making me peel potatoes and if there's any job I hate!"

When Roy came hurrying out of the house, the taxi-driver shifted gears quickly and tried to get away, but Roy jumped on the running-board.

"Wait a minute, buddy," he said.

The taxi-driver was a tough-looking, redheaded fellow with heavy shoulders and his cap on the side of his head, but the sight of Roy's face was enough for him.

"O.K., pal. Just following orders."

Marie was in the back seat. Roy was so stunned he couldn't speak. He heard a dog barking and turned. Pard was standing up in the coupé, trying to attract his attention.

Roy opened the taxi door.

"Well?"

"Hello, Roy. Sore?"

"I was."

"You looked it. I thought you was coming right through the glass."

"I thought somebody was tailing me."

"I've been tailing you ever since you left me uptown."

"What're you sitting out here for?"

"I thought maybe you'd take her some place. Out to eat or something. I wanted to see her. She sure lives in a nice neighbourhood."

"Yeah. So you want to see her? Well, come on in."

"Look, Roy. I shouldn't've done this. You'll probably be off me for life."

"Oh, I don't know. Come on. Get out. I'll pay the guy. You can drive back with Pard and me."

There was something in his manner she couldn't quite make out. She didn't trust him entirely. He didn't look like Roy Earle to her. He looked like a man who had seen a ghost.

"You feeling all right, Roy?"

"Sure I'm feeling all right. How much, buddy?"

Marie got out and stood waiting. When the taxi-driver told Roy what the bill was he whistled, but paid it without a word and gave the driver a good-sized tip.

The driver shrugged and winked.

"Dames!" he said, shaking his head.

Pa had come out on the porch and was standing staring at Roy and Marie with his mouth slightly open. They came up the steps arm in arm.

"Pa," said Roy, "this is a friend of mine, Marie Garson. She knew I was out here, so she drove out. She's going back in my car."

"Howdy do? I'm Jim Goodhue. Come right in, Miss Garson."

Ma was standing in the hallway, wiping her hands on her apron. She ran her eyes over Marie quickly and her lips tightened with disapproval. Marie's long, bushy black bob was pushed back over her ears and hung to her shoulders. Her skirt was very short, revealing a pair of extremely good-looking legs in sheer

98

stockings. She had on a wide-shouldered little jacket and a red scarf around her neck. Feeling self-conscious, she put on her boldest front. Her dark eyes flashed and her teeth gleamed. She looked predatory.

"Miss Garson," said Pa, "meet the wife. This is Ma."

"Howdy do? Any friend of Roy's is welcome. Won't you come in and meet my granddaughter?"

"I'd love to."

Velma had removed all trace of weeping from her face and had fluffed out her thick blonde hair. She looked very young and innocent sitting there with the comfort around her knees.

Marie glanced at her, then at Roy, while the introductions were going on.

"How do you do?" said Velma. "Sorry I've got to stay in bed, but I just got out of the hospital."

"Oh," said Marie, glancing at Roy again. "What was the matter?"

"I had an operation on my foot. Won't you sit down?"

"No," said Roy. "We're going in just a minute."

The girls looked each other over carefully. They both smiled and were very friendly, but neither thought the other amounted to anything. To Marie, Velma was a pretty little weak-faced ninny; to Velma, Marie was overdressed and obvious, like a girl she knew in Barrowville that every male from sixteen to sixty handled familiarly whenever she was within reach.

"What kind of an operation did you have?"

Velma flushed slightly.

"There was something wrong with my foot. The doctor made it well."

Marie was thinking: "I don't like the way her eyes turn up and the way she makes cute little mouths. What does she think she is, a goddamned angel? If men don't beat the devil! Roy going for that act. I'll bet she's a pushover."

"You mean you were crippled?" asked Marie, smiling sweetly.

"Clubfoot," said Pa, jumping a little as Ma kicked him. "But she's all right now, thanks to Roy."

"Yeah," said Roy, laughing uncomfortably. "She sure is."

Strange emotions were tugging at him. He was jealous of Velma; he couldn't keep from thinking about that guy back in Barrowville. He hoped Velma would be jealous of Marie, who, after all, did look mighty cute today.

He put his arm around Marie, and he felt a glow when he saw Velma's lips tighten in disapproval.

"We better get going," he said. "I'm hungry. How about you,

Marie?"

"I could eat. Always can."

"We'd ask you to stay," said Velma, "only . . ."

"Sure, sure," said Roy. "Well, we'll be going."

"When will we see you again, Roy?" asked Velma, smiling sweetly. "I'll be walking in a few days."

"Yes," cried Pa, "you must come and see her walk. You sure must."

"I'm going to be pretty busy," said Roy. "I'll try to make it."

When they had gone, Ma said:

"I don't think so much of Roy Collins as I did. That girl!"

"Good-looker," Pa put in. "Yes, she is. A man couldn't go wrong with her!"

"That's just what a man would do," snapped Ma. "I know her kind."

"And I do, too," said Velma. "She's like Nona Braden back home."

"I don't know what men are thinking of," sighed Ma.

Pa laughed.

"You see, Velma? Don't look like Roy's going to go moping around much. Naturally wouldn't, a fellow like him."

"She came running out here after him," said Velma. "Can't fool me."

Outside, Roy was standing with his foot on the running-board, waiting for Pard to empty out. He saw Marie laughing.

"For crying out loud," she said. "A gimp!"

Roy shrugged.

"I like her people."

"Can't get any place, hunh? You got the wrong technique. Take my word for it. She can be had."

Roy flushed with anger and turned to call Pard. Marie was right, at that. Velma *had* been had. The little dog jumped into the car and sat on Marie's lap.

"He likes his mamma," said Marie. "His papa is a dope."

"Oh, shut up," said Roy, getting behind the wheel and driving off. "You would come busting out here where you wasn't wanted."

Marie was silent so long that Roy turned to look at her. He saw tears in her eyes. He put his arm around her and hugged her.

"It looks like you and me," he said.

Marie slid down and put her head on his shoulder.

"She's not your kind and you know it, Roy. What good would she be to you? She'd just be a drag."

"Yeah," said Roy; then he stared at the street in silence.

CHAPTER TWENTY-SEVEN

Roy was appalled at the change in Big Mac's appearance and sat studying him covertly. Mac had lost a lot of weight and the skin under his chin hung in pale folds. His hands shook and he kept drinking glass after glass of straight whisky.

". . . it sure was a surprise to me," Mac was saying. "A chiselling copper turning out to be a right guy. But you take my word for it, Roy; Kranmer's all right. He's sure give me a lot of real tips. He knows what's what. I got confidence in him."

"You're crazy, Mac," said Roy. "You never saw a right copper in your life and you know it."

"First time for everything. Just mark my word. The guy's valuable to us. Course he's a little hungry, but who ain't! All right, Louis. Speak your piece."

Louis smiled and sat up. He'd been sitting there in silence, resenting Roy, who, for some reason, made him feel small. Big hick at that! But he was looking better; he'd lost that pale, flaccid look he'd had when he first came out; he was sunburnt and seemed hard and fit. But his dark hair was shaggy, his tie was crooked, his shoes scuffed, and his clothes looked as if somebody had stood across a room and thrown them on him. Louis was wearing his expensive sports coat and he was hurt that neither Mac nor Roy had noticed it.

"It's like this," he said. "I been waiting till we were full up. Things aren't so good as they ought to be at this time of year. But the last few days things showed signs of picking up, so I think we better go for the dough any time now. There's a couple of things I want to ask you about, Roy."

"Shoot."

"Well, there's been some petty thieving going on in Tropico, something we never had before, so now the merchants have hired a watchman and he goes the rounds all night long. Even comes to the hotel every hour."

"Is he tough?"

Louis laughed.

"Lord, no. He's a fellow about fifty. Shell-shocked or something. Wears glasses. I guess he was starving, so they gave him the job. He used to be a policeman in some little town in Iowa."

"O.K. Write him off as long as you know just when he'll turn up."

101

"He generally hits us on the hour till five in the morning. He's never later than ten after. So quarter after the hour would give us at least forty-five minutes."

"That's plenty. I hope this watchman don't decide to prance. Old guy like that."

"I'm not going to cry over him," said Mac.

"But that's not all," said Louis. "Three days ago a Los Angeles copper arrested some guy on the streets of Tropico and it turns out he's a burglar, wanted in three states. The copper tailed him to Tropico. So the editor of our paper, the *Desert Sun*, gets a brainstorm and puts an editorial on the front page about the undesirable guys that are beginning to come to Tropico and how the citizens of the richest little town on earth have to be protected. Stuff like that. So now we got two coppers on duty all night."

"Radio car?"

"Well, the radio car's parked out in front of the station so if a call comes in they can get going right away. They used to put the car in the garage at midnight and only leave one man on duty."

"Where is the car parked?" asked Roy.

"Right in front of the station."

"Can they see it from inside?"

"Not unless they stand right at the window and watch it."

"That's simple. We'll just let the air out of a tyre or so. They only got one car, ain't they?"

Louis and Mac both burst out laughing at once.

"Yeah," said Louis.

"By God," cried Mac, "that's the best one I've heard in years. I'd like to go along with you guys just to let the air out of the tyres. I'd like to see the faces on those chiselling bums when they come out and see their tyres flat. That calls for a drink."

Roy and Louis refused.

"I see I got to drink by myself. Well, no novelty in that. So, Roy, you think things don't look bad?"

"Not from here."

"How are your boy friends?"

"They're tame. We're all pulling together."

"All right," said Mac, slapping his thigh, "in a few days we'll go for the coconuts. Louis'll call you."

CHAPTER TWENTY-EIGHT

"Yeah," said Roy, "I'm sure glad I went down and cased the place again yesterday. I got to thinking we ought to know just where everything was, so we wouldn't be running into anything. The radio-car business kind of got on my nerves. But it's a cinch. They park it under a big pepper tree a little bit beyond the loading zone in front of the station. It's in the shadows. The streetlight's down quite a way from it. Red, you and Babe park your car about twenty feet ahead of it and I'll come along slow and park about fifty feet behind it; then one of you guys let the air out of a tyre. That town'll be dead as a doornail around three in the morning. It's a walk. If there's a rumble the guy in the car drives away and I pick up the other guy. O.K.?"

"Sounds good," said Red. "Only I speak for the job of letting the air out. Babe can drive. Oh, boy! What an idea! I'd like to see the faces on them coppers!"

"Got everything checked?" asked Roy.

"Yeah, I think so," said Babe. "One gun apiece for Red and me. Here's the three hammers. You think we'll need that sledge, Roy?"

"I don't know. I never busted into no safety-deposit boxes before. We'll try the ballpeen hammers first; then if they won't do the job, we'll have to try the sledge. You can stick them hammers down inside the waistband of your pants. With them short handles they won't be no trouble."

"O.K.," said Babe. "But I still don't see why Louis can't open them boxes."

"In the first place," said Roy, "it takes two keys: an office key and the key the guy whose stuff is in the box carries. In the second place, it would be a tip-off it was an inside job. They'd pinch Louis and he'd sing, or I don't know nothing about guys."

"Yeah," said Red. "I thought about that. You know, Roy, this is a loud one, and the coppers are really going to give somebody a going over, them bastards! Think he can take it?"

"He's got to. Anyway, we'll be clear by that time. I ain't going to worry about that. Hell, I wish Marie would come back. What's keeping her?"

Babe and Red began to stow the hammers and the other equipment, including a shoe-box for the jewellery with the lid glued on and a hole cut in the top, into a big sack. Roy checked each item and scratched it off a list, which he afterwards threw into the fire.

"I'm glad you're taking Marie," said Red. "She's all right. Got more guts than most men."

"And more sense," said Roy. "She can look after the cars and keep the motors idling. She wanted in, so I finally told her O.K. We'll make up her share between us. That's fair, ain't it?"

"Yeah," said Babe.

"You bet," Red put in. "I'm going to feel a hell of a lot easier with somebody out there looking after the heaps. I'll never forget what happened to a guy I knew, Petty Garrison. Small-timer, he was. He and another hood waltzed in to heist a grocery-store. They left the heap out in front with the engine running. When they come busting out a couple of jumps ahead of a shotgun blast some so-and-so had stole their car. They ducked down an alley and run right into a big copper who'd heard the blasting. Brother, what a mess!"

"What happened?" Babe demanded, turning from his work.

"The copper throws a slug into Petty's pal and kicks Petty in the groin. They both go down and now they're picking daisies up at San Quentin. That was a tough copper."

"Yeah," said Babe, "he sure was. Damned if you can't think up the prettiest stories when we're going out on a caper."

"They was just small-timers," said Red. "Not like us."

"We wasn't so big till this one," said Babe. "I don't feel big."

"Roy feels big and that's what counts."

"What's keeping Marie?" reiterated Roy peevishly. Then he began to pace the floor.

Neither Red nor Babe spoke. They just glanced at each other. They knew that Roy was feeling bad. He'd sent Marie up to the store with Pard so Algernon could keep him locked up till they got away. That little bugger was sure hell for following Roy's car. He'd had to take him into Tropico with him the day before.

The door opened and Marie came in.

"Well?" said Roy.

"Algernon's going to look after him. It's funny. Pard knows there's something up. He kept scratching at the door."

Roy got very red in the face.

"Oh, that little old dog's just a damn nuisance. Now, look, fellows. In a few minutes we're going for the coconuts. Let's get things straight. Red, you and Babe drive ahead of us. When you get to the police station you know what to do. After we get to the hotel park your car on the south drive facing west and when we come out it's a straight shoot. Marie'll look after the heaps.

We walk right in. You guys just get behind the desk and go to work and leave the rest to me. Stall a little on account of the night bellboy. You know. Make it look good for Louis. He'll open the safe. He says we won't get much out of it, but it may run over a grand and that's money. Then bust open the boxes. Put all the bills in your pockets and dump the jewellery into the shoe-box. Everything you see that looks like glass, stick it in the box. That's what Big Mac's after. All right. If we don't get no rumbles we're a cinch. I take the shoe-box and Marie and hit for L.A. You take the dough and go back to the lake. That way we won't be ganging up together. When you get word from me, you come in with the dough. Any questions?"

"What about the watchman?" asked Babe. "Suppose some of the people who stay at the hotel come in late?"

"Don't even look up, no matter what happens," said Roy. "That's my job. And keep working till I say scram. We sure been a long time on this caper and we don't want to boot it now. Nobody's going to bother you, and I mean nobody! If some smart copper walks into us, that's his tough luck."

Babe and Red both grinned and sighed with relief. Brother, this Earle guy didn't have his reputation for nothing like some so-called big hots you ran into! He had what it took. It wasn't just wind or a pep-talk. He meant it.

"All set?"

"Yeah," said Marie. "All set, I guess. I got our grips in the rumble-seat. Load up the junk you're taking for the job and we're ready."

"It's late," said Roy. "If you guys get any kind of a break nobody'll ever know you were away from the lake tonight. Marie and me don't matter. Everybody knows we're leaving. I paid my bill today. Now, guys, don't forget. When you leave here pay your bill. Many a wise guy had ended up in clink because he outsmarted a hotel or an auto-camp out of a few bucks. Small-time stuff."

They all went out, loaded up the cars, and locked the cabin doors.

The night was cold and clear. There was no wind. In the bright moonlight Roy could see his breath, a white vapour, which rose slowly in the thin air. The lake was still as a pavement and a wide shimmering path of moonlight stretched from shore to shore. A lone gull cried down by the boathouse. Far off they heard barking, followed by a sharp, insistent yelp.

Marie glanced at Roy, who turned away and said:

"Well, goodbye, Eagle Lake. I've seen the last of you."

A dog began to howl in the stillness, making Roy's hair stir slightly. It was a high-pitched, unearthly wail which died away slowly. Babe crossed himself involuntarily.

"I told you he knew," said Marie. "That's Pard."

"Shut up and get in the car," said Roy. "Get going, you guys. What're you standing there for?"

"O.K., Roy."

"And when you guys get back here, let that dog stay with Algernon. Don't let him come fooling around the cabin."

"All right, Roy."

Red drove off.

"I wish that dog'd stop howling," said Babe. "I don't like that. It gives me the creeps."

"All right, panty-waist!" said Red.

Marie jumped in beside Roy and slammed the door. Roy began to swear. The gears wouldn't mesh properly and he jerked on the gear-shift and kicked the clutch in violently. Finally he got the car turned around and headed for the settlement.

"I got an idea," said Marie. "Why don't you get Red and Babe to bring Pard in with them when they come?"

"No," said Roy. "I got to keep moving from now on. I can't be bothered with no dog."

"I'd take care of him for you, Roy."

"No. He's better off up here. Now keep still. I got other things to worry about."

Roy drove quickly past the store where Algernon slept, looking straight ahead. The howling had stopped. The moonlight was so bright in the settlement that the trees and houses were casting long, dark-blue shadows. Marie turned in her seat to take a last look at Eagle Lake. She gave a gasp. A little dog was running down the middle of the road after them, kicking up dust.

"What's wrong with you?" Roy demanded. "You bawling?"

Marie hesitated, then bent over and began to laugh hysterically.

"It's Pard. He got loose. Here he comes."

Roy stepped on the gas.

"He can't follow us far at night. Ain't like daytime."

"Roy! You can't do that."

"The hell I can't."

There was a short silence, then Roy jammed on the brakes and pulled over to the side of the road.

"I don't see him," said Marie.

"He'll be along. What a damn nuisance of a dog! What I

106

ought to do is put a bullet in his head. Ain't I got enough trouble without a fool dog . . ."

Marie sat huddled up against Roy, waiting. Men were such brutes. Even Roy. She was afraid and shivered a little. It seemed impossible to her, but maybe she didn't know Roy as well as she thought she did; maybe he *would* shoot the poor dog.

Pard came up panting, jumped on the running-board, and tried to leap into the car; on the second attempt he missed his footing and rolled on his back in the dust.

"Pard," said Roy.

The little dog sat up and barked sharply. Marie opened the door on her side and Pard was round the car like a shot and in between them on the seat.

"Poor little devil," said Marie. "Got no home. Got nobody. Just like I used to be."

"Shut your door, for Christ's sake," said Roy, driving off. "Of all the fourteen-carat saps! Starting out on a caper with a woman and a dog. We should've bought that canary after all. What in hell are we going to do with him?"

"You just tend to your business and I'll look after him," said Marie.

"If he spoils this caper, I'll . . ."

"Oh, you're full of talk, I think you're glad."

There was a long silence, then Roy reached over and patted Pard.

"Maybe I am. I don't know. I'm getting crazy, I guess. A fellow back in stir once told me everybody in California was nuts. It's the climate. So good you can't stand it." Roy laughed and Marie put her arm around him and kissed him. "Yeah, I end up with a family. Pard, old boy, looks like we're going to have to make a hood out of you. You're on the loose now. Say, how much did you give Algernon?"

"Five dollars. Why?"

"Why, that cheap crook. He took your five dollars and then let Pard out. He couldn't get out without help. I ought to go back and cut his ears off."

"Maybe he got scared," said Marie, placatingly. "You know, Algernon was mighty relieved when Pard began hanging after you. Algernon's superstitious. He thinks Pard's bad luck."

"Aw, that's malarkey. That's an act. Algernon's a born chiseller. He pulls the sob stuff about Pard so he can clip suckers."

"Well, he's our dog now."

"Yeah."

As soon as they got onto the main road Roy drove very fast

till he caught sight of the tail-light on Red's car; then he slowed down and followed it, keeping a two- or three-hundred-yard interval.

When they made the hairpin turn near Broken Creek Summit, Marie leaned across him to look out. It was almost as bright as day. The abyss was full of velvety-blue shadows, but Marie could see the jagged rocks and, far down, the dark expanse of the pine forest.

Crossing the tableland, the gaunt lonely mountains towered above them, their rocky summits, covered with snow, a pale blue in the moonlight.

"Some country," said Marie, shivering.

"Yeah," said Roy. "I'll bet it looks like this on the moon."

"You can have it."

Marie slid down in the seat and they rode along in silence. Between them Pard slept and from time to time his feet twitched and he gave pathetic little whimpers.

CHAPTER TWENTY-NINE

The stars were sparkling over Tropico when they parked the two cars on the south drive. Red got out laughing, but when he saw the little dog in Roy's car he started.

"W – where did he come from?"

Marie explained briefly.

"Look, Babe. The pooch!"

"That Algernon!" said Babe. "He ought to be taken care of."

"You forget it," said Roy. "You don't know anything about it, see?"

"I get you."

Red laughed again.

"Oh, boy," he said, "that was the best ever. Wait till them coppers try to drive that heap away. I got both front tyres. Brother, did you ever see such a dead town? Like a graveyard. Wow! Look at the size of that hotel. What a joint!"

Glancing around, Roy saw Babe furtively cross himself.

"All right, guys," he said. "You know what you're supposed to do. Now do it. Marie, you keep the motors idling and shut Pard up if he barks. Got the sack? O.K. You guys do the carrying. I've got my hands full with the chopper. But I'll take the shoe-box on the way out."

The moonlight was as bright in Tropico as it had been at

108

Eagle Lake. The trees and bushes of the immense lawn of the hotel cast long shadows. The great rambling building, dimly lit and faintly bluish in the moonlight, awed Red and Babe, who faltered a little and glanced apprehensively at each other. The thick grass muffled the sound of their footsteps.

Roy walked a little ahead with the machine-gun partly hidden under his coat. He was not excited and didn't feel nervous. This looked too easy. It was another matter to walk into a bank, crowded with patrons and employees, in broad daylight. This caper was almost like prowling, something he'd never done in his life. He glanced back and noticed that Red and Babe were lagging.

"Come on. What's holding you?"

"Jeez," said Red, "it's sure big."

"Yeah," whispered Babe, trembling slightly, "I never knew it was this big."

"Step on it," said Roy in a cold, cutting voice. "And when we get in, work fast. Stop worrying about whether it's big or small. It's in the bag."

The plaza was deserted. There wasn't a car in sight. As they crossed the wide veranda, they could see into the huge, spacious, dimly lit lobby with its great divans and its enormous stone fireplace, where a log fire was burning and casting flickering reflections on the white walls. Louis was leaning on the desk, looking at a magazine. He seemed very casual and Roy was pleased. The night bellboy was yawning on his bench and scarcely looked up when Roy entered, followed by Red and Babe. Suddenly he gave a jump and a squeal. He'd seen the machine-gun.

"Oh, my God! Louis . . ." he cried.

"Shut up," said Roy.

The boy jumped again. He wanted to hide. His face was ghastly. He lost control of himself to such an extent that he couldn't sit upright, but sagged from side to side.

Louis was standing with his hands in the air.

"Lie down on your face, sonny," Roy called to the bellboy in a voice that chilled him to the bone, "and don't move or I'll fill your pants full of lead. And keep your head down. Don't try to see what's going on."

"Yes, sir. I will, sir. Don't you worry about me, sir."

Red and Babe were behind the counter now. Shoving a gun into Louis's back, Red forced him towards the safe, the door of which was standing ajar. Louis winked and jerked his thumb at the safe.

"Open it, you son-of-a-bitch," shouted Red for the boy's benefit.

Louis pushed the safe door open with his foot and showed them the money, neatly stacked on the floor. Red and Babe stuffed their pockets full, then got out their ballpeen hammers and began to bang away at the safety-deposit boxes. Babe took the shoe-box out of the sack and put it on a chair behind the desk. The head of Red's hammer flew off, sailed over the desk, and crashed into a huge ornamental brass urn, which rang like a gong. Roy turned slightly at the sound, then ignored it. Red threw the useless handle away and went to work with the sledge. The racket they made was deafening, and the bellboy finally put his hands over his ears. He was half-delirious and hadn't the vaguest notion what all the noise was about.

Roy stood with his back to the desk, running his eyes over three sides of the lobby, where there were many windows facing the veranda. The fourth wall had no windows in it as the great fireplace took up most of it.

Without turning, Roy shouted above the noise:

"How's it going?"

"Having a little trouble with the boxes," Red shouted back, "but I'm getting it. Plenty of rocks, Boy!"

Out of the corner of his eye Roy saw Red and Babe swinging away at the boxes. Louis was standing in an angle of the receiving-desk with his hands in the air. As it was a chilly night all the windows on the veranda were closed. Roy began to wonder how it sounded outside. Suddenly he thought about Marie and Pard and glanced at the clock. They'd been at work three minutes.

"How you doing?" he shouted.

"Got a few more," came Red's voice with a note of triumph in it. "Boy, is this a haul!"

Turning, Roy saw a shadow on the veranda. He stiffened. A man and a woman were hurrying towards the lobby. They were in evening clothes and the woman was bundled up in a beautiful white wrap. The man banged back the big door and they came in quickly.

"Oh, I'm frozen," said the woman. "Look at the fire, Bob. Doesn't that look –" Suddenly she turned. There'd been a momentary lull behind the desk. The hammering broke out again, louder than ever; and Red was swearing above it.

"Nice time of night to build a house," said the man. "What is this, a game?"

Roy watched them narrowly. They were both tight and a little bewildered by a situation they couldn't comprehend. Then the woman saw the machine-gun and screamed:

"Bob! Look!"

"Yes," said the man, staggering a little. "I see. Look, my friend. You can't do this. I mean, you can't – you –" His face began to turn greenish.

"My rings!" screamed the woman. "The safety-deposit boxes they – Bob, you've got to stop them. My rings!"

"Go sit by the fire, both of you," said Roy, "and you won't get hurt."

The woman gave a loud squeal and her legs began to buckle.

"Take care of her, you chump!" said Roy, gritting his teeth at the silly antics of the man, who came to himself and caught the woman just as she was sagging to the floor. Her weight overbalanced him and they fell side by side on their backs.

"Don't shoot, for God's sake," cried the man. "Give me time. I'll get her over to the fire. Take it easy now. I'll get her . . ."

"Stay where you are," said Roy. "Lie down and stay down. That's perfect. Now be quiet or I'll fill your guts full of lead."

"Oh, my God," sighed the man, lying back.

The man and woman lay quiet. The hammering gradually ceased. Roy heard a loud metallic ripping sound, then Red said:

"Couple more and we got it. This is a big box. Tough going."

Roy glanced round. Louis was pale as death and his teeth were chattering. The strain was beginning to tell on him. Red and Babe were as busy as monkeys, working away as carelessly as a couple of hands in a factory.

"Nice going!" Roy thought.

The stillness began to bother him; after the terrific racket it seemed a little ominous. He stood straining his ears trying to catch outside sounds. The bellboy groaned as if in his sleep. The man in evening clothes was talking to his wife in a low, distracted voice, begging her to wake up and say something.

"She's out cold," said Roy. "Don't worry. She'll be all right."

"Her heart's bad," said the man. "I'm scared. I don't know . . ."

"You lie still and don't give me no trouble. We'll be through here shortly."

"You'll suffer for this."

"O.K.," said Roy.

The silence continued, broken occasionally by a single blow of a hammer followed by a sharp metallic rip.

"With you in a minute," called Red.

There was a long interval of intense silence, then a dog

barked, a single yelp, and somebody touched a Klaxon which gave off a quick sharp peal. Roy's muscles tensed up all over his body. He put his back against the desk and ran his eyes slowly over the windows facing the veranda. Pard had barked for some reason, and Marie had touched the klaxon. It was no accident. It meant trouble.

He gave a start, then controlled himself. A tall man in a khaki uniform was walking rapidly across the veranda towards the north entrance. He had on a big Western hat and a Sam Browne belt. Roy saw a leather holster swinging at his hip.

"Watchman," said Louis.

"Shut up, you chump," hissed Roy without turning.

The man had a hard leathery face and a closely clipped grey moustache. He walked straight into the lobby, unbuttoning his holster-flap. Roy swung the machine-gun on him.

"Get your mitts up, buddy, or I'll blow your guts out."

The man peered at Roy as if he didn't see very well, then he slowly raised his hands. His moth was compressed into a hard straight line.

"He ain't got his glasses," said Louis.

"Will you shut up?"

"No, Louis," said the watchman. "I ain't. Just my luck. I busted them this afternoon. What's going on here?"

"It's a hold up," said Louis.

"They'll never get away with it."

"O.K.," said Roy. "Just keep your mits up."

"Be right with you," called Red. He and Babe were stuffing money into every pocket. Red glanced over the desk. "Jeez, the whittler! A rumble, Babe."

"Keep your shirts on," called Roy. "It's nothing."

"Let's get going, for Christ's sake," cried Babe in a high-pitched voice. "There may be more of 'em."

A roll of money with a rubber band around it bounced from the desk to the floor and fell at Roy's feet. Keeping his eye on the watchman he bent over to pick it up. Just as his hand touched it, the woman lying on the floor sat up and screamed piercingly. Roy started, dropped the money, picked it up again, and glanced momentarily in the direction of the scream.

A gun roared loudly in the stillness and a bullet clipped a big splinter off the top of the desk just to the left of Roy's ear. Acting instinctively, Roy swung the machine-gun around towards the watchman and pressed the trigger. Louis, Red, and Babe all fell down behind the desk.

The quick stuttering blast of the machine-gun was deafening

112

in the lobby and echoes rolled from wall to wall. The revolver flew out of the watchman's hand and went fifteen feet as if jerked by a wire. He gave a loud cry of surprise and pain, then he began to slap at his legs as if a swarm of bees had attacked him. Finally he fell to the floor with a groan and tried to crawl away, but his legs wouldn't work. His head sank and he lay on his side with his face towards the veranda, groaning.

"Sorry, Pop," said Roy. "I guess you ain't killed. I shot low enough."

The woman was still screaming, wild hair-raising screams, as if she was being tortured. The man had fainted.

Roy turned.

"Come on, guys. Get going."

He started across the lobby. Red hurried over to him and shoved the shoe-box under his left arm. Babe rushed up out of breath, followed by Louis, who looked like a dead man somebody had dug up.

"Where you going?" Roy demanded.

"I'm going with you. I'm all shot. I couldn't face the police now."

Roy studied him for a moment, then he said:

"O.K. Come on."

They crossed the lobby quickly and went out the south entrance. Behind them the woman was still screaming and in between screams she shook her husband, trying to rouse him. The bellboy raised his head cautiously and when he saw the four of them just going out the door he lay down again. The watchman had managed to crawl to the north entrance and was yelling for help.

They crossed the immense lawn rapidly.

A lone car was parked in the plaza, but there was nobody in it. The moon was hidden now by the gigantic mountain to the west and it was dark as a pocket once they got beyond the circle of light from the lobby windows.

Red stumbled and swore. Louis was blubbering.

"I never thought we'd have to shoot anybody."

"Little boys that plays with guns sometimes get hurt," said Red with a forced laugh.

"You sure cut him down," said Babe. "I hope he don't croak. I don't want to be jumping around just a boot ahead of a murder rap."

"I shot low," said Roy. "Clipped his legs out from under him. It didn't do him no good, though. If he don't lose a leg he'll be lucky."

"Damn, it's dark," said Red. "Are we going right? I don't remember. . . ."

"I hope he don't die," said Louis. "He wasn't a bad old guy at all. Used to keep me company."

"Quit whining, Louis. This was your own caper. You thought it up. Now take it and like it."

"God, I feel awful. I'm going to faint, I think. I can't see nothing. I got pains all down my legs. . . . I guess I better go back. I don't know if . . ."

Roy kicked him sharply and he straightened up with a jerk.

"Get yourself together, Louis. We got enough trouble without you blowing your top."

Far away at the end of town they heard the muffled scream of a police siren.

"There's the rumble. Them bums can sure change a tyre quick," said Red. "Where the hell's the heaps?"

"Roy!" Marie called guardedly.

She grabbed his arm. He heard the motors idling.

"You're a sweetheart," cried Red, hugging her. "Let's go places, Babe, and fast! Come on, Louis. Hop in."

The three men disappeared into the darkness. The motor roared, then the car moved off. Babe switched on his parking-lights to get the lay of the road, then he turned them off.

"He's crazy," said Roy, "driving without lights. If the moon was up it'd be different."

"Come on, Roy. Hurry, for God's sake. The siren's getting nearer."

"O.K. Here we go. Is Pard all right?"

"He's in the rumble-seat. I was afraid he'd get lost when we started to blow. When I saw the copper crossing the plaza I knew you'd come running."

"I had to take care of him."

"Yeah. I heard the shots."

Roy switched on his lights and drove off. They could just barely make out Red's car ahead of them.

"He better switch on them lights."

"Don't worry about him," said Marie. "Worry about us."

Roy was driving very fast now and the wind was whistling around them. Behind them and to the right the siren came nearer and nearer, screaming shrilly. Ahead of them, Babe switched on his lights. They were at a crossroad. The highway to Los Angeles made a slight jog to the right. A paved mountain road, which wound off through the canyons to San Diego and Mexico, swept sharply to the left. Roy yelled loudly when Babe swung

114

his car to the left and just barely made the turn, careening, his tyres shrieking.

"Where the hell is he going?"

Roy slowed down and stared up the mountain road. There was a loud crash of a collision, followed by a shattering, jolting, ripping series of sounds, then silence punctuated by the faint tinkle of broken glass.

"My God!" cried Marie.

"Now they done it," said Roy. "What do you suppose they hit? Lost their heads, the damn fools. Small-timers for small-time jobs. This was too big!"

Somebody yelled: "Help! Help!" in an agonized voice.

Roy hesitated, but behind them the siren drew nearer and nearer.

"Damn it! It's bungled. I done the best I could."

Setting his jaw, he drove off in the direction of Los Angeles. At a turn in the road they saw a red glow on the rocks, then a few flames sprang up into the darkness.

"Up in smoke," said Roy. "Their car's on fire. Well, it's a break for us, anyway. It's a cinch them coppers will see the fire."

They drove along for quite a while in silence.

"And they got all the dough," said Roy suddenly. "But I got the glass and that's what Big Mac wants. I done my share. That's all a guy can do." He thrust his hand into his coat pocket and found the roll of bills bound up with the rubber band. He grunted. "I couldn't remember if I stuck them in my pocket or not. Just as I was picking it up this monkey started blasting at me. He didn't miss me over two inches."

"Roy –"

"Yeah?"

"I'm about ready to pass out," said Marie quietly. "No fooling. I –" She slid sideways and fell against him with a groan.

Roy got her head on his shoulder and without slackening pace managed finally to manoeuvre her into a comfortable position.

"Done her part all right," he said. "Not a bad kid. I didn't do much better myself on my first caper. Done everything wrong but faint."

When Marie came to they were driving through a good-sized town. She stared in bewilderment at the red neon lights, then she turned suddenly to see if it was Roy beside her.

"I fainted, I guess."

"You sure did. Say, I'm going to stop. You get Pard out of

the rumble-seat and put him in between us. The word's gone out by now. Guys that stick up places don't carry dogs around with 'em. Get me? You feel all right?"

"Kind of wobbly."

Half an hour later Roy stopped at a traffic light in another town. A highway patrol cop was sitting on his motorcycle at the intersection, scanning the cars which were drawn up. He looked grim. As Roy drew abreast of him, he ran his eyes over the car, then looked in. Pard jumped up and began to bark. The cop grinned.

When they got out on the dark highway, Roy said:

"I hope none of them coppers start rarin'. Nobody's going to stop me getting into L.A. today."

Time passed. First Pard went to sleep, then Marie. Roy felt a little lonely driving through the night and smoked one cigarette after another. At last it began to get light. A blue twilight hung like smoke among the branches of the tall eucalyptus trees along the highway. Houses, barns, and trees began to stand out, then to take on their proper colours. Roy heard roosters crowing. He saw a man, yawning and stretching, leisurely taking the boards down from in front of his roadside orange-stand. A thin white mist was rising from the ground and there was a chill in the air. Finally, behind him, the sky began to glow and a faint golden light spread out all over the awakening countryside.

"I still like to see that sun come up," said Roy aloud, and Marie started awake.

"It's day," she said, rubbing her eyes.

"Yeah. It won't be long now. We'll be in soon, then I'll turn the glass over to Mac and he'll hand me a big roll. We got a fortune in this car, Marie. God knows how much."

"I'll feel better when we get rid of it."

CHAPTER THIRTY

When Roy drove through Los Angeles, people were just going to work, the street-cars and buses were jammed, the traffic heavy. The sun was beating down on the crowded streets and it was already very hot, owing to a dry desert wind which was blowing in from the east.

"This is worse than the desert," he said.

"Yeah," said Marie. "This is the kind of weather when they have brush and forest fires. I nearly got caught in one down around Santa Monica. It was just this time of year. It got so dry my lips cracked. A strong offshore wind was blowing and you could see for miles. All of a sudden the brush caught on fire. I was staying in a hillside house with a —" She hesitated. "With a couple of girl friends. We just got out by the skin of our teeth." Marie fell suddenly silent and stared at the street. She was remembering that weekend party. At the time she thought it was swell. Now it seemed lousy, awful lousy. Things were different now.

Roy turned to look at her. She was pale, and as she hadn't made up recently, her lips looked a little bluish and there were dark shadows under her eyes.

"Tired, kid?"

"Sort of. Roy, I haven't said nothing. I didn't want to bother you. But what do you suppose happened to Babe and Red?"

"That sounded like quite a crash. If they didn't kick off, the coppers have got 'em by now."

"They may talk."

"Nope. I don't think so. But Louis will."

"You're in a spot, ain't you?"

"Oh, I don't know. It ain't worrying me any."

Marie looked at him with admiration.

"I believe you."

"I'm not bragging. I'm used to jams, that's all."

"I know. Roy, if that watchman dies —"

"He dies. He asked for it. If he hadn't come prancing he wouldn't of stopped lead. I can't understand a guy like that. A bunch of chiselling merchants probably give him forty a month and he gets himself shot up for it. He's a sucker."

"He sure is."

They stopped at a traffic light. There was a policeman on the corner. Pard jumped up and barked at him and the cop grinned.

Driving on after the light changed, Roy patted Pard.

"Cop-hater, eh? You'll get yourself in a jam yet, dog."

They were in the centre of Hollywood before Roy spoke again. He glanced at Marie. She looked haggard. Too much strain for a girl. She had no business getting mixed up in such stuff. Most men couldn't stand it, even.

"Look," he said, "after I see Mac I'll have a roll. I'm going to stake you because I'll be blowing pretty soon. Going back east, I guess."

"I'll go 'long."

"Don't be a sap. You got no record. They don't want you. If you run around with me you'll never be in anything but trouble."

She turned to look at him.

"Are you trying to ditch me on account of that gimp you spent your hard-earned dough on?"

"It's not that. She's out anyway. You look tired, kid. You been through a lot. You can't take it. . . ."

"Could she?"

"Of course not. No girl could. I mean . . ."

"I bet I can do a better job of it than any woman you ever met before."

"That's no lie."

"All right. I stick."

Roy glanced at Marie. Her lips were pressed into a firm line. As far as looks went, she wasn't at her best now by any means; in fact she looked plain. But that didn't matter. She was some girl.

"They may be gunning for me before long, kid. If you stick you may stop lead and that's no picnic. I know. I'm still carrying some."

"I'll take a chance. Anyway, who's going to look after Pard?"

"You're crazy. I can leave him at the pound."

"I got a picture of that." Marie put her arm through Roy's and sat up close to him. "Don't think you're going to shake me so easy. I never been so happy in my life. I'm a different girl. I don't feel so much like a bum any more. I feel clean."

Roy looked at her with surprise. Women were sure funny.

"I think you're nuts."

"You think what you like. I'm going wherever you go and that's final. Course you can kick me out. I can't stop you from doing that, But I'll take Pard if you do."

Roy laughed. He felt good. He put his hand on Marie's knee and squeezed it.

"Well, we'll see. If the going gets too tough I may have to park you for a while."

Marie gave a little laugh.

"I'm glad you said 'for a while.' That makes me feel good. If I really get in your way you can park me. Is it a deal?"

"It's a deal."

Roy stopped in front of the Berwyn Arms, wrapped the shoe-box in an old newspaper, then got out.

"I don't like to leave that chopper with you," he said. "But I can't take it with me."

"It's under the seat. So's the ammunition. Don't worry. I'll be all right."

When Roy started away from the car Pard tried to jump over

the door to follow him, but Marie caught the little dog, held him up, and playfully spanked him. He turned, growling, and began to snap at her, baring his teeth. She was startled for a moment, then she laughed, realizing that he thought she wanted to play with him as Roy did.

"You sit down and behave, Pard. Papa will be out in a minute."

The apartment-house lobby was cool and deserted. There was no receiving-desk and nobody was ever on duty. Roy stopped for a moment and shifted a small blunt automatic from his left pants pocket to his right coat pocket. His .45 was in the waistband of his trousers under his vest. He didn't think much of automatics, as they were always jamming, but a little one was a mighty handy weapon at times. It was nicely hidden in a coat pocket; you could slip your hand in casually without anybody suspecting that you were armed.

Mac's door was immediately opened when he knocked. Roy took a step backward. Kranmer was grinning at him from the threshold.

"Hello, Earle."

"Hello. What're you doing here?"

"Looking after things for Mac."

"How come? Where's Mac?"

"He's in bed asleep. Mac's an awful sick man. He collapsed. Got a bad heart. I'm helping him out."

"Yeah? O.K. You walk ahead of me into Mac's bedroom and don't play no games on the way in."

Kranmer laughed.

"Mac said you didn't trust me. It's all right, Earle. Don't get nervous."

"Don't you worry about me getting nervous," said Roy, locking the hall door behind him, "but if you're putting the finger on me you're going to be the first guy to hit the carpet."

"Look, Earle. Mac's paying me. I'm in. Caper turned a little sour, didn't it?"

"Did it?"

"There's an extra out. I knew about it nearly two hours ago. Tough about the two guys."

"It was their own fault."

"Well, their troubles are over."

"Both dead?"

"Yeah. Louis broke his collar-bone and got knocked cold, but he'll be all right. That's the best part of it. The police think Louis was kidnapped. They're looking for the third guy, that

119

did the shooting, but they don't know who he is yet. They ain't even identified Red and Babe. They carried the watchman over to the morgue to look at them and he said neither one of them did the shooting. It was an older fellow."

Kranmer took a crumpled newspaper out of his pocket and held it for Roy to look at. The headlines read: "TROPICO STUNNED BY HALF MILLION DOLLAR ROBBERY . . . early this morning the most daring crime in West Coast criminal annals . . . three men already dead, two injured.

"Who's the third guy?" Roy demanded, impatiently pushing the paper aside.

Kranmer laughed shortly.

"That was sure a funny one. When the alarm went out, the boys at Tropico had two flat tyres on the radio car. Smart work, Earle. So they called the sheriff's substation at Alcott, a little joint in the mountains just west of Tropico. Two deputies jumped in a car and come busting down the mountain and ran smack into Red's car. One of them was killed; the other one never even got a scratch. . . ."

"What a break!" Roy was beginning to feel a little easier with Kranmer. If the guy was a fink he could have had a dozen coppers laying for him as he drove up. Maybe the guy was all right.

"Yeah, they found all the money scattered around the two cars. About fifteen grand, besides nearly ten grand in traveller's cheques. But, Earle, you really nicked 'em on the jewellery. They claim you got about half a million. A lot of famous stuff. Let's go show it to Mac. It may pep him up. He sure had me worried last night. You got it there in the shoe-box?"

"Yeah. And it sure is heavy."

Kranmer pushed open the bedroom door. Big Mac was lying on his side with his face turned away from them. In spite of all the weight he had lost he still made quite a mound under the covers. Roy shut the bedroom door behind him and began to unwrap the shoe box. He felt excited. Five hundred grand! What a beautiful knockover! With a grin he began to shake the jewels out on to Mac's night table – rings of all kinds, pendants, necklaces, brooches, bracelets, ear-rings, a fabulous glittering heap.

Kranmer shook Mac gently.

"Wake up, boss. Earle's here. He clipped them for half a million."

"Yeah," said Roy, "I sure come through for you, Mac. You didn't spring me for nothing."

"Mac," Kranmer insisted, "wake up. Wake up. Earle's here."

Suddenly the detective glanced up blankly at Roy. "This guy's dead."

"He's what?"

"He's dead. My God, Earle, he's cold as a mackerel. Kicked off in his sleep. I just had a feeling last night . . ."

Roy was stunned and stood rubbing his chin. Poor old Mac! Couldn't quite make it. There he was, lying cold, and on his bedside table was a half-million dollars' worth of jewellery. Big Mac! The guy they all used to look up to. The biggest fixer in the Midwest, who used to pay off governors and judges, hobnob with the rich people at Saratoga and Belmont, race his own horses in the handicaps and stakes, and give parties where even a U.S. Senator might appear. Cold as mutton, a worn-out old man!

"Yeah," said Roy, reflectively.

"This is a mess," said Kranmer. "I don't know where he keeps his dough, and he owes me plenty. Let's frisk the joint."

"No," said Roy. "I got business to tend to." He began to gather up the jewellery, turning over and over in his mind Mac's letter of instructions in Jump code, which he had learned by heart.

He turned. Kranmer was watching him. There was a furtive look on the copper's face.

"What're you going to do with all that stuff?"

"I got to turn it over to another guy. I guess Mac had a feeling he'd never make it. He told me just what to do in case something like this come up."

"Don't be a sap," cried Kranmer, getting pale. "Mac's dead. You done the best you could for him. Look, Earle. We're rich. I can get a fence to handle it. We may not get what Mac would have given you for it, but we can clear fifty grand apiece and when the heat dies down we can blow. Don't you get it? We're rich. We don't never have to do a tap of work again. My God, man, use your head! This is the biggest break you'll ever get in your life." Kranmer was sweating with excitement.

"No," said Roy. "You go frisk the joint and see what you can find. I got to use the phone."

"My God, man! You don't mean to tell me —" Kranmer's voice broke; he was overcome. He saw an immense fortune taking wings before his eyes and flying away from him. It was too much to bear.

Kranmer got himself in hand. His face stiffened. He shot a look at Roy, who ignored him.

"O.K., Earle," he said. "I just got a little upset. I guess. Maybe you're right. I'll take a look around."

He went out into the living-room, leaving the bedroom door wide open.

"Don't lam on me," called Roy, "or I'll come and get you. You stay right in this apartment till I say go."

"Say, I'm a right guy," said Kranmer with a whine in his voice. "I don't see why you can't figure that out."

"Yeah," said Roy, dialing his number. He stood facing the bedroom door. He heard Kranmer moving about in the next room, opening drawers and banging things around. "Is this Pico 7179? Like to speak to E. D. That you, E. D.? This is R."

"What do you want? Don't you know you're hotter than a wood-stove? You oughtn't to be calling me up."

"Did they identify me?"

"No. But they will. They all know that the rodman was a big-timer and they know you're out. Tell M. to blow by plane right away."

"M.'s dead. It said in the letter to call you. You're supposed to do the handling."

"Not me. I wouldn't touch that stuff for a million bucks. Boy, what a noise! Every newspaper in town's got ten men out. This is the biggest thing since the Lindbergh case. You better hit for Mexico and crawl in a hole. What happened to the Big Boy?"

"His heart."

"I was afraid of that. You better hang up."

"Wait. It said in the letter if you couldn't handle it, I was to contact Art, you'd give me his number."

"He's got no phone. At least I haven't got his number. But here's his address." Roy wrote it down on a scrap of newspaper. It was a boardwalk address in Ocean Park.

The man at the other end hung up with a bang. Roy gathered up the rest of the jewellery and began to wrap the newspaper around the shoe-box. He heard the shuffle of a foot and turned. Kranmer was standing in the doorway with a big automatic in his right hand. His face was pale and twitching. It took guts to tackle Roy Earle and he was suffering under a terrible strain.

"What's the matter?" said Roy sharply.

"You'll never get out of here with that stuff," said Kranmer. "I didn't find but two hundred dollars in the joint. I want my end."

Roy smiled easily.

"Why don't you look in here, Kranmer? Maybe Mac keeps his roll close to him."

"The hell with that. Hand over the shoe-box, that's what I want. If you give me any trouble, I'll fill you full of lead and turn you in. I'd get a medal."

"That's right," said Roy. "Well, this stuff's pretty hot at that. You're welcome to it."

Picking up the box with his left hand he offered it to Kranmer. But his eyes betrayed him. They looked merciless and hard as flint. He slid his right hand into his coat pocket.

"Don't!" cried Kranmer weakening, his face pale as death. His trigger finger jerked convulsively and Roy saw a spurt of flame and felt a sharp tearing pain in his right side. He shot twice through his coat pocket and Kranmer reeled, clutched at the door-jamb, then slid slowly down, fell over backwards with a loud clatter, and began to flounder. Roy took careful aim and fired one more shot. Kranmer lay still.

"I don't even like to see a bastard like that kick," said Roy.

He picked up the shoe-box, stepped over Kranmer, unlocked the hall door, and glanced out into the hallway. Nobody in sight. He shut the door behind him and started walking quickly down the hall. His side felt as if somebody had touched him with a red-hot poker and he could feel the blood running down his leg.

"I'm getting old," he muttered, "letting a rat like that put the blast on me."

A woman with blond hair opened her door and looked out into the hall. Seeing Roy, she said:

"Did you hear shooting?"

Another door opened and another woman looked out before he could reply.

Roy took off his hat.

"Why, no, ma'am. I didn't."

"I thought I did. It sounded close. But I've got the windows up, so maybe it was outside. Those crazy kids are always driving those cut-down Fords around the streets in this neighbourhood. If they don't stop it I'm going to move."

Another woman looked out and a man peered over her shoulder.

"Might have been a truck," said Roy. "Personally, I didn't hear a thing."

He smiled and walked slowly down the stairs.

Marie was pacing up and down beside the car. Her face looked greyish.

"My God, Roy . . ." she began, but he opened the car door, hustled her in, and drove off. "You still got the jewellery?"

"Yeah. Mac's dead."

"What was all that shooting? I thought somebody had killed you, Roy. I was getting ready to go look for you."

"You damn fool. Never do anything silly like that. When we get to that drugstore down there, you go in and call the Nu-Youth Health Institute and tell Mr. Parker Roy's coming in to see him right away, to be ready."

"I got it. What's wrong, honey? You look bad."

"I got a slug in me, I think, and I want to get it took out."

Marie stared at him, but said nothing. Pard kept whimpering and glancing at Roy; Pard was uneasy; he smelled blood.

"I never saw a caper go so haywire before," said Roy. "I sure never did."

"Don't worry," said Marie. "We'll be all right, honey."

CHAPTER THIRTY-ONE

While Roy was stripping to the waist Doc locked the door and got out his instruments.

"You know, Roy," he said, "I wouldn't do this for anybody but you. That was a dumb caper and you're going to be hotter than a firecracker in a day or so. Did you really crack 'em for five hundred G's?"

"I don't know, Doc. They always kick up the price after a heist. But we got lots of rocks. Look. Before you start cutting I got to tell you something. You got to trust me on the dough angle. I ain't got but fifty-six dollars."

"Didn't get your end yet, eh? All right, Roy. But I figure this is going to cost you five hundred when you do get it. I'm taking an awful chance. Get up here on this table."

Roy lay down and Doc began examining the wound.

"Five hundred is O.K. with me. When I need help, I need help bad, and I'm willing to pay for it. That's the reason none of us guys ever end up with any dough, though. Fall money for the mouthpiece. A wad for the croaker. Another wad for coppers and turnkeys. All we can get our mitts on for a spring if we need it. It's worse than running for office."

"Yeah," said Doc, absentmindedly as he swabbed the blood away; then he laughed. "You're lucky, Roy. The slug tore a hole in your side and went right on past. A little farther down and a little to the left and you'd had a shattered pelvis. Nothing to this if it heals right. But the five hundred still goes. It's the chances I'm taking, not the work."

Roy smoked a cigarette while Doc bandaged him, then he got up and Doc helped him with his clothes.

"That stuff burns like hell, Doc," said Roy, wincing.

"You ought to be glad I didn't use iodine. Here, take this bottle with you. Change the dressing every day and don't take any chances. The guy that put the blast on you was certainly aiming for your belly. He really wanted you down. But what were you doing, Roy? Running around in your underclothes when you caught lead?"

"What do you mean? Oh, I get it. No. I changed clothes in a filling-station toilet. I couldn't be walking around with bullet-holes in my coat."

Doc put his hand on Roy's shoulder.

"Listen, son. Get out of town and stay out. You got nothing to worry about as far as that wound's concerned. Take a tip from old Doc. The heat's really going on in this town. It's going to be mighty unhealthy for a lot of people from now on. The bunch that runs things is in for a trimming and they know it. Ed Seidel's the A-one guy here, you know. And I heard this morning he's taking it on the lam. Going to Honolulu for a vacation and it'll probably be a long one. The fix has slipped. The Bookie Syndicate is in for a pasting. Even the small-time chisellers and the con-men are blowing. I'm glad I'm in an honest gyp-racket now, Roy. But I don't feel natural about it. In the old days when the heat was on I had to hole up like the rest. I can thumb my nose today. It's certainly funny to see the boys running for cover and me holding the fort." Old Doc laughed. "Yeah, Big Mac's luck ran out on him. In the old days if it rained soup he had a wash-boiler in his hands. Now he hasn't even got a fork. If you guys get a rumble and they take you they'll send you up for life and ninety years. So blow and blow fast. But don't forget my five hundred."

"You don't think I'd welsh, do you?"

Doc laughed.

"I'm not even going to answer that one."

Roy grinned.

"Doc, I took your advice."

"How's that?"

"I got a dame can stand the gaff and I'm taking her with me."

"What about little Verna? My friend, the surgeon, says she's O.K."

"Velma's her name. I don't know, Doc. It was just one of them things."

Roy seemed slightly embarrassed, so Doc didn't press the point.

"Yeah. Well, you better get going, Roy. If you'd get taken here I'd be sunk. They'd start looking me up and I'd be keeping you company in San Quentin. I'm sixty years old. A short jolt would finish me."

"Don't worry, Doc. I'm going. So the heat's really on. I thought this town was a playhouse. That's what I heard in Chi."

"It has been for years. And how! But it's all over, Roy. All over."

They shook hands and Roy went out. Doc left his office and walked to the big front windows. He saw Roy get into his car, saw a black-haired girl pat him and handle him possessively, then he started.

"What! They got a dog in that car!" Old Doc stood shaking his head, then he laughed. "Just a big farmer. Give him a dog and a woman and he's satisfied. He should've stayed back on the farm. He'd live longer and have just as much fun. Never could dope Roy out. Some years back it was Myrtle and that chow that bit everybody, even Johnny. I thought that would be the end of the chow and it suited me all right. But Johnny just laughed it off. Kind of a good-natured guy, at that. Of course maybe he was scared of Roy. I'd be."

A buzzer sounded over his head and he glanced up. Corson again. Wanted help. Old Doc sighed and turned.

"Mrs. Hansen's probably got a fever. If she has it's over that new young doctor I signed on today. He doesn't know straight up, but he's got curly hair and he's twenty-five years old. He ought to bring me in a lot of business."

CHAPTER THIRTY-TWO

When they got out into the far south end, Roy suddenly turned off the boulevard and drove down a side street.

Marie sat up abruptly. She'd been riding with her head on the back of the seat and her legs stretched out, perfectly relaxed. She bumped Pard and he jumped up, too, and barked sharply, still half asleep.

"Where you going, Roy?" But before he could reply, she knew. "So that's it."

"It's right on our way."

"So what? Fine time you pick to go calling. We got a machine-gun and a shoe-box full of jewellery. Suppose some nosey cop would come smelling around?"

"He'd be sorry."

"So would Ma and Pa and little Eva and all the rest of your sucker friends."

Roy set his jaw.

"You said a mouthful, Marie. But when I get rid of this stuff we're going to blow. The heat's on bad, Doc says. I may never get another chance to say hello to the folks. I promised to come and see Velma walk, didn't I? You heard me."

"You didn't promise. I remember exactly what you said. You said you'd try to make it."

"Well, I was sore that day. Pa knows I meant I'd come. My God, Marie, it was my own idea. If it wasn't for me Velma'd still be a cripple."

"I couldn't bear it, the poor little thing!"

"You're just jealous, that's all."

"All right. If you get knocked over visiting them people, you deserve it. Course I'll go up, too, but that's nothing. And Pard'll go to the pound and get gassed."

Roy squirmed.

"It'll only take a minute. I'll tell 'em I'm going back east."

"Tell 'em you're taking me back with you and I won't say another word. Only I'm going in."

"It'll look funny," said Roy, still squirming. Marie said nothing. "All right. You win."

When Roy parked the car, he saw a shiny new sedan in front of Velma's house. Marie laughed.

"Looks like competition."

Roy patted Pard, then locked his car thoughtfully.

"Do you suppose that director guy . . .? No, he wouldn't know where to find her."

"What are you mumbling about?"

"This bit director, Marty Pfeffer, saw Velma in Tropico and he told me himself she had a very interesting face."

"He told you! Oh, so you run around with the Hollywood crowd now, hunh? That's the first I ever heard of it."

"It's a long story. It couldn't be him. He'd never know where to find her."

"That's tough. He's probably got the militia out looking for her."

"You shut up."

"All right. I'll shut up. But I hate to see a guy like you making

127

a sap of himself over a little fluff like that. We used to have babes like her around the dance-hall. The pimps got 'em all."

Roy stopped and turned.

"Marie, if you don't . . ." He saw that she was about to cry and hesitated. "O.K. It'll only take a minute."

"No matter what happens, I won't let you stay. I won't."

"I don't want to. Anyway, I can't."

When Roy knocked he heard music and several people laughing. Velma's mother opened the door. He hardly knew her. She'd had a permanent and her face was made up like a girl of eighteen. She had on a snappy new dress, much too young for her, and she was smiling happily. But she frowned at Roy.

"Oh, it's you."

"Yeah. How do you do, Mrs. Baughman? Meet my friend, Marie Garson. I'm going back east, so I thought I'd drop in and say goodbye."

"How do you do?" said Velma's mother, nodding coldly to Marie. "So you're going back east? Well, come in. I know Pa'll be glad to see you."

Roy hardly knew the house, it looked so clean and neat. In the living-room a Victrola was playing and he heard Velma laughing.

"Oh, you're getting it now, Velma," came Pa's voice. "That's it. That's it."

Roy heard the shuffling of feet, followed by more laughter; then they went in. Ma was sitting placidly on a sofa, dressed in her best. Even Ma had been to the beauty parlour. Her white hair was carefully waved, making her look a little unnatural. Pa was standing in the middle of the room with a cigar in one hand and a glass of wine in the other. He had on a starched collar, which was obviously sawing his neck, and his sparse grey hair was plastered down and neatly parted. A strange young man was teaching Velma a new dance step.

Velma hesitated and looked over her shoulder. At the sight of Roy she started slightly; then he saw for the third time that weak smile he didn't like.

"Roy! We thought you'd gone. Where have you been?"

She came running to him, laughing, her mouth slightly open with excitement. But she didn't stumble now. She managed her extremely high heeled shoes expertly. And she looked neither sad nor pathetic. Her face was glowing, her eyes shining. She also had been to the beauty parlour. Her coarse blond hair was arranged in symmetrical waves. She looked mighty cute and pretty. But to Roy this wasn't Velma at all. This was a blonde kid that you'd try to make quick or let alone. You'd never lie thinking about her at night.

"Hello, Velma," he said, shaking hands with her.

"Did you see me? I can dance. I'm learning, I mean. Oh, excuse me, Roy, this is Mr. Preiser. He's from back home."

"Howdy," said Roy, shaking hands with the young fellow.

"Oh, hello," said Velma, turning to Marie. "Lon, this is Miss Garson. Does she remind you of anybody back home?"

"Glad to meet you, Miss Garson," said Preiser, bowing slightly. "Why, yes, she does. Nona Braden."

Velma glanced triumphantly at Pa and Ma.

"That's what I said."

"Only better-looking," said Preiser. "Much better."

"Thanks," said Marie. "Of course I never saw your friend Nona, so I don't know whether it's a compliment or not. Was that the shag you were trying to do a minute ago?"

"Yes," said Preiser, "that's what they call it back home."

"You haven't got it right," said Marie. "Let me show you."

"Delighted." Preiser started the record over and took Marie carefully about the waist.

He began haltingly, a little intimidated by Marie, but in a moment they were doing the intricate, syncopated steps in perfect unison.

"You know," said Marie, flashing him a brilliant smile, "you're not half bad."

"Thanks," said Preiser, beaming. "You're wonderful, if you don't mind my saying so."

Velma looked on a little bewildered, then she went to sit beside Ma, who patted her shoulder and glared at Marie. Pa came over and put his arm around Roy and hugged him.

"He's going to marry her," he whispered. "Ma and I are going back for the wedding."

"Yeah?" said Roy. "Why, that's fine, Pa." But he wasn't paying much attention to what the old man was saying. He was getting sorer every minute. What the hell did Marie think she was doing, rubbing up against the guy like that! Once a bum, always a bum.

"You better let Velma dance with him, Marie," he said trying to hide his irritation. "She's just learning. You know all the steps."

"Wait till the record's over, please," said Preiser. "I'm learning now, too. I had it all wrong, I guess. What a wonderful dancer you are, Miss Garson!"

"Chump!" thought Roy. Was this the guy he'd wanted to put

129

the blast on? This nice-looking, curly-haired, polite young fellow, harmless as a mosquito? Look at him there getting all fuddled because a bum was pulling the dime-a-dance rub on him!

And suddenly Roy didn't give a damn about Velma, or about Pa and Ma. He realized that they had never been real people to him at all, but figments out of a dream of the past. He began vaguely to understand that ever since the prison gate clanged shut behind him he'd been trying to return to his boyhood, where it was always summer and in the evenings the lightning-bugs flashed under the big branches of the sycamore trees and he swung on the farm gate with the yellow-haired girl from across the road while the Victrola on the porch played *Dardanella*. . . . Pa and Ma were replicas of his own folks merely, and Velma wasn't really Velma, a slim, ordinary little blonde, but the ghost of Roma Stover, the yellow-haired girl swinging on the gate. . . .

The music stopped. Preiser bowed slightly and thanked Marie for her expert teaching. He looked a little heated. He was flushing and a damp lock of dark curly hair had fallen over his forehead. Ma gave Velma a push.

"You dance now, pet."

After a while Velma's mother brought them all in a glass of wine.

"Yes," Preiser was saying, "I was tickled when I found out the Exhibitors' Convention was going to be in Los Angeles. Velma was out here and I was trying to think up some excuse to get out to see her. I hated to leave my business, but along came the convention and so . . ."

"You boys have quite a time on them conventions, I hear," said Marie.

Preiser laughed and flushed.

"That's what they tell me. But that's out, as far as I'm concerned."

Velma smiled and threw a triumphant glance at Marie.

"I'm going back east, too," Marie was saying. "Roy wants me to ride back with him and I guess I will."

"Tell them, Lon."

"Velma and I are going to get married."

"Oh, really?" said Marie. "Now, that's nice. Isn't it, Roy?"

Velma glanced at Roy. She saw the hard glitter in his eyes and paled slightly. Roy shook himself.

"Yeah. Yeah. That's fine. Congratulations." He managed a counterfeit grin with difficulty, then he shook hands with Prei-

130

ser, who winced. "Best of luck." He turned to Pa and Ma. "Sorry, Pa, but I guess we'll have to be going. I'm hitting east and I want to get started. That's why I dropped in."

"Well, don't rush off, Roy. Ain't it grand the way Velma can walk and even dance?"

Preiser interposed. He looked embarrassed.

"Mr. Goodhue told me all about what you did for Velma and I want to say that I feel I ought to reimburse you ... I mean, after all, that's a lot of money ..."

"Forget it," said Roy. "Think nothing of it." He was in a hurry to get out of this house. He was like a man walking in his sleep who suddenly wakes up and wonders how he got where he is. These people didn't mean a thing to him now, not a damn thing. All he could think about was getting Marie outside and giving her hell.

"Yeah," said Roy.

He and Marie shook hands all around. Pa kept detaining them, making little jokes, squeezing Roy's arm, till finally Roy pulled away rudely and went down the steps. Marie saw the hurt look on Pa's face and patted him on the back.

"Roy's a little upset, I guess," she said. " 'Bye, Pop. Don't take any wooden nickels."

When they had gone, Velma turned and, frowning at Preiser, said:

"Did you have to dance that close to her?"

"Was I dancing close? I didn't know it. I was trying to get those steps down pat so I could teach them to you, Velma."

"Now, Velma," said her mother.

"I don't care. Roy noticed it, and he was furious."

"Then he shouldn't go around with such a girl," said Ma. "Don't you blame Lon. It wasn't his fault. What can a man do when a girl grabs him like that? A man has to be polite."

"Oh, he was polite, all right," said Velma.

"I wouldn't mind a turn or two with her myself," said Pa, pouring himself another glass of wine. "But Roy was mad as a hornet. Yes, he was."

"Maybe that wasn't what he was mad about," said Velma, raising her nose at Preiser and giving a little shrug. Then she went out into the hall and Preiser followed her.

"Now, Velma ..."

"I'm not crippled any more, Lon Preiser, and don't you forget it. Don't you ever let me see you dancing with another girl like that or you'll go back to Ohio alone and I'll stay out here. I like California and I may stay anyway."

"Oh, Velma, it wasn't my fault."

"It was. You wouldn't even stop when Roy told you to. You know what Roy was mad about? He was mad because I'm marrying yóu. He's crazy to marry me."

"I know," said Lon, sadly.

Velma turned to look at him, then she put her arms around him and said:

"Oh, honey, I'm so jealous. Are you?"

"Yes," said Lon. "I'm glad that man's gone."

CHAPTER THIRTY-THREE

Instead of bawling Marie out as he had intended, Roy sat staring at the road, driving in silence. From time to time he reached down and rubbed Pard's ears absentmindedly. Marie watched him out of the corner of her eyes. He was silent so long that she finally said:

"Want me to light a cigarette for you, Roy?"

"No."

He was gradually cooling off. The only thing for him to do was to keep his mouth shut until he could talk calmly. No use letting Marie know he was jealous of her. Women were all smart when it came to men; Marie especially so. She had put on the act for a reason; not because she wanted to cuddle up to a guy she'd never seen before. She was either trying to put Velma in her place or to make him jealous, and she'd done a pretty good job both ways.

"Still sore?" asked Marie.

"Not particularly. But you sure gave 'em an eyeful."

"And made a chump out of her boy friend. Why, I could twist him around my finger. I guess your little Velma ain't so much."

"Yeah? Well, she don't throw herself at a guy."

"She's scared to."

"O.K. Have it your way."

"You never saw me dance before, did you? I'm good. I admit it. Can you dance, Roy?"

"A little."

"Some night we'll go dancing. They've got dine-and-dance places all along the roads out here."

"Maybe."

Marie turned suddenly and, putting her arm around him, kissed him on the cheek.

"I'm nuts about you, Roy. Don't be mad. I was just trying to show you how easy it is for me to get a man. Sometimes you act as if you thought nobody would look at me but you."

Roy turned and kissed her fiercely on the mouth.

"If I catch you rubbing up to another guy like that I'll cut your ears off."

Marie laughed and drew away.

"If I do, you won't catch me."

Roy sat swearing under his breath. What a chump! In spite of himself he'd walked right into it.

"I was kidding," he said. "You can get out of the car right now and go about your business. That's what I think of you."

"I won't, though," said Marie. "Anyway, I don't believe you."

Roy lit a cigarette and they drove along in silence. Marie sat petting Pard and glancing at Roy.

In a little while they saw the Pacific Ocean at the end of a street. It was a grey day. A white fog-bank was massed far.

"Funny how different it is at the beach," said Marie. "Back in town it's hot and dry. I don't like the beach in the fall. It makes me feel funny. I don't know."

"So that's the Pacific," said Roy. "I'll take Lake Erie."

He drove into a little parking-lot near the boardwalk and got out.

"Don't be long," said Marie.

"I'll make it snappy. You better let Pard empty out, because when we leave here we're going to keep moving." He put the shoe-box under his arm and hurried away.

A stiff wind was blowing from the northwest and as Roy walked up the boardwalk it pasted his clothes against him and tugged at his hat. He turned to look at the water. Towering waves were rolling slowly in, seething and throwing spray high into the air; they broke with a roar on the beach, and the boardwalk shuddered under him.

"Ten thousand miles across that water to China," said Roy. "I'll stay here."

Most of the concessions along the beach were closed. There was hardly anybody about. The place looked dismal and deserted.

He found the number finally and knocked at a battered door beside a shooting-gallery which had its front boarded up. The door was immediately opened and Roy stared into a narrow hallway which was black as a pocket.

"That you, R.?" came a voice.

"It's me. Did Ed get in touch with you?"

"Yeah. Sent a man over. Come on back."

Roy followed a little man back through a long narrow passageway which was like a tunnel. A door opened and light sprang out into the darkness. Roy saw a cozy little room with a couple of expensive sofas, a big radio, and a tile-top coffee-table loaded with bottles, glasses, and siphons. There were pictures of bathing beauties, prizefighters, and race horses on the walls. A single big lamp gave off a mellow light.

"I'm Art," said the little man, turning to shake hands. He had a sharp, rather handsome face and a wise, friendly air, but his pale eyes were too close together and he had a big mouth with thick lips.

"Howdy," said Roy.

They sat down and Roy put the shoe-box on the coffee-table. Art picked it up, hefted it, then began to spill the jewels out. His eyes got bigger and his mouth sprang open.

"If I didn't know where they come from," he said, "I'd think they was phonies. Wouldn't they turn on the heat when we got our mitts on something like this?"

"I heard the heat was on."

"On? I'll say it's on. Ed's lamming for Honolulu. You got a picture of him running out with this kind of take in his lap if things wasn't sizzling, ain't you? He's got plenty dough in this job. Mac didn't have a red."

"Mac was broke, eh?"

"Not only broke; he owed everybody. Why, that guy had a million bucks at one time, but he threw it away on horses and blondes. Was he a sucker for a blonde! Couple of years ago I introduced him to a young kid named Saisy. She was an usher in a movie house, making a little dough on the side. Strictly a one-night-stand type. What does Mac do? He takes her to Paris with him and she comes back with a chinchilla coat. A five-dollar-a-throw dame!"

"Poor old Mac," said Roy. "There he was dead and half a million bucks right beside him."

"This ain't no half a million."

"That's what the papers said, but course they always heist it."

"It's plenty, though," said Art.

"Well, it's all yours now. I want my end."

Art shook his head.

"You're going to have to wait for that, Roy. I got no dough to speak of. I'm in twelve hundred as it is and I hate to think how far Ed's in. Mac was an all right guy, but it cost him like hell 1 operate. He had to spring you. He wouldn't listen to nothing else. Then he bought two cars, yours and Red's. New ones, too. Kept you guys while Louis waited for the plunge. One thing and another. It was sure an expensive caper, and did it turn sour! I hope Louis keeps his trap shut. He's clean as a whistle if he'll just stay smart."

"Look. I got to have some dough."

"Can't help you much. Fifty's my limit. Roy, I guess you know that Max, in Kansas City, is the big noise behind this caper. He and Ed, that is; and Ed's out now. Mac was the engineer, that's all; and I'm strictly petty larceny with a cheap cut-in. You leave the stuff with me and lam. Stick around close. I got a secret telephone number. I'll give it to you. In a couple of days call me up. Max'll be here then and we'll figure your end."

"You wouldn't pull a fast one on me, would you, Art? I don't like fast ones."

Art fingered his chin nervously. He wasn't used to dealing with big-time heist guys like Roy Earle. He was used to pushing the small fry around.

"All I can say is, Ed sent you here. Mac knew I was in. What's my percentage in pulling a fast one on you? Anyway, Max wouldn't let me if I wanted to; not that I do. Max is a right guy."

"I heard different."

"Take the stuff," said Art. "It's like carrying a bomb around, anyway. I just got a feeling I'll end up in S.Q. over this one."

"Give me a hundred bucks," said Roy. "You keep the stuff. But if I don't get my end I'll come gunning for you; and Max, too. He ain't too big for me."

"All right. Hundred it is. And here's my number," said Art, shoving a card at Roy. "Learn the number by heart and throw that card away. Roy, you got no cause to get sore. I'm just doing the best I can. If I was smart I wouldn't touch this stuff with a fishing-pole."

"I just want you guys to know where I stand, that's all."

Art took ten ten-dollar bills out of his billfold and put them on the coffee-table. Roy picked them up, shoved them into his pants pocket, but hesitated and began to finger the jewellery. Art looked on without comment. Finally Roy selected an unpretentious platinum ring with a single, medium-sized diamond set in it.

"That's the one I want," he said. "Nobody would take a second look at it on a dame's finger. A copper could see some of

135

them headlights fifty feet away. It would be like wearing a sign. O..K, Art. I'll give you a buzz in a couple of days. So far I'm in the clear. Nobody's looking for me. I'll stick around pretty close."

Art got up quickly and shook hands with Roy.

"Don't you worry about your end," he said. "We like your work. May want you again. Max may have a good job for you."

"That's O.K. with me. So long."

"I'll go out to the boardwalk with you. You might get lost in here, or some of the dames that live upstairs might tackle you. Business is terrible. Even the coppers ain't making any dough."

At the door they shook hands again. Roy glanced out to sea. The wind had died down. The white fog-bank was moving slowly towards the beach. It was cold and gloomy.

Suddenly a feeling of loneliness came over him and, turning, he hurried towards the parking-lot where Marie and Pard were waiting for him. Suppose they'd got a rumble? Suppose some nosey chiselling copper had come smelling around? Sweat broke out on his forehead and he stumbled over a loose board in his haste. But when he turned the corner there they were. Marie was sitting with her head against the back of the seat, calmly puffing on a cigarette, and Pard was leaning out looking at the sea-gulls.

Marie smiled when Roy got in. He didn't say anything. He just took her right hand and slipped the ring on the first finger he got hold of.

"Why, Roy!" cried Marie, and her face lit up and she gave him such a look of gratitude and joy that he felt uncomfortable. It was like that time at Tropico when he'd helped Pa. Pa had looked just like that. And suddenly Roy was ashamed of the way he had acted at Velma's and he wanted to go back and shake hands with the old man and say something to him.

"Present," said Roy with a grin.

Marie flung her arms around him and began to cry.

"Oh, I'm glad you're not sore at me, Roy, for the way I acted. It was only on account of you. I just wanted you to see how men felt about me. I just . . ."

"Sure, sure," said Roy, soothingly. "Look. We got to get moving."

"Course you'd put it on the wrong hand," said Marie.

CHAPTER THIRTY-FOUR

It was a perfect desert night. A cool gentle breeze was blowing up from the south, ruffling the sagebrush. The sky was vast and far away, and thousands of stars were glittering like jewels in the thin, dry air.

Marie and Roy were sitting out in front of their auto-court cabin, smoking and watching the cars zip past on the highway. Pard was lying at their feet, dozing.

"Swell night," said Marie.

"Yeah."

"Funny. I never used to notice the nights much. I'm happy I guess."

"Yeah," said Roy. "Me, too. I ain't much for just sitting around ordinarily. But I don't care if I don't move till bed-time."

"I feel great. Funny thing. I never used to feel like this. All I thought about was getting my hands on a big piece of change."

"Well, we'll soon have our hands on quite a hunk and you know it. Maybe that's why you feel great."

"No," said Marie. "We ain't got that money yet, and I never count my chickens before they're hatched. It's just because I got you and Pard, Roy. I never really had anybody before. Nobody I ever cared a hoot about, I mean."

"I know. When I was a young fellow I thought that all you needed to be happy was a wad of dough. And then when I got my first big wad (ten G's, it was) I wondered why I wasn't happy. I didn't feel no different at all. I was just the same guy. The same things bothered me like they did before. Course I could gamble and buy good clothes and fly around some, but it's a funny thing how little that means to a guy. Then I met Myrtle and things were different for a while. Flush or broke, I was happy. But it didn't last."

"Yeah. You got to have somebody you care about, that's all."

"Yep. Money sure is a funny thing. I used to know a guy named Ed Tuttle. He was a swell fellow. He had a farm and pegged along making a living just like the rest of the farmers in them days, but not saving anything. He didn't give a damn. But one day the railroad bought him out on account of a right of way or something. And there he was with forty grand in cash. He got so tight he wouldn't even buy his family enough to eat. He just spent his time watching his dough. One day he got scared and decided he'd put all his dough in Liberty bonds, where it'd be safe. So he goes to the county seat and has a talk with a chiselling banker over there by the name of Kramm. Kramm tells him he's a chump for putting his money in Liberty bonds, on account of they don't pay enough interest. So he sells Ed forty grand worth of gilt-edge Chicago hotel bonds which paid six or seven per cent. In two years them bonds wasn't worth the paper they was printed on and Ed's broke. He'd got so nobody would even speak to him; his own kids hated his guts. But he turned right around again, leased a farm, and went to work. Last time I saw him he was just like he used to be and everybody liked him. Yeah, dough's a funny thing."

"Yeah," said Marie, thoughtfully.

Pard woke with a start and looked about him wildly for a moment; then he got up, yawning and stretching, and put his head on Roy's knee. Roy rubbed his ears.

"What's the matter, Pard? Seen a ghost?"

"He was dreaming. I never paid no attention to dogs till I got to know Pard. I didn't know they had dreams like people."

"Sure. I used to have an old dog called Sport. He used to sleep in front of the fire on winter nights and his feet would move like he was running and he'd bark, sort of. That dog chased rabbits in his dreams all night long."

"I wonder if they ever have silly dreams like we do that don't mean nothing."

"I guess they do. Pard was sure scared there for a minute. I don't know."

"You like dogs, don't you, Roy?"

"Yeah. I sure do. You know, it's funny about us guys. People get the craziest notions. If you believed what you read you'd think we went around kicking old ladies in the face and torturing animals. One time I read a book in stir that Barmy gave me. It was all about the old gangs of New York. There was a gangster in it named Monk Eastman. He was crazy about animals and when he got old he opened a pet-store. The guy that wrote the book couldn't get over it. He thought it was wonderful." Roy laughed and shook his head. "I wish he could've seen some of the guys in stir. The toughest guy I knew in clink, Doby Lemon, had a trained mouse. It'd come in his cell every night and it'd sit on the palm of his hand and eat stuff he'd saved for it. Doby was sure crazy about that mouse. But something happened to it; one night it didn't turn up and Doby never seen it again. His cell-mate told me that Doby had used to talk about that mouse with tears in his eyes. Half a dozen guys had pet cock-

138

roaches; some of 'em carried the bugs around in little tin boxes. One guy, Zeke Patman, had a pet rat. They say it used to roll over on its back and do other tricks. I never seen it. It used to crawl up a drain-pipe with him. Yeah, people sure got funny ideas about us guys."

There was a long silence. Finally Marie asked:

"Roy, when we get all that money what are we going to do?"

"I ain't sure. But I know one thing: we'll hit east. Maybe stick around Chicago awhile and see some shows. Might go on to New York. It's quite a burg. I got the roof of my mouth sunburned looking at the tall buildings once."

"You didn't!"

"That's an old gag. I'm surprised at a sharp kid like you falling for it."

"Some gags are so old they're new."

"Yeah," said Roy, reflectively, "that's right. The first time I seen New York was fifteen years ago. You was hardly out of diapers."

"What do you mean? I was ten years old." Marie jumped up and mussed his hair. He made a grab for her but missed and she bounded into the cabin and stood in the doorway taunting him, but hesitated. Roy was grimacing and pressing his hand to his right side.

"Wow!" he said. "I got to quit jerking around like that."

"Does it hurt bad?" asked Marie, coming back and putting her hand on his shoulder.

"It'll ease off."

"Come on in, Roy. I'll change the dressing."

"No. Wait till we go to bed. You can make me some coffee now. Boy, oh, boy! Well, I'm old enough to know better. I got to move easy after this."

Marie bent down and kissed him. He put his arms around her and hugged her; she excited him more every day.

"Love me, Roy?"

"I sure do. You bet. I guess you're right, Marie. I guess we better change that bandage right now."

Marie laughed.

"Come on."

Pard watched them go into the cabin, then he got up on the top step and lay down. In a little while he fell asleep and began to dream.

The little dog whimpered in his sleep while the stars marched in a slow procession over his head and meteors blundered into

139

the earth's atmosphere and burst into white-hot flames, leaving short-lived silvery trails in the velvet darkness.

One by one the lights of the little desert town went out; traffic on the highway slowed down until there was nothing but an occasional lone car. A heavy silence throbbed round the autocourt. Finally, far off, a coyote set up a dismal howl, and Pard jumped straight out of his dream with his hackles up and his teeth bared. Behind him the door opened and Roy's voice said:

"Come in, you little bugger, or that wolf'll get you."

CHAPTER THIRTY-FIVE

When Roy came in, Marie was setting the table and Pard was perched on a chair, watching her.

"Well?" said Marie, studying Roy's face and noticing that he looked tired and irritable.

"Same old song. Max ain't showed yet. I'm going to run out of dough calling that guy, Art, long distance." He fell down into a chair, took off his hat, and tossed it into the bedroom, where it lit on the bed. Then he began to rub Pard's ears absentmindedly. The little dog turned his head slowly from side to side as Roy rubbed first one ear then the other.

"Look," said Marie suddenly, "your hat's on the bed. I don't like that." She ran in quickly, picked up the hat, and put it on the dresser.

She came back and began to bustle about the table. She looked so fresh, strong, neat, and capable at her work that Roy had a twinge of envy as he watched her. He was feeling old, nervous, and off his feed.

"You and your superstitions!" he grumbled, wanting to hurt or irritate her. "That's just plain dumb. A kid knows better than that."

"Yeah?" said Marie. "All right. But I've been to fortunetellers lots of times and you'd be surprised if you knew the things they told me."

"Malarkey."

"All right. That's what you say. But sometimes things like that work out. Look at Pard."

"O.K. Look at him!"

"You know what Algernon always said. He was bad luck. Well, ain't he?"

"If you say so," said Roy, in an irritating voice, patting Pard.

"Well, ain't he?"

"No," cried Roy. "Pard's got nothing to do with it. Blaming things on a poor little old dog! Things were stashed up to go haywire and they did. That's all. Babe goes up the wrong road and he and Red get killed. Old Mac kicks off. A chiselling copper walks into one that he's been breeding for a long time. Max starts out, his plane makes a forced landing on account of a storm, and he gets his arm busted. All on account of Pard. Nuts!"

"It ain't natural for everything to go wrong, is it?"

"I don't know whether it's natural or not. It happened, so maybe it is. You know what a friend of mine used to say? With stupid people superstition is a substitute for religion. That's what he said."

"My, what big words! I'll bet it was Barmy Johnson said that. If you don't stop talking about him, some day I'll scream."

"Oh, so you don't like the way I talk. O.K. Any time you get so you can't stand it any longer, beat it. Scram. Nobody's holding you."

Marie had a plate in her hand. Gritting her teeth, she banged it against the sink and broke it to pieces.

"All right," she said. "Right now's as good as any time."

She went into the bedroom and slammed the door shut. Roy sighed, pulled his chair up to the table, and, leaning on his hands, stared out the window into the gathering dusk of a mountain evening. They were staying in a cabin at Paulson's Camp, an isolated spot six or seven miles off the main highway. It was late in the season now and there were very few people around. But the altitude at Paulson's was only about five thousand feet, so the weather was still fairly good, though the nights were very cold. A hundred yards from the cabin was Granite Lake; there was still a faint light on it and Roy could see it glimmering coldly between the black tree-trunks. From time to time a gull cried and the sound drifted up softly, sad, lonely, and remote.

Roy groaned and turned in his chair. His wound was bothering him, had been for days; if he didn't begin to feel better pretty soon he'd have to make a dash in to see old Doc. But he hated to do that, as he still owed him five hundred dollars. Besides, things were hot in the city. The newspapers were playing up the Tropico business and the mysterious deaths of Kranmer and Big Mac as if ten thousand criminals had suddenly descended on the community and nobody was safe, not even in his own home. City detectives, men from the sheriff's office, D.A.

dicks, private investigators for the insurance companies, and a horde of newspapermen were combing southern California for clues to the identity of the older man who had done the shooting at Tropico. Some shrewd bird in the D.A.'s office, in a newspaper interview, had said that in his opinion the deaths of Kranmer and Big Mac were definitely hooked up with the Tropico knockover.

Red and Babe had long been identified and buried. Roy discovered that Red's name was Joseph Potter; and Babe's name was Arnold Francis Milnik; he was twenty-three years old and had been an honour student in grammar school; he had a great grandmother, ninety-four, who had seen the Germans march into Paris in 1870. Her picture was in the paper. It was anything for copy. The reporters had been rooting around all over California trying to dig up stuff they could use to keep the case hot. All the newspapers, except one, were fighting the city administration, which was on its way out, but still putting up a battle for power. The police were held up to ridicule. High officials were laughed at openly and charged with malfeasance. And the Tropico case and the deaths of Kranmer and Big Mac were so many clubs in the hands of the insurgents and they swung them viciously.

"Don't look like things will ever cool off," said Roy with a sigh; then he glanced down.

Pard had put his head on Roy's knee and was staring up at him inquiringly with his pale, shrewd eyes.

Roy patted him.

"He knows, that little devil," he said. "Can't fool him."

He heard a faint noise and turned. Marie had opened the bedroom door an inch or two and was peering at him.

He wanted to make up with her. He didn't want her to leave him. He depended on her more and more every day. But not being able to get any definite word from Art had made him irritable and he'd taken it out on her just because she looked so young and capable when he felt so old and fumbling. He'd been a chump not to take the jewellery with him. They'd be looking him up if he had.

"Roy," called Marie.

"Yeah?"

"I'm about ready. Will you take me down to Ballard so I can get a bus?"

"Come and get my dinner."

There was a long silence, then Marie came out with an embarrassed look on her face. She wasn't ready at all. She still had her apron on.

142

Roy laughed.

"Bluffer!"

"Well, you're so mean to me sometimes. If you keep it up some day I *will* run away. I'll take the car, and Pard, too; then we'll see how you like it."

"What do you want with Pard? He's poison, that dog. Why, he killed Mac and God knows what all."

"I didn't mean what I said about Pard. I was just arguing. Sometimes you irritate me so I can't stand it. You think when you say a thing, that's that. Nobody knows nothing but you."

Roy winced slightly and turned away from Marie to hide it.

"Roy! It's hurting you again. You come right in here and let me change that dressing."

Roy got slowly to his feet and Marie put her arm around him and helped him into the bedroom.

"I'd like to see you, if I run away from you," she said. "Why, you're just a big baby. How you got along without me all these years I don't know."

He playfully mussed her hair, grinning feebly; then his face got serious, he kissed her on the cheek, and said:

"I don't either, kid. No fooling. I don't."

When he was stripped to the waist he lay back on the bed and Marie began to take off the bandage which was wrapped round and round his waist.

"Ooo!" said Marie, making a face. "It's stuck."

"Give it a yank. Oh, Christ! You sure take a guy at his word, don't you?"

"Can't take it. Getting soft."

"Oh, my God! Doc said it was a good thing he didn't use iodine. What's that stuff? Liquid dynamite!"

"You ought to see your face," said Marie with a laugh. "To hear the papers talk you'd think you was the toughest guy in the world. 'The hard-faced, commanding bandit with the machine-gun.' That's what Vince Healy called you. He ought to see you now."

"Vince Healy! That fink. I'd like to know how much dough he's getting for blasting the administration. That's all he is. Just a plain fink, and they call him a newspaperman. He's nothing but Edgar Hoover's little poodle. The big brave G-men! It took forty of 'em to knock Johnny off and he didn't even have a gun on him. It's the God's truth."

"Don't get so excited."

"And an East Chicago copper shot him at that!"

"Shot who?"

"Why, Johnny. It's a wonder them G-men didn't kill forty people the way they was blasting. At that they shot a couple of women in the tokus. Crossfire!"

"Is that tight enough?"

"Yeah."

"It don't look so good, Roy. It's all red way up under your armpit. You got any fever?"

"I don't think so. Maybe I have. I ought to go in and see Doc, but . . ."

"No, you can't do that. They might kill you. You can't trust nobody. Not even your friends. Ten thousand dollars is a lot of money."

"You ought to turn me in and live easy the rest of your life."

"If you wasn't a sick man I'd punch you in the nose."

Roy tried to pull her down on the bed with him, but she squealed and wrenched herself away.

"No. I got to finish dinner. You wait till you see what I'm cooking for you. Lay right there till I call you."

She turned off the light in the bedroom and went out, leaving the door open. Roy lay in the darkness dozing and listening to the pleasant kitchen sounds. Marie had on felt bedroom slippers and she moved about soundlessly, but Pard, who was hungry, followed her back and forth and Roy could hear his toe-nails clicking on the linoleum.

Suddenly he felt good all over. His wound had stopped hurting. He lay smiling in the darkness.

"I'm a chump to be mean to her," he told himself. "A man's lucky to have a kid like that to take care of him. Hell, what good am I, after all? A goddamned has-been. Why kid myself? Yeah I should get up on my hind legs and r'ar and tell her off! A lot I got to kick about. Lucky, that's what I am."

"Honey," he called, "how you doing? Can't I help some way?"

There was a long silence, then Marie said:

"You *must* have a fever! Just relax, honey. I'll call you when it's ready."

CHAPTER THIRTY-SIX

Marie had insisted on going into the little dine-and-dance joint in the desert town they were passing through.

They had moved down from Paulson's Camp after the blizzard and were living at an auto-court in Ballard. Roy had wanted to stay in and read the newspapers, but Marie had been restless and had put up such a howl that he had taken her for a ride.

They sat in a booth and ordered some drinks, then Roy picked up his newspaper and, holding it in front of his face, began to read. Marie squirmed and twisted and got madder and madder. A nickel music-machine was playing in the next room, which was used for dancing, and she saw two couples moving to and fro past the door.

Roy folded his paper and slapped his hand on the table.

"Them Japs!" he said. "They're going to ask for it till they get it. Just like the Germans. Guys that go around with chips on their shoulders always get 'em knocked off." He frowned indignantly.

"Do tell," said Marie.

"Yeah. That's the way the Kaiser done and look what happened to him. England holds off till she can't get out of fighting no longer; then she really goes to town. I've known guys like that. And you better look out for 'em. They're the worst kind."

"My, my," said Marie.

"Say, what's wrong with you?"

"Nuts to you and your Japs."

"Now look here. I wanted to stay home and read. But, hell, no! We got to go riding all over hell and gone. . . ."

Her face tightened and he saw tears glistening on her long black eyelashes.

"O.K., honey," he said quickly. "That's all right." Boy, you sure had to handle Marie with gloves at the wrong time of the month. He seldom remembered it and went raring around making himself obnoxious.

"You and your Japs. What do you think I care about Japs and Germans and all that hooey! I care about you and me and having some fun; that's all I care about."

"Sure, sure," said Roy. "How about a little dance?"

Marie jumped up quickly, her eyes sparkling.

"Now you said something."

They went into the next room and began to dance. After a while Marie said:

"For crying out loud! You dance like a polar bear."

"I know it. I'm not very good."

"Not very good! You're lousy. Look. Take it easy. Relax. Don't grab hold of me like I was a sack of wheat. There. That's better. That's fine. You're getting it."

Roy grinned and his grin widened when he saw the two other

145

men in the room staring at Marie. Nice doll he had, all right. Guys always on the make for her.

The music stopped and one of the fellows put in another nickel. A new record swung up off the turntable and a mellow baritone voice filled the little room.

"Crosby," said Marie. "He's sure swell."

"He sure is," agreed Roy. "He's about the only singer I like. I hate singers. They ought to have on skirts. But not that guy. He's got a real voice and I hear he's right all the way."

They danced in silence for a moment to the slow time of *Little Lady Make-Believe*; then, without thinking, Roy said:

"You know, that piece reminds me of Velma."

"Yeah?"

"It sure does. That's what she was. I mean, that's the way I felt about her. I mean . . ."

"Get it straight before you say it. Stop stuttering. I'm thirsty. Let's go get our drinks."

Roy followed her back to the table, still trying to put into words how he felt about Velma and why that song reminded him of her. They sat down.

"Roy," said Marie, "tell me some more about the Japs."

He compressed his lips and said nothing. This was no place for a brawl.

On the way back to the auto-court, the road took a sudden turning and they saw cars lined up, and hurricane flares, like small lighted bombs, were throwing a weird red glare out into the darkness, through which moved the black figures of men.

"Coppers," said Marie. "Searching every car. How come?"

"You got me," said Roy. "Wait. I know. It's the brake-testing dodge. That way they get a good look at everybody. Boy, the heat's really on."

"Let's go back. Turn around quick, Roy, before you get too close."

"Hell, no. Don't be silly. We got Pard in the car. They ain't looking for me yet. Them descriptions in the papers were malarkey. Not even close."

"Oh, please, Roy. I'm scared. I can't stand it. I might scream or something. You know how I am when . . ."

"O.K."

Roy made a U-turn and started off in the opposite direction.

"Oh, Lord," sighed Marie. "I feel better. Gee, Roy, I'm sorry I . . ." But she stiffened and grabbed his arm. A siren was screaming behind them and, turning, she saw the light of a motorcycle. "Oh, now I've done it."

"Sit tight," said Roy. "I'll show you the old cat-road trick. Pull that gun out of the waistband of my pants and put it between us just in case."

"Oh, honey . . ."

"Do what I say."

She obeyed him.

Roy stepped on the accelerator and the car shot away like a projectile; the speedometer needle spun, trembled at 80, then went up to 85, hung for a moment, then went on to 90. The car swayed as if ready to leave the ground, and the cold desert air shrieked past them drowning out every other sound. Marie put her hands over her face and held her breath. Behind them the siren was still going, but fainter now. Pard barked loudly as the wind tore at him; then he lay down and cuddled up to Roy fearfully.

A filling-station flashed past. Roy saw the lights of a little town ahead of him. He slowed down, cut his lights, and in a moment swung the car to the right up a little paved road which led towards the mountains.

He drove for miles without slackening speed, then gradually he slowed down.

"We lost him," he said. "Cinch, eh?"

"Yeah," said Marie, heaving a long sigh and lying up against him. "You got guts, Roy. Sometimes I forget it when you go mumbling on about the Japs and things like that. I'm crazy about you, Roy. You ought to give me a spanking."

"It's an idea. Well, settle back. We got a long ride ahead of us. I got to swing clear around to the right and angle back. I can miss the hold-up line that way."

That night just as Roy was falling asleep Marie asked suddenly:

"You don't think about her much, do you?"

"Who? What?" he stammered.

"Velma."

"No. She's nothing to me. It was just that piece Bing was singing. It made me think about her. I mean, that's the way she . . ."

"This is where I came in," said Marie. "Oh, go to sleep."

CHAPTER THIRTY-SEVEN

They were still at the auto-camp in Ballard. That night, after two or three days of semi-confinement, Marie had wanted to go to a movie or to a dine-and-dance joint, or, in fact, to any place just to break the monotony. But at sundown a fierce dry wind had begun to blow in from the east, rattling windows, banging doors, tearing furiously at awnings through the court, whirling scraps of paper high up into the gathering darkness. Sand was blown against the windows with such violence that it sounded like heavy rain.

The wind and the blowing sand made her very uneasy and she got up and began to pace the floor. Pard was uneasy, too, and walked about, sniffing at the windows and the door, giving little whimpers, and from time to time looked at Roy, who was sitting in his shirt-sleeves, with his chair tipped back, reading a newspaper.

"We might as well be out in the Sahara," said Marie. "First time I ever saw a sandstorm."

"Good night to be in," said Roy. "We're snug as a bug in a rug. Listen to her blow! Wow! I'd hate to be out in that. How about heating up the coffee you got left over?"

"You're drinking an awful lot of coffee lately, Roy. No wonder you don't sleep good."

"Coffee's better than liquor for you. How'd you like it if I drunk liquor all the time?"

Marie made no comment. She lit a gas-burner and put the coffee-pot on it.

Roy threw down his paper with disgust.

"Sometimes them guys burn me up. Always talking about criminals. What the hell do they know about it? Some guy rapes a little girl. He's a criminal. Another guy kills some dame with a hammer. He's a criminal. A woman kills her baby. She's a criminal. A conman ootches some chiselling sucker out of a big roll. He's a criminal. I knock over Tropico. I'm a criminal. Hell, that's not sense."

Waiting for the coffee to get hot, Marie said:

"What do you mean, Roy?"

"I mean they lump us all together. One guy's just as bad as another. That's just plain goddamn silly. Take when I was in stir. Why, we had rapists and guys like that all around us, and

148

we wouldn't even speak to 'em. I'd just as soon smack one of 'em on the jaw as look at him. I'd rather. Them guys ain't criminals. They're screwballs. Daffy. Now you take a smart conman. Nothing's wrong with him. He's got more brains than any seven coppers and he's clean and neat and behaves himself. What makes him so bad? He don't do nothing but clip a few suckers who are just begging to be clipped. You can't cheat an honest man. Anybody will tell you that. No matter what you hear, any guy that gets took by a conman is trying to commit larceny himself. That's why most of 'em don't squawk.

"Take my pal, Barmy. He was the smartest there was. Used to be rolling in dough. But he got old and they caught up with him. Like we all get caught up with some day. He worked with Blonger, the Big Guy, in the old days, and he used to make sometimes as high as two hundred G's a winter in Florida. In the summer he worked Denver, where the fix was perfect. He got tired finally, so he took a trip to Europe. He was hell for gambling and dropped his wad at Monte Carlo. That's a laugh. He worked out a perfect system that couldn't lose and clipped himself for half a million." Roy bent over to laugh. "One thing about Barmy. He never got downhearted. So he went over to London and started in on the con. But he couldn't get no place because the British are honest. Not like the Americans. Barmy was a Canadian himself and he knew all about foreign people such as French, British, Italians, and so on. He said the Americans were the crookedest people in the world and the biggest suckers for the con. In this country nobody's straight. There ain't one official out of a hundred that ain't got his hand out. Coppers are so crooked they can't lay straight in bed. Even judges can be had. I know. They cost me enough when I was hiding high. Yeah, Barmy said he practically starved to death in London. He said he'd get some john steamed up how they could make a hundred thousand dollars between them, but as soon as the British john found out he had to gyp somebody to get it, he backed out. An American just says: 'Lead me to it!' "

Marie brought Roy his coffee and sat down to listen. Sometimes what he had to say interested her; at other times, when he got to talking about politics or the stars or things like that, he bored her stiff.

"Yeah, Barmy couldn't make a dime in London, but he borrowed passage money, came back to the U.S.A, and pretty soon, with the same old act that'd flopped in London, he made dough so fast he had to hire guys to help him spend it.

"Barmy wasn't no criminal. I mean, not like they talk about

149

criminals in the newspapers. He was just a smart guy, that's all. Why, I heard him talk to a university professor by the hour when them guys was going around measuring our heads, and he made that professor look silly. Maybe that professor knew how to measure heads and write a book, but get him out in the world with other guys and he couldn't button up his own pants.

"Take me, for instance. What's wrong with me? I just waltz in with a couple of other guys and knock over a bank for dough. Nobody gets hurt if they don't get tough and nobody loses nothing except the insurance companies, and who's going to cry over them! I've shot a few guys in my time, though I ain't sure I ever killed anybody except Kranmer. I blasted *him*, all right. Now what makes me such a low-down skunk they class me with a rapist or some screwball like that?"

"They're nuts," said Marie.

"Sure," said Roy. "Outsiders are all nuts. Take the way they do things. I know a guy that busted into a garage and stole a couple of tyres; they gave him ten years. Look at Johnny. When he was a kid nineteen years old he and another guy cold-cocked a man and clipped him for five hundred. First offence for Johnny. He was tight at the time. He got ten to twenty and served nine of it. The guy with him on the caper was out in fifteen months. And they wonder why Johnny was so tough! Yeah. On the other hand, there was a banker in our town named Henry. He lost the depositors' money in the stock market, and the bank folded. Lots of farmers and poor people dropped every cent they had. Dough they'd been saving up for years. What happens! Mistrial the first time. The second time he was convicted, with recommendation for mercy 'cause he was a sick man. He served ten months. Sick man, my fanny. He weighed two hundred pounds. And he done all his time in the hospital at that! Look at that judge in New York. He's been taking money to fix cases for years – a guy that the people elected to look after their interests. So they catch up with him and convict him, and what does he get? Two years. The guy that stole the tyres got ten. Talk about criminals. They ought to shoot so-and-so's like that.

"You take me. I never pretended I was trying to help nobody but Roy. I steal and I admit it. But if I was a judge that the people elected I'm goddamned if I'd be crooked and gyp them. I'm not kidding. I mean it.

"That's what these guys can't understand. They talk about criminals. They ought to stick some of them in clink and they'd find out. You got to earn your way there, brother. A man ain't got no standing at all in prison till he proves himself. Don't make no difference if he's a bank president or what he is (not counting screwballs, of course, who ought to be in the hatch); if he's a fink, it'll come out. The biggest rat we had in prison was a preacher who'd gypped his congregation out of the dough he was supposed to build a church with. Us 'criminals' wouldn't touch him with a ten-foot pole.

"Look at it another way. If a guy was a heist guy or a con-man or something like that, he always had friends, providing he was right, of course, which most of 'em are. But suppose now he was a kidnapper. Something like that. We thought he stunk. ... Yeah, that's what busted things up for everybody finally. Some of the big boys got so dough-crazy they went into the kidnapping racket. And that's a sucker racket if there ever was one. That and the killing at the Kansas City railroad station put the kibosh on everything. Johnny wouldn't even listen when somebody talked about a snatch. He thought it was a silly caper and he didn't have no use for anybody that'd get mixed up in it.

"You know it's funny. Take what I was talking about: a gypping banker; a crooked judge; coppers raking the community for a racket they can get a take on; a big-shot official selling jobs – stuff like that. Why do people stand it?

"Look. A few guys have got all the dough in this country. Millions of people ain't got enough to eat. Not because there ain't no food, but because they got no money. Somebody else has got it all. O.K. Why don't all them people who haven't got any dough get together and take the dough? It's a cinch. A bank looks pretty tough, don't it? O.K. Give me a chopper and a couple of guys and I'll loot the biggest bank in the U.S.A. I'm just one guy. What could ten million do?"

"They're all scared," said Marie, beginning to yawn. "Anyway, that's communism or something."

"O.K. So what? Like in prison. A guy would get to talking like I am and some guy would yell: 'Communist!' and it would shut him up. But that don't scare me. Call it what you like. It's still good sense."

Marie laughed.

"Drink your coffee and stop saving the world. Lord, I wish that wind would let up."

In a little while Roy was off on a new tack. He got to talking about his boyhood. Marie was always surprised when he got on that subject. Roy was a big tough-looking man. What could it matter to him what things were like thirty years ago?

"... yeah," Roy was saying, "they don't raise women like her any more. Aunt Minnie was sure a peach. She was always baking

151

cookies for us and making ice cream and stuff like that. No matter what happened, we always went to her. When we fell down and got hurt. When we run a nail in our foot or got stung by a bee. When the old man whipped us or we caught hell at school from Ed Simpson, the teacher. Yeah, she was some woman. Churchy, kind of, but no blue-nose. Best woman I ever laid my eyes on. Never had a bad thought in her life. Kind to everybody and everything. Couldn't hardly stand to have a chicken killed for dinner. . . ."

"What do you mean, never had a bad thought in her life?"

"You know what I mean."

"Married, wasn't she?"

"Sure she was married."

"Have any kids?"

"You bet, and what a mother! !"

"Well," said Marie, "maybe I don't know what you're talking about. I thought you meant maybe she was pure or something."

"Why, of course she was pure."

"Let it lay."

Suddenly Roy caught on. He stared at Marie for a long time. Then he began to understand. Like Velma and Pa and Ma, Aunt Minnie was another figment. It gave him a start when he realized that even Aunt Minnie had had a private life. He had thought of her only as a kind-faced little woman who gave him cookies and patted his head when he cried; a ghost of a woman who had no existence apart from himself. Marie was right. Aunt Minnie had had her fun like all the rest of the human race. And why not? Only the thought was unpleasant to him.

"Ever hear of a guy called James Whitcomb Riley?"

"No," said Marie. "Where did he tend bar?"

Roy laughed.

"Wise-guy, hunh? Well, he wrote poetry. He was from my home state. One time he wrote a poem called 'Out to Old Aunt Mary's.' And you'd think he was writing about Aunt Minnie, just as if he'd known her all his life. Yeah, I used to know that poem by heart, but, hell, I can't remember it now."

Roy got up yawning and stretching, then he winced and bent over.

"There you go."

"Goddamn that copper," snarled Roy. "He sure marked me good and plenty. Oh, brother! I never should've stretched like that."

"Want me to change the dressing?"

"No. Wait till we go to bed."

Roy sat down and, drumming nervously on the table with his fingers, tried to control his face. His side felt as if somebody had stuck an ice-pick into it and was now twisting it round and round.

"Brother!" groaned Roy, taking out his handkerchief and mopping his brow.

Marie came over quickly, put her arms around him, and kissed him on the top of the head.

"Poor old honey."

"I just got to get this looked after. I'm hot as hell all over. Look at me sweating."

"It was just because you jumped up like that, Roy. It'll quiet down."

"Wow! I wish I had a toothache instead."

"You wouldn't say that if you had one."

Roy mopped his brow again.

"Boy, listen to that wind. Can't it howl, though? I hope this cabin holds together till morning."

"Me, too. Look at poor Pard. He don't like that wind at all. You know, Roy, I've felt funny all day. I just knew something was going to happen. Felt awful uneasy. You know what I mean. Like something was hanging over me. Funny thing. Pard's been acting like he felt that way, too. It was the storm on its way, I guess. Feel better?"

"Yeah. It's easing up. Oh, boy, what a relief. It sure feels good when it stops, like the guy in the asylum said. I'll bet I don't go stretching myself again like that. But, no fooling, I got to get it looked after. I guess I can wait, though, till I go in to get my cut."

"If ever."

"Yeah. Getting kind of low on dough, ain't we?"

"We still got some."

"Good thing I bent over and picked up that roll from the floor at Tropico even if I did almost get bumped on account of it. We'd be strapped."

"Yeah. You should've took that dough Velma's boy-friend offered you. Four hundred bucks! But no. You got to be the big shot. 'Think nothing of it.' That's what you said." Marie laughed. "Sucker!"

Roy grinned sheepishly.

"Yeah. But I thought I'd have a big wad."

"It just goes to show you. Feeling all right now, Roy? If you are I got to look after my other boy."

"I'm O.K."

Marie left him, opened the dish-cupboard, and took out a little cardboard box.

"Here, Pard," she said. "Look what Mamma's got for you."

The little dog came over and sat up. Marie fed him from the box. His pale eyes sparkled as he chewed.

"What you got there?" Roy demanded.

"Something I saw at the market today."

"What is it?"

Marie hesitated and looked a little embarrassed.

"Dog candy."

"For crying out loud! Have they got special candy for dogs?"

"Yeah. It tastes kind of sweet, but it don't hurt them like real candy."

"Well, I'll be!" Roy bent over to laugh. "It's sure funny. When I first met you, you thought Pard was a damn nuisance. Now you buy him dog candy. Candy for a dog! That's a hot one."

"All right, laugh. You'd never think of it. All you think about is yourself."

After Marie had changed the dressing, Roy put on his pyjama coat and lay back with a loud yawn.

"Looks better, hunh?"

"Yeah," said Marie, brushing her hair, "lots better. The red don't go up so high."

When she was ready for bed she took the .45 out of the dressing table drawer and quickly slipped it under her pillow. Roy turned.

"Thought you'd get away with it, hunh?"

"Oh, Roy!"

"How many times do I have to tell you? Not under the pillow. Under the covers."

"You always kept it **under** your pillow at the lake."

"I wasn't worried **about** a rumble then."

"I don't like to sleep with that thing under the covers."

"Look. Some copper gets suspicious of us. He don't say nothing. He waits till we go to bed. Then he jimmies the door and comes in. I hear him. If the gun's under the pillow I reach up for it and he plugs me. If it's under the covers I just lay there and he can't see my hand. If he asks for it, I blast him through the blanket and that's that."

"Take it on your side, then. You think I want to get shot in the pratt turning over."

"It's got a safety catch."

154

"Yeah. I've heard that one before. Also the one about it wasn't loaded."

Roy took the gun on his side. Pard jumped up on the bed and lay between Roy's feet. Gradually they all settled down and Roy began to drift into sleep. The wind wasn't blowing as hard as it had been and the sand was no longer being driven against the windows.

Roy turned over with a sigh, carefully arranging his feet so Pard would be comfortable; then Marie cuddled up to his back and put her arm across his shoulders.

"Night, honey."

"Night, baby."

There was a long silence. Then Marie jumped up with a squeal.

"My God! What's that!"

"What –! Wha –!" stammered Roy.

She shook him awake. He heard a distant sound, like thunder on a hot night in Indiana, but somehow it wasn't quite the same; more muffled, more jarring.

"First time I ever heard thunder under the ground," he said sleepily.

"Oh, God! An earthquake!"

Roy sat straight up. Pard jumped down from the bed and ran from window to window, snarling and barking in an unnaturally high-pitched voice. The joists in the little cabin began to creak and groan; the window-panes rattled; and the bedroom door swung back and banged against the wall. The ground began to heave and sway. The bed tipped under them; plaster fell.

They heard a loud jarring rumble, then it was over. A dead silence followed. Then they heard a little child shrieking somewhere in the court. Lights sprang on.

"Wow!" said Roy. "I . . ."

He heard the subterranean thunder again and swallowed hard. Marie flung her arms around his neck and kissed him repeatedly.

"I don't care," she cried, hysterically. "As long as I got you. Let 'er quake. I mean it, honey. Sometimes maybe I nag at you, but I mean it."

"Me, too."

They sat with their arms around each other and Pard jumped back onto the bed and lay up against them. He was trembling all over.

The ground quivered and bucked, then a long jerking tremor moved from north to south, making the whole cabin dance and creak. The jarring rumble passed under them and rolled southward. A big piece of plaster hit the floor with a clatter.

Marie was almost choking Roy and he breathed loudly with his mouth open.

"I guess it's over," he said in an unnatural voice. "Man, oh, man! I've heard about earthquakes all my life, but I never felt one before. I hope my hair didn't turn white."

"There may be another one," said Marie, holding tight.

But nothing happened, so they lay back and listened to the noises in the court. Men were talking loudly and running to and fro; a baby was crying; half a dozen dogs were barking frantically. They heard the roar of a motor; a man's voice called:

"Come on! Come on!"

"Some guy's blowing," said Roy. "But he's a nut to do it. That's one thing you can't run away from. There's no place to go."

"That's the awful part."

"Yeah. Barmy used to talk to me about earthquakes. He said the old earth just twitches its skin like a dog. We're the fleas, I guess."

They lay with their arms around each other.

"I meant what I said," said Marie. "Every word of it."

"Me, too," said Roy.

CHAPTER THIRTY-EIGHT

Roy came out of the corner drugstore smiling. It was sure funny what a difference a few little words made. Last night the world had looked black; he and Marie had had a row over Velma; Pard had got in a fight and had his ears chewed; and Roy's wound had bothered him so much that he hadn't been able to get to sleep till just before dawn. Now everything looked rosy. Over the telephone a voice had said: "Max got in. How soon can you make it?"

"Yeah," Roy told himself on the way to the auto-court, "I guess I just had a feeling without knowing it. I'm sure glad I angled back. Now I can get a good night's sleep and still be in early tomorrow morning. I was getting damn sick of that desert, anyway. We all was. It gets on your nerves. Even Pard. I never saw him rare before like he done last night. Boy, he really give that big collie a going-over. And Marie give me a going-over. She's got a temper, that girl. And she used to be nice as pie." He laughed to himself as he walked along.

They were staying at an auto-court in a good-sized highway town between San Bernardino and Los Angeles. It was a beautiful early winter afternoon, and Roy stopped on a corner near the auto-court to look around him. Across the road was a big orange grove, row after row of dark-green trees filled with red-gold fruit and giving off a sweet heady odour which filled the countryside. The California town with its one-storey white houses roofed with red tile seemed to sleep in the warm sunlight. And far beyond to the north loomed a hazy blue mountain range with here and there a snow-capped peak. After the dry, burnt up, windy desert this place looked like paradise.

"Yep," said Roy with a grin, "just like on the post-cards."

His wound gave a twinge, but he ignored it. Tomorrow he'd have his cut; God knows how much, but four figures sure; he could go see old Doc, pay him what he owed him, and get his wound looked after; then he and Marie and Pard could hit for the East and that would be that.

"Things went so haywire for a while," said Roy, as he turned towards the auto-court, "that I was beginning to got to thinking that Art and Max were giving me the old oil. It's been done before. Funny how a guy's mind will keep feeding him wrong ideas, and how's he going to know they are wrong? Boy, it sure is easy to be wrong in this world."

"Evening."

Roy turned. The little man who had showed them to their cabin last night was nodding and smiling. He had a rather pleasant face, Roy thought, except for a sort of foxy look about the eyes.

"Howdy. Nice day."

"They're all nice out here mostly. Back east where you come from I guess this seems like a wonderful day. But it's just another day to us."

"I guess that's right."

"Your dog get hurt much?"

"Got his ears chewed a little. He's all right."

"I've told that fellow time and again to keep that collie out of this court. Some day he'll tackle the wrong dog. That little tyke of yours did pretty good."

"He's tough."

Roy nodded and went back to the cabin, where the door was open and he could see Marie bending over, putting salve on Pard's ears.

"Baby! Our troubles are over."

"Did Max come?"

"Yeah. They told me to drive in in the morning early. They'll have my cut ready then. How's that?"

Marie threw up her arms and whirled around.

"Oh, boy! That's great. Now we can hit east where we'll be safe."

Roy came in and, taking Marie in his arms, kissed her repeatedly. Pard caught the excitement and rushed about barking and leaping at them. Finally he seized the cuff of Roy's pants in his teeth and worried it, growling fiercely.

"Go ahead," said Roy. "Tear it to pieces. I don't care. I'll be heavy with dough tomorrow."

But in spite of the good news and the feeling of ease and relaxation it had brought, Roy had a bad night. For the first time in months he woke up drenched with sweat, his nerves twitching, and a terrible depression weighing him down. He turned from side to side. Presently he began to have shooting pains in his wound. They got so bad finally that he could not restrain himself from wincing violently and kicking his feet.

Marie started up.

"Roy! That you?"

"Yeah."

"Pains?"

"Yeah."

"I told you it didn't look so good tonight. But don't you worry. Doc'll fix you up tomorrow."

"Tomorrow's a long way off, and I got to drive in."

"I'll drive."

"Nothing doing. Suppose we'd get a rumble?"

"We won't. They're not even looking for you yet. And if they was they wouldn't know you now."

Marie had insisted so irritatingly and so stubbornly that Roy should disguise himself that he'd raised a moustache which was thick and black as ink; Marie had cut his hair short (so short, in fact, that his hat no longer fitted him); and she had got him a pair of cheap glasses with plain lenses. In spite of the pain, Roy smiled at the memory of the first time he'd got a slant at himself in the mirror in his new rig. Why, his own brother wouldn't recognize him, it made him look so respectable and kind of harmless!

"All the same, I'll drive."

"Well, try to get some sleep."

"I feel like hell."

"Poor honey," said Marie, soothingly, but she was a little irritated with him and wished he'd turn over and let her sleep.

Men were such babies. If they had a pain they wanted everybody to stay awake and watch them suffer. She'd like to see Roy go through what she went through at times. "All alike," she told herself. "Even Roy."

"When I was a young fellow," said Roy, "I didn't know what the word 'nerves' meant. I thought only dames had 'em. It was that goddamn prison.... Oh, man! There she goes again. You suppose I got blood-poisoning?"

Marie stared up, suddenly afraid.

"No. Course you haven't. You'd know it by now."

"Yeah? I been shot two-three times. I still got lead in my left leg. But I never had one hurt like this before."

"Want me to get you something? How about a drink? Or I could heat you up some hot milk. My old lady used to drink that so she could sleep."

"No. What I need is a shot of something to ease off his pain a little."

"I'll get you an aspirin. Maybe that'll help."

Roy took two aspirin tablets, lay back, and tried to sleep. Marie got in beside him, curled up in a ball with her knees to her chin, and in a little while he heard her breathing regularly. It irritated him and he turned and twisted. There she was, sleeping like a baby; no troubles, no pain. It wasn't right when he hurt so and felt so lousy. Suddenly he got sore at himself and muttered:

"You big yellowbelly! Lay still and let the poor kid sleep. It's all your own fault letting a small-timer like that put the blast on you!"

Pard jumped down from the bed to scratch and Roy called to him softly. The little dog got up beside him and put his head on Roy's shoulder. Roy sighed and slowly began to drift into a fitful sleep. Once he woke Marie by talking loudly. "Oh, yeah?" he cried, in an unnatural voice. "I can lick two like you, Fat Evans. You give me that ball bat. It's my turn. It is so. Ain't it, Elmer? ..."

"There he goes again," said Marie. "Even when he's asleep he's thinking about when he was a kid. That's sure funny."

Roy woke with a start. The edges of the blind were bright with morning. He looked at his watch. Seven o'clock.

"By God," he said aloud, "I got some sleep after all." He turned. "Marie! Seven o'clock. We better get up. This is our big day."

Marie opened her eyes and yawned loudly. Her hair was hanging down over her face and she looked all tousled and rumpled.

159

Roy reached under the covers and spanked her, then he got gingerly out of bed. There was a dull ache in his right side, but no more shooting pains. Marie got up, too.

"Just heat up the coffee," said Roy, "and we'll eat some bread and butter with it. Let Pard out, too, when I'm gone. I want to get a paper. See how it's going."

"Don't be long. I get the jitters when you're away."

Roy kissed her, flung on his coat, and hurried down to the little all-night restaurant two blocks away. A sleepy Greek stared at him foggily. The Greek had been on his feet for twelve hours, all through the long night while Roy wrestled with himself in the cabin, and he was wondering why the hell George didn't come to relieve him. Roy tossed a nickel on the counter and picked up a paper.

"Brakfuss?" said the Greek automatically. "We got . . ."

But Roy didn't answer. He was trying to control his face. A picture on the front page of the paper leaped up at him and hit him between the eyes. The caption read: "America's New Public Enemy No. I." It was an old Bertillon picture of himself, taken about six years ago. It looked leaner, stronger, more formidable, and even the fuzziness of the newspaper reproduction could not disguise the hard, rebellious light shining out of the eyes.

". . . we got nice rulls. Whit keks wit syrup. You like brakfuss food? We got grep nots. . . ." Suddenly the Greek's face lit up. "Hallo, George. Where you been?"

"What a party!" said a voice behind Roy. "I ain't had a wink of sleep. I hate to think about that twelve-hour stretch I . . ."

Roy turned and went out, banging the door behind him. He found Marie in the kitchen, standing with her hands on her hips, humming a new dance tune, as she waited for the coffee to heat up.

"I let him out like you told me. He won't go far. He's got sense, that dog."

"Yeah," said Roy, "listen to this. ' "The hard-faced commanding bandit with the machine-gun" turns out to be none other than big-timer Roy Earle, recently pardoned from the Michigan City, Indiana, Penitentiary, and believe it or not, he's travelling with a moll who answers to the name of Marie and a little white mongrel dog who answers to the name of Pard; at least he was, when last seen by Mendoza leaving the grounds of the Tropico Inn on the night of the hold-up. . . .' "

"Louis!" cried Marie.

"Yeah. He squawked. I should have took care of him when he followed us out. I knew he was that kind. It says here some guy
160

in the D.A.'s office suspected him from the first. Wait a minute. 'And by playing on the vanity of this small-timer who wanted to be a big-shot . . .' Oh, the hell with that! Look at the name they hung on me. Mad Dog Roy Earle! Them newspaper rats!"

"My God, Roy! What're we going to do?"

"Honey, I got to park you like you said."

"Like who said?"

"Like you said. Remember? You said it was a deal. When the going got too tough I could park you."

"No. I can't leave you, honey. I don't care what happens to me. Let's stay together."

"It can't be done. You got to take Pard. I got to go in and get my cut. I'm going to need it. I'm practically broke. Ain't got a cent outside of what's in my pocket and your purse."

"No. Let it go, Roy. The hell with it. Let's hit east. We'll make it. Then you'll be safe."

"Safe and busted. We'd end up heisting filling-stations like a couple of high-school kids and getting shot in the pratt by some hick cop. It takes dough to get back east. I got maybe ten grand coming to me and I'm going to get it. Listen, I got an idea. You can get a bus out of here for San Bernardino. You can wait there for me. I got it. We'll get a big basket with a lid and put Pard in it. You take him with you. I'll go in and get my end, then I'll come after you and we'll hit east. Where the hell is that dog?"

"Roy! No. I can't go alone. I'm scared."

"You got to, honey. You think I'm going to drag you in with me and get you shot? Brother, when they hang that No. 1 tag on you they shoot first and argue afterwards. I know. Mad Dog Earle! How do you like that? Go call Pard. No. For God's sake. Don't call him. Just whistle."

Marie went to the door.

"I don't see him."

"Whistle! Whistle!"

"I can't. My lips are too dry." Marie burst out crying.

Roy stamped up and down impatiently.

"Louis sure give 'em the works. I'm wanted for murder. They'll hang the Kramner killing on me if they get me. But, brother, they won't get me. You heard me. I've done all the time I'll ever do, and you take my word for it. I've seen them poor so-and-so's in the death cells. Not for me. . . ."

"What do you mean, Roy?"

"I mean they'll never take me, that's what I mean. Will you whistle for that dog?"

Marie turned away and put her hands over her face. Roy went to the window and pulled back the curtain. The little man who ran the auto-court was standing in front of one of the cabins, making "come here" motions with his hands which puzzled Roy. Then he saw Pard a few feet farther along, staring warily at the man, his pale shrewd little eyes non-committal. There was a morning paper in the man's pocket. Roy started slightly, then tiptoed over to the door and opened it.

"Nice doggie," the man was saying. "Nice boy. Nice little Pard."

Pard came to him, wagging his tail.

Roy leaped out the door and came up behind the man, who turned around quickly and jumped sideways.

"I want to see you," said Roy.

The man's face turned greenish.

"I'm busy. Got a lot to look after this morning. N – nice dog you got, mister. I was just trying to make up with him."

"What makes you think his name is Pard?"

"Didn't I hear you call him that yesterday? Maybe I'm wrong."

"Did you read your paper this morning?"

The man began to wilt. Roy took him by the arm and hustled him into the cabin. Marie was in the bedroom, hastily throwing her clothes into a suitcase.

Roy locked the door, then he called:

"That's it, kid. Pack your stuff. Leave mine alone."

Marie glanced up and started when she saw the auto-court man, who was swaying slightly, his face livid with fright. Roy jerked the .45 out of the waistband of his pants.

"You know who I am, don't you?"

"No. I never saw you before. Not till you come here. . . . Honest to God!"

"What you so scared about, then?"

The man held his hands out in front of him as if to ward off a blow.

"Oh, my God, Mr. Earle. Don't kill me."

"Looking for that reward, hunh?"

"No. I swear I wasn't. I was only going to call my nephew."

"Your nephew! Copper?"

"No. I'm Paul Healy. Vince Healy, the big reporter, is my nephew."

"He'd get the coppers on me fast enough after he got his story telephoned in, the rat!"

162

"Don't shoot him, Roy," cried Marie. "Please don't. I can't stand it."

Little Mr. Healy wavered on his feet, then fell in a faint. Roy looked down at him and shrugged.

"Marie," he called, "you run down to that store on the corner and get a big basket with a lid on it. I'll take care of this guy, then I'll get you on that bus."

"All right, Roy. I was wrong to act like I did. I'll do what you say. Only please don't hurt that poor little man. He was good to Pard last night."

"I ain't going to hurt him. I'll tie him up and stick him in that closet so we can get a good head start. I don't think nobody in the court noticed nothing, do you?"

"I didn't even myself."

CHAPTER THIRTY-NINE

Marie was so nervous and distracted that Roy kept a firm hold on her arm. Roy had parked the coupé in a little side-street just off the main highway and they sat waiting for the bus. Pard was in a big wicker basket at their feet.

Roy kept repeating his instructions and from time to time Marie would nod, but her heart wasn't in it.

"Virge Ray's pool-hall. You can't miss it. Don't ask where it is. Look for it. Just mention Art and Virge'll look after you. I'll be with you by tomorrow night at the latest. Got that?"

Mari nodded, then she leaned against him and began to cry.

"I've just got a feeling ... Roy, please take me with you. I can't stand to be alone any more. . . . I . . ."

Roy said nothing. He sat trying to control himself. It would be so easy to say: "O.K., kid. Come on," and they'd feel mighty happy over it – for a while. But it just wasn't good sense. If he got a rumble and the coppers started blasting, he had a machine-gun under the seat and plenty of ammunition and he could take care of himself. If he was alone, that is. But what could he do with Marie and Pard on his hands?

"Can't be done."

"I know."

Marie sat with her head on his shoulder, and she winced when she remembered how irritated she'd been with him last night because his wound was paining him and he couldn't sleep.

"I was mean to you last night, Roy."

"Mean? You were not."

"I was. I was thinking mean things. How you wouldn't let me sleep just because . . ."

"Hell, I was thinking them myself. Why should you stay awake because I had a pain in my side?"

"I wish I had now."

"Look. That woman's waiting for the bus, too. She's moving out. I guess it's coming." Bending down he kissed Marie, but pulled away when she clung to him. Her face was pale and her lips were twitching.

"I can't, Roy. I can't. You're all I got in the world."

"Come on, kid. See you tomorrow night."

Roy had the suitcase in one hand and the basket in the other. He walked so fast that Marie had to run to keep up with him.

The big bus stopped with a squealing of brakes; the door sprang open.

"Make it snappy," said the driver.

"Goodbye! Goodbye!"

Roy glanced up, took one look at Marie's pale, tear-stained face, then turned his back abruptly and hurried towards the coupé. He tried to keep his eyes to the front but he couldn't do it. He turned. The bus was just disappearing past a corner drugstore. A woman's hand was waving out of one of the windows.

A wild panic seized Roy. He was alone. Marie was gone. Pard was gone.

"I can't stand it," he told himself. "I just can't make it alone no more."

He jumped into the coupé and started the engine. He had a wild desire to run the bus down and take Marie and Pard off of it. Hell! Why not? Let the money go. They'd get back east some way. Then maybe he could promote a stake. He made a sharp U-turn and got onto the highway. The bus was out of sight.

"Boy, they really ramble in them big crates," he muttered, stepping on the gas.

But a motorcycle cop came out of nowhere and ran him into the curb. Roy quickly unbuttoned his vest and slanted his .45 so he could get it out easily.

The cop kicked the stand under his motorcycle, then pushed his hat back, mopped his brow, and came slowly over to Roy.

"Out of state, hunh?" he said.

"Yeah," said Roy with a grin. "What's wrong?"

"You can't make a U-turn like that. You know better than that. And you were really stepping on it."

"Was I? I didn't know it."

The cop took off his cap and carefully scratched his head. His face looked pale and haggard and seemed to sag with weariness. "I ought to give you a citation for this. But since you're from out of state . . ."

"Thanks, officer."

"O.K. You got the right attitude, too. Some of these guys burn and tell me they'll get my job. Hell! Them's the kind of guys I like to hang it on. Boy, I been up all night and I'm tired."

"Yeah?"

"Yeah. And I got to stick right on the job till relieved. Orders. Every policeman in southern Cal's out looking for that Earle guy. Read the paper this morning?"

"Yeah. Tough guy, I guess."

"That's what I hear. Well, get going, and mind your P's and Q's. Some of the boys that've been up all night are fit to be tied. Tangle with them and they'll haul you to jail."

"Thanks, officer."

Roy drove off. What a lucky break! If it hadn't been for that copper he'd've taken Marie and Pard off the bus sure. What a damn silly thing that would have been!

He turned up a side-street to make up his mind what to do. Suddenly he snapped his fingers.

"The pass!" he said. "With every copper in southern Cal looking for me I'll never get in over them main highways. Healy's going to get himself untied some time. He may be loose now. I'll just beat it in the opposite direction, go through the pass, and swing back on the wrong side of the mountains. I hear the weather's been good lately. Boy, I'm glad I thought of that."

He swung out into the highway and headed back for the desert.

CHAPTER FORTY

In the south end of Los Angeles a heavy sea-fog was rolling up the streets, blotting out the sun. At Baughman's a gas-grate was burning in the living-room and the house was stuffy and filled with the salty damp smell of the fog.

Velma's mother was lying on the couch, her face pale and drawn, and a wet towel pressed to her forehead. Baughman was pacing up and down, sweating at every pore, and pulling at his sparse hair.

"Oh, I can't get over it," said Mrs. Baughman. "I'll never get over it. That awful man in this house. Imagine! Poor little Velma going downtown to a movie with him. It makes me sick just to think of it. He might have kidnapped her or killed her or something. They call him a mad dog. Oh, thank God, Velma's gone back to Ohio. I wouldn't have a minute's peace if she was here. He might come and –" She sat up with a squeal. "Carl! He don't know she's gone. Oh, my God! Call the police. Do something. Don't just stand there. Tell them to send an officer over to protect us. Hurry, hurry. He might be mad because Velma's gone. He might – Oh, Carl! He was furious that last day he was here. Remember, I told you? Oh, please, Carl. . . ."

"Calm yourself, Mabel," said Baughman, shaking all over. "Be calm. We can't call the police. Don't you see? They'd arrest us for harbouring a dangerous criminal. Ten thousand dollars! Just think of it. All that money just for one man. Well, it shows what a big shot he is. Yeah. No matter what you say, Roy Earle's a big shot and he was right here in this living-room."

"You fool," cried his wife, lying back and groaning. "Oh, God! If we can't call the police, what are we going to do?" She sat up abruptly and the towel fell to the floor. "We'll get out of here, that's what we'll do. We'll go down to Helen's and stay all night. Maybe they'll catch him before tomorrow."

"Look out there at that fog," said Baughman. "You think I'm going to drive to Long Beach in that fog?"

"Well, then call the police. They can't arrest us. We didn't know. . . ."

"That's what everybody who knew him will say."

Mrs. Baughman lay back but sat up immediately.

"Oh, Lord! What will Lon think? I wish Velma had him safely married."

CHAPTER FORTY-ONE

In a little apartment in Barrowville, Ohio, Ma was darning socks, her face expressionless and her old fingers nimbly manipulating the needle; Pa was pacing the floor with a look of blank incredulity, stroking his stubbly chin from time to time and hemming and hawing loudly. Velma sat stunned. Every once in a while her babyish mouth dropped open and her eyes widened.

"I knew," she said finally, with conviction. "Pa, don't you remember? I told you he looked at me as if he could kill me."

"A person has to be so careful nowadays," said Ma in an unnaturally calm voice.

"It's him all right," said Pa. "Yes, sir, at first I couldn't quite ... but it's him."

"He was so nice to me," said Velma. "Only that one time he wasn't. I saw the little dog in the car, too. A little white dog. What did it say his name was?"

"Pard," said Pa.

"Some good in him," Ma put in, "or he wouldn't be carrying a little dog around with him."

"Some good in him!" Pa exploded. "Look what he done for Velma."

"He wanted Velma," said Ma. "That's all. And he didn't want her with a lame foot. I guess he must have plenty of money. He ought to, robbing people of five thousand dollars that way."

"Five hundred thousand, you mean," cried Pa impatiently.

"Well, whatever. I'm trying to say four hundred dollars didn't mean anything to him. But to carry a little dog around with him ..."

"I'm as cold as ice and I've got goose-pimples all over me just thinking about it," said Velma. "It was late that night we was riding around. If I'd only known ..."

Pa scratched his head and yawned from nervousness. He got so agitated that finally he took out a plug of tobacco and bit off a big hunk.

"Pa," said Velma, "you know you mustn't chew tobacco any more. I thought you said you'd given it up. Look, Ma. He's chewing tobacco. Lon thinks it's such a filthy habit. Nobody who is anybody ever chews tobacco. That's what Lon said."

"Jim Goodhue," snapped Ma, "you swore to me you'd never ..."

The front door burst open and Lon dashed in with his hat on the back of his head and a crumpled newspaper in his hand. He looked about him wildly and made such violent gestures that his hat fell off unheeded.

"Look! It says in the paper. ... It's that man. I know it is."

"Yes," said Velma, "it is."

"But we didn't know it at the time," said Ma. "He was so kind to us, we ..."

Pa had his mouth full of tobacco juice and couldn't say anything.

Lon sat down beside Velma and put his arm around her.

"Only think ..."

167

"Feel how cold my hands are."

"I got so scared when I read it. He might've — People! We must never say a word about this to anybody. We never heard of him. You know how things are in Barrowville. Everybody would be scandalized." He kissed Velma twice on the cheek. "Just think! I almost gave him back that four hundred dollars. I'm glad I didn't. A thief like that!"

CHAPTER FORTY-TWO

About noon Roy stopped at Lone Mountain, a good-sized desert town on the Ballard road. He parked near a corner so he couldn't be hemmed in in case of a rumble, and went into a ten-cent store, where he bought some stationery.

When he came out he drove up a side-street and sat in his coupé under a big oak tree and wrote in pencil a note to Art, then one to Marie.

Dear Art

If you don't hear from me in four days, send my end to Miss Marie Garson who is staying with V. Ray in San Bernardino.

Yours truly,

R.

"Well," mused Roy as he sealed up the letter, "it's the best I can think of in case I get knocked off. He *might* send it to her."

Dear Marie

Hi, kid. It's the old man broadcasting.

I'm sitting here under a tree in Lone Mountain writing this. I can see Mt. Whitney and it sure is some mountain.

I will get back some way. Don't you worry, kid. Tell the little white nuisance hello for me.

The Old Man

Roy had some stamps in his billfold. Looking for them, he discovered that in the excitement he'd given Marie more money than he had intended to. All he had left was a five-dollar bill and some change. He stared blankly for a moment, then he drove down to the mail-box on the corner and dropped the two letters in.

He sat scratching his head. He didn't have but five gallons of gasoline in the tank and that was only good for about eighty miles. In this region gas was high and he had around five hundred miles to travel, maybe a little more.

"That's what comes of doing things in a hurry," he grumbled. "Now I'm in a spot. I got to have dough. Suppose I'd bust up the car, or something. Wouldn't that be sweet? It's going to cost me four and a half to fill up the tank. That'll leave me about a dollar. Brother, there's no help for it. I got to pull a small-time heist. That's what it means not to have no capital. Walk right into a joint you never cased and get a belly full of lead. What a sucker! Why didn't I let that boy-friend of Velma's pay me back the dough I spent on her? Then I'd be sitting pretty. But, hell, I thought that was just chicken-feed. I thought I was going to have a wad."

Sitting in his car, he studied the corner drugstore carefully. Not bad at all. It was a sultry afternoon; the sun was beating down on the little town; very few people were moving about; no coppers in sight. They'd be nothing but whittlers, anyway; unless a highway cop happened to barge in. There was a good spot where he could park his car and not get it hemmed in. He might do worse.

"Yep," said Roy as he drove off, "I'll get the tank filled up, then I'll knock that little joint over. I might get fifty. That'll take me in."

The man at the filling-station was very talkative and Roy sat listening. The man was a former packer and had been to the top of Whitney twice. Things weren't so good in the tourist and mountain-climbing line, so he'd been forced to get a job selling gas. He didn't like it. It was sissy stuff. Roy nodded. He knew what the man meant.

"A guy couldn't drive over them mountains this time of year, I don't suppose," said Roy.

"No chance. The pass you can see from here has got ten foot of snow on it. Won't be open till next June. See that little V way up there between them two mountains? That's the pass and it's nearly twelve thousand feet up. Brother, it's a dinger to drive even in the summer! Farther up north you can get through all right, I hear. If you're thinking about trying it, turn in at Blue Jay Lake, go right on past Eagle Lake, then keep moving. I hear the pass is still clear up there, late as it is."

"Thanks, buddy."

Roy drove down a deserted side-street, parked, and got the machine-gun and the ammunition out from under the seat. He fitted the loaded drum in place, then put it on the floor. He didn't need it for the heist, but if he got a rumble afterwards it

169

might come in handy. He examined his .45, then put it back in the waistband of his pants.

Driving around and observing the lay of the town, he'd worked out a plan. As soon as he came out of the store, he'd drive back towards Los Angeles till he came to the jog in the road; then he'd turn left, angle back down a side-street, and at the far end of town he'd turn left again and he'd be on the main highway with a straight shoot for Blue Jay Lake. That way he might throw them off entirely.

"Yep," said Roy, parking near the drugstore, "it looks easy. Well, here goes nothing."

The drugstore was deserted. A little man with glasses was standing behind the tobacco counter, reading a magazine. He looked up.

"Can I help you, mister?"

"Yeah. Pack of Camels."

The little man lowered his eyes and reached below the counter for the cigarettes; when he raised his eyes he was looking into the black muzzle of a .45. He turned white but kept control of himself.

"Don't give me no trouble," said Roy, "and you won't get hurt. Hand me the dough in the cash-register."

"Yes, sir," said the little man. "Don't get nervous with that gun. You got nothing to worry about. I'll never get myself shot up over money." He began to take bills out of the drawer.

"Got a sack?" said Roy.

"Yes, sir. Here you are. That's all there is except for the pennies. I take it you don't want pennies."

"You're all right," said Roy, stuffing the sack into his pocket. "You got sense."

Their eyes met and Roy smiled slightly. Suddenly the man seemed to wilt and Roy saw a look of horrified recognition on his face.

Just as Roy was backing away somebody came in the front door and made a grab at him.

"Oh, my God! Don't, Tom," cried the druggist. "Let him alone. Let him go. That's Roy Earle."

Tom turned and tried to get away, but Roy knocked him down with his left fist and, stepping over him, made a break for the street. A gun went off and he heard a bullet smash against the front of the drugstore. He jumped into the coupé, made a wild U-turn, and swung out into the highway with his tyres screaming and the car careening under him.

"Yeah," said Roy to himself. "I had it all worked out, but I

170

got no time for it now. I got to hit north and keep moving. I wonder who that bastard was that put the blast on me. Where did that other guy come from, anyway?"

Because of his exertion his wound began to hurt him and he bent forward to ease it.

Back in Lone Mountain people were converging on the drug-store from all directions.

"Yeah," Tom, a big fat man with a badge, was saying, "Ed and I been watching that guy ever since he lit. Something about him and the way he was acting looked funny to us. Yes, sir. But, John, you're plumb crazy about that fellow being Roy Earle. Why, he's got half a million dollars' worth of jewellery with him. What would he be holding up a drug-store for?"

"Yeah, that's right. Never thought of that. But it sure looked like his picture except he's got a moustache."

"Doggone! I wish you'd never yelled at me. I'd've had him. But when you yelled 'Roy Earle,' my legs kind of got weak."

Everybody laughed.

A highway patrol officer came roaring up and jumped off his motorcycle.

"What is all this?"

When the druggist explained, he said:

"Well, we'll take no chances. Went north, did he? If it's Earle he's trying to get back into L.A. over the pass at Blue Jay. It's the only one open. We'll get him. I'm going to use your phone, John."

CHAPTER FORTY-THREE

Roy was crossing the wind-swept plateau at Broken Creek Summit now. He knew every turn of the road. It was almost like being in his home country. But he was worried and he had shooting pains in his side.

"Flushed me for sure now," he muttered. "I never should've throwed my glasses away. But, hell, I knew Healy would get loose and tell everybody I was wearing glasses and a moustache. I'd've shaved off the tickler if I'd had time. Yes, sir, Roy, you're really in a bad jam this time. Pert little guy, that druggist was. He makes a heist a pleasure. Course a smart guy like that would recognize you!"

He slowed down for the hairpin turn, then stepped on the gas again. But a powerful wind was blowing beyond the summit and he couldn't make any time. His car swayed as the whistling wind met it head on and he had a hard time holding it on the road.

As he approached the turn-off to Blue Jay Lake, he saw a car coming towards him. It had an official look to it somehow. He stepped on the gas and his coupé almost shot from under him. Gritting his teeth he took the turn on two wheels and disappeared into the pine forest east of Blue Jay.

"I don't know," he said. "Maybe I should've went on. They kind of got me bottled in here. If I can't get over the pass I'm sunk." He started slightly. A siren was going behind him. "Wow! Here comes trouble. That car didn't look right to me and it wasn't. Well, it's probably full of game-wardens. They'll wish they never tackled me."

He came out into the open. The dark pine forest disappeared behind him. He caught a flash of Blue Jay Lake glimmering off there between the trees, then he was rushing past Eagle Lake; and he thought about how the night of the hold-up he'd wondered if he'd ever see it again.

The siren was still going, but he was gradually losing it.

Ahead of him the road started to climb. He drove through a mighty forest of huge old pine trees, which shut out the sun and made a green twilight. Trout streams plunged along at the side of the road through clumps of birch and tangles of underbrush. He saw little birds flying low, chirping. And at one place he saw a man in a red coat, carrying a rifle. The man turned and stared at the coupé roared past.

Suddenly he came out into the open. He had passed timberline. His heart jumped up into his mouth at the sight before him. The sun was blazing down on a vast, upended world; gigantic, stony peaks rose one above another, lonely and monstrous under the naked blue sky. On a high shoulder at a bend in the mountain road he saw two ancient, riven juniper trees, then nothing but rock piled on rock.

On his left hand was a stony wall, on his right hand a terrible abyss which made the canyon at the hairpin turn near Broken Creek Summit seem like nothing at all. The road wound up and up. Snow began to fall and an arctic wind blew down through the huge fissures above him, whistling and howling.

Suddenly his car gave a jump, swerved towards the left, staggered, then crashed into the stony wall with such an impact that Roy was thrown violently against the steering-wheel. Stunned, he sat staring straight ahead of him for a moment; then he got out groggily, trying not to look at the abyss at the edge of the road.

A big stone had fallen onto the road from above. He'd hit it and broken his left front wheel.

"This is it," said Roy. "I'm done. Too bad she didn't go the other way. Then my troubles would've been over."

He could hear the siren again, coming closer and closer. He picked up the machine-gun, loaded his pockets with ammunition, then stood staring at the coupé for a moment.

"If I had time I could change wheels and make it. But, hell, I got no time. Here they come, them dumb game-wardens."

Roy ran up the road, which wound higher and higher, looking for a place where he could climb the wall. The siren was very close now, and suddenly it stopped.

"Found the car, I guess," said Roy.

In the middle of a sharp turn he discovered a crevice in the solid rock. He climbed up slowly, panting and grabbing his side. Pains were shooting all the way up to his right armpit and spreading across his chest.

"She'll stop when I can rest a minute," he told himself. "Can't stand much of this. Boy!"

Finally he was at the summit. He sat down and put his back against a big rock. He waited for a long time with his machine-gun in front of him, but nothing happened. He relaxed and lit a cigarette.

"My God, what a place!" Roy muttered. He bent over to look, but jerked back suddenly as a wave of dizziness swept over him. A thousand feet below he had seen Sutler's Lake, like a silver dollar embedded in green velvet. "Baby, am I up there!"

He heard a strange flapping sound and looked up. A huge bird was flying over him, headed towards the abyss – an eagle!

"Brother," said Roy, watching the eagle's lazy effortless flight over the terrible chasm, "I wish I had wings!"

Somewhere below him a stone rolled and he caught a glimpse of a sombrero. He fired high and violent stuttering echoes rolled from peak to peak, then died away. A bunch of stones rolled and clattered, then there was a long silence.

Finally a voice was wafted up:

"I told you it was Earle. Watch yourself, boy. He's tough as a boot."

"You, up there!" someone shouted. "You got no chance. We don't want to kill you. Come down. We won't do no shooting."

"Come get me, buddy. Come get me."

Roy pushed back his hat and leaned forward to ease the pain which was still shooting in all directions from his wounded side. Why had he said that? Why didn't he give up? He was like old

173

Mac. He'd just keep going till he run down like a kid's toy. There was no sense to it. But, hell, what was there sense to?

He heard another car drive up and stop. They were talking about him down there. There was a medley of voices, but he couldn't catch any of it except a word or two. "... Earle! You sure?" "... machine-gun! Tough...." "... no risks, fellows. ..."

"You, up there!" someone shouted. "Better give up. You got no chance in the world."

In a sudden flash Roy saw the tiny death cells at Michigan City; remembered the way the lights used to flicker when they burned some guy. "No, thanks," he told himself. "I'm done right here. I know when my goose is cooked."

Leaning over he shouted:

"Come get me, boys. There's plenty of you down there. What's the matter, yellow?"

"Let's go get him!"

"Keep your shirt on. Lou. He can't get away. I'm bossing this and I say we'll wait till the sheriff gets here."

"Yellow!" shouted Roy. The pain had stopped. He felt much better. He lit another cigarette and leaned back against the rock.

There was a prolonged silence, then he began to hear scraps of conversation.

"... who did he say?"

"... don't say. Deer-hunter. High-powered rifle. ..."

"... well, maybe, but ..."

Time passed. The sun began to get low in the sky and the giant peaks turned golden, then red. The big eagle flew lazily back across the chasm, sailed over Roy's head, then disappeared above him up among the rocks.

Suddenly a voice shouted:

"Earle! Come down. This's your last chance."

"Nuts to you, copper," said Roy, leaning forward.

There was a short silence, then far off to Roy's right a rifle cracked. At first he sat without moving. The gun didn't even fall out of his hands. The rifle cracked again and the echoes rolled off sharply, bouncing from rock to rock. Roy stood up, threw the machine-gun away from him, mumbled inarticulately, then fell forward on his face.

... Aunt Minnie was shaking her head at him reproachfully.

"Look at you," she said. "Wet as a spaniel and trying to make me think you didn't go swimming in the creek. You're a bad little boy, but I won't tell your father on you if you'll milk

Sarah for me tonight."

"Look," Roy wanted to say, "I may be a little boy to you, but I'm really a man. I've got grey in my hair and I'm in trouble. Bad trouble!"

... It was all over now. He was falling down that black abyss. Suddenly a huge green and white ball of fire swept across in front of him and a hand reached out and took his hand. But the hand was not little and soft as it had been that other time. It was lean and firm. Marie! The hand checked his fall.

CHAPTER FORTY-FOUR

Vince Healy had his overcoat collar turned up and his hat pulled low. He was trying to make these deputies and game-wardens think that he felt perfectly at home up in this God-forsaken place.

"How'd you get here so quick, Healy?"

"Flew to Ballard. Say, for Christ's sake, where did this guy get to? He must be part mountain goat."

"There he is."

Healy started slightly, then controlled his face.

"Big-shot Earle! Well, well. Look at him lying there. Ain't much, is he? His pants are torn and he's got on a dirty under-shirt. Let me down out of here. I need a drink. *Sic transit gloria mundi,* or something."

CARROLL & GRAF

FINE MYSTERY AND SUSPENSE
TITLES FROM CARROLL & GRAF

- [ ] Brand, Christianna/FOG OF DOUBT — $3.50
- [ ] Boucher, Anthony/THE CASE OF THE BAKER STREET IRREGULARS — $3.95
- [ ] Carr, John Dickson/LOST GALLOWS — $3.50
- [ ] Coles, Manning/NIGHT TRAIN TO PARIS — $3.50
- [ ] Dewey, Thomas B./THE BRAVE, BAD GIRLS — $3.50
- [ ] Dickson, Carter/THE CURSE OF THE BRONZE LAMP — $3.50
- [ ] Douglass, Donald M./REBECCA'S PRIDE — $3.50
- [ ] Hayes, Joseph/THE DESPERATE HOURS — $3.50
- [ ] Hughes, Dorothy/IN A LONELY PLACE — $3.50
- [ ] Innes, Hammond/THE WRECK OF THE MARY DEARE — $3.50
- [ ] MacDonald, John D./TWO — $2.50
- [ ] MacDonald, Philip/THE RASP — $3.50
- [ ] Mason, A.E.W./AT THE VILLA ROSE — $3.50
- [ ] Rinehart, Mary Rogers/THE CIRCULAR STAIRCASE — $3.50
- [ ] Rogers, Joel T./THE RED RIGHT HAND — $3.50
- [ ] Woolrich, Cornell/BLIND DATE WITH DEATH — $3.50

Available at fine bookstores everywhere or use this coupon for ordering:

Carroll & Graf Publishers, Inc., 260 Fifth Avenue, N.Y., N.Y. 10001

Please send me the books I have checked above. I am enclosing $_____ (please add $1.75 per title to cover postage and handling.) Send check or money order— no cash or C.O.D.'s please. N.Y residents please add 8¼% sales tax.

Mr/Mrs/Miss _____

Address _____

City _____ State/Zip _____
Please allow four to six weeks for delivery.